Come
and Go,
Molly Snow

For Cathy,
with many thanks for
your reading of my work.

Come
and Go,
Molly Snow

A NOVEL

Mary Ann Taylor-Hall

Mary Ann Taylor-Hall

7.21.10

UNIVERSITY PRESS OF KENTUCKY

The University Press of Kentucky
Scholarly publisher for the Commonwealth,
serving Bellarmine University, Berea College, Centre College of Kentucky,
Eastern Kentucky University, The Filson Historical Society, Georgetown
College, Kentucky Historical Society, Kentucky State University, Morehead
State University, Murray State University, Northern Kentucky University,
Transylvania University, University of Kentucky, University of Louisville,
and Western Kentucky University.

Editorial and Sales Offices: The University Press of Kentucky
663 South Limestone Street, Lexington, Kentucky 40508-4008
www.kentuckypress.com

A section of this novel was published in a slightly different form as a story,
"One Main Sound," in *Ploughshares,* vol. 16, no. 4, winter 1990–91, edited
by Gerald Stern, and later in *Ground Water, a collection of contemporary
Kentucky fiction,* edited by Scot Brannon, Marguerite Floyd, and Charlie
Hughes, The Lexington Press, Lexington, Kentucky, 1992.

13 12 11 10 09   5 4 3 2 1

The Library of Congress has cataloged the hardcover edition as follows:
Taylor-Hall, Mary Ann.
    Come and go, Molly Snow / Mary Ann Taylor-Hall.
       p.   cm.
    1. Young women—Kentucky—Fiction. 2. Bluegrass musicians—Kentucky—
Fiction. 3. Man-woman relationships—Kentucky—Fiction.
    I. Title.
    PS3570.A983C66 1995
    813'.54—dc20   94-20841
ISBN 978-0-8131-9216-1 (pbk. : alk. paper)

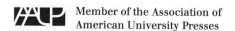

To the memory of my mother,
Mildred Rose Dubina Taylor,
and my father,
Edmund Haynes Taylor—
the music and the words.

Contents

ONE

Full of Holes

One

The day after I graduated from high school, I cut out. Left my mama weeping in the carport. "I'll be back, honey, don't cry," I yelled out the window of my inheritance, Daddy's old Riviera. But she knew what I meant: back for Christmas, back for the Shorter family reunion. In all other respects, goodbye flat dirt and frozen-out orange groves, hello I-75. If you want to play the fiddle in a bluegrass band, that's one of the roads you'll *be* on. Renfro Valley to Dayton, Ohio. Live Oak, Florida, to Knoxville, Tennessee. "Doin' 75 on I-75" is the name of a song I wrote that day, on my way to what I mistakenly thought was the bluegrass music capital of the world, Lexington, Kentucky.

That song doesn't have much in the way of words. It's mainly a real fast breakdown.

Pardon the expression. A real fast breakdown is what's landed me where I am *now*, a dozen years later, out in the deep country, at a round cherrywood table, peeling peaches with two semi-old ladies. Sometimes I have to laugh out loud at myself—Ms. Roughhouse, Ms. Grab It and Growl, letting her temples be dabbed with orange water. I don't know for how long. The time being, is how we put it.

The table is in front of two long windows. The morning

sun lays a gold rectangle over the linoleum. They're trying to see if they can trust me with a knife.

There's been a misunderstanding here, but I don't know how to make myself clear. The best policy is to keep my mouth shut and go on cutting up peaches in a responsible way.

We dunk them in boiling water, we slip off their skins. Then we split them down the groove and on around, taking the red pit out, slicing them into the big stainless-steel basin. The gold, moist slices, red at the inner edge, gather the light to them. They look like light itself, as if to say, "You want to believe in something, believe in peaches."

We live a tidy life out here in the middle of nowhere. They give me little things to do. Keeping me occupied is their main goal in life these days.

Ona's main goal, anyway; Ruth works me in. She's got a busy schedule. She's going to Lexington this afternoon, for instance, on the trail of a three-piece travel outfit, which she's been telling us the ins and outs of for about a half an hour. How long would it take for a nice lightweight jersey to dry in the desert air is the question before us at the moment.

Ruth's retiring from the bank at the end of the month, and then she's going to the Holy Land. Don't ask me why— Ruth's quite a load of mouthy woman to be walking those Stations of the Cross on her knees. I think she's just drawn to all the old places where history happened. She's not the type to let a little thing like current events throw her off. In fact, her contingency plan for old age or terminal illness is to fly to all the dangerous hot spots. I don't think she's actually hoping to get hijacked, but if she does she's going to talk back to them and not do what they tell her, so they'll shoot her and get it out of their system. She thinks they'll just kill her and throw her down on the runway, not beat her up beforehand—she's heard those Arabs respect old ladies.

"I'd die sudden and happy. It could save some young person's life," she explained to us. "It'd be more up my alley than dwindling off in the nursing home from Loony Tunes or one of them bad cancers. And I'd get my name in all the papers—you *know* they'd give me the Medal of Honor, honey."

Ruth's Senior Trust Officer in charge of Estate Planning at the bank. She's professionally trained to look ahead.

Now Ona over there thinks Oxford County, Kentucky, is an old place where history happened. According to her, this right here is the Holy Land. Seek no further.

I don't know if Oxford County is as holy as the Holy Land, but it's as dry these days. Drought's mainly what we talk about now. Ona and Ruth tell each other over and over, as though there's some comfort in it, the names of all the things that are dying. A chant going on over my head all day—pignut hickories, young poplars. Toads and crickets and lightning bugs. Snakes, crawdads, box turtles, clover, all grass, most wildflowers. Everything but grapevine, thistles, pigweed and hackberry shoots, poison ivy and brambles—you begin to think that survival of the fittest is nothing but a vicious circle: Fittest for what? For survival. There's got to be more to life than that.

The drought's been on since late May. Now it's the first of August. It hasn't rained once in this whole month I've been out here. The ground's got big cracks in it. We throw our bathwater by the bucket on the tomatoes and roses. We've given up on almost everything else. Whatever's managed to hold on, grasshoppers chew away on. Every step you take, grasshoppers spray out around you, mouths on legs.

Last week, Ona bought a flat of begonias and planted them in a shallow basin, just to remind herself of what things used to look like, she said. The next morning, I came out and found the plants all dug up and lying on their sides this way and that. I thought the dogs had knocked them over. I poked my hand into the dirt to right the plants, and touched something cool—a toad, splayed out as flat as it could get at the bottom of the basin, the only damp place it could find, probably. It gathered itself fast and leapt out from under my hand. A toad's skin has to be moist a certain percentage of the time or it dies of dehydration, Ona told me. I keep thinking of that toad hopping off, panicky, across the sharp yellow grass.

And Barney, Ona's old three-legged dog, her darling, is out there in the grass, rolling around on his back and groaning, about to itch himself to death. We comb him and put flea powder on him every morning, but it's not working. I get up and open the screened door, and he scrambles up the steps and in the door, hopping across the linoleum, bright-eyed and raggy-tailed. Ona fills his water bowl and bends from the waist to place it right before him. "Worthless thing," she says, scratching his ears.

I'm going to start putting out some pans of plain wet dirt, for the toads.

NOW RUTH'S TELLING what she read in her Holy Land book last night, that back in the last century the pilgrims from Russia used to go into the Sea of Galilee in white gowns that they dried out in some sacred way and wrapped up and took home with them, to get buried in.

"Was it just the old people or who?" Ona wants to know.

"Just Russians, was all it said."

"Because it looks like the younger ones wouldn't have cared to fool with it. Imagine if you were just twenty, having to lug that thing around with you from then on. It would give me the willies."

"It would keep your mind focused, anyhow. I might just sneak in myself, when nobody's looking, in my nightgown."

"Not you. You'd wait till you had you an audience."

"I'll bring it back and give it to you to keep for me, Ona. You could stow it up there in the attic and bring it down when they're laying me out."

Ona looks up at her briefly, then back at her peach. "Time they lay you out, I'll be long gone, honey. And you can bury *me* in any old thing. These old brown pants will suit me fine."

Ruth flicks a glance at them. "They're about ready for it, I'd say." They both throw their heads back and hoot.

The beauty part of Ona and Ruth is, they stay so cheerful themselves it's hard for them to remember dangerous areas, so they forget to pussyfoot around them. It works out fine, because most words don't get through to me anyway. I'm kind of a brick wall, things bounce off of me, shrouds and Sea of Galilee and Church of the Holy Sepulchre and the name of everything that's died in the drought. Words, I just don't know. *Red brain red brain red brain*, I'm thinking. Whatever words turn up in my mouth, it seems like someone else put them there. *Red brain* ticks back and forth like a busy clock until I can't stand it anymore. "Peach pits look like red brains," I blurt out then.

There's a pause, the air pricks up its ears, then Ona glances at the pit. "Now *I* always thought," she says in her sprightly, interested voice, "that them hedge apples looked like brains." Now she pushes up out of her chair to throw another batch of peaches into the boiling water. She puts her hand on her hip and waits, then fishes them out again, one by one, with her slotted spoon

I throw the pit into the bucket with the others, ashamed of myself. I don't have much say in what I say these days. Words get into my mouth, round and hard as marbles. I hope I won't spit them out; I tell myself not to, and the next thing I know, there they are, bouncing across the table.

There's a difference between *those* words and the ones I myself think, which are all hooked together. A crazy speed-boat in my head going around in circles with nobody at the wheel. I never run out of gas.

I know how to draw silence up around the place I can't bear in the center of myself. I'm a past master. But the words are less trouble. And less danger, too, as I now know. I just wish I could stop when I want to. I'm like the girl in *The Red Shoes* who cannot stop dancing. I don't know whether it goes on in my sleep or not, but I wake up exhausted.

And then, of course, this steady racket makes it hard for things other people say to get through to me.

Ona and Ruth have fast hands, nimble ones. They're flying through these peaches. Next to them, my hands look clumsy and slow to get the message. I can't imagine how I managed to play the fiddle. But I did.

Ona and Ruth would be great banjo-pickers, both of them. I can see it—"The Barkley Sisters." Boots and long suede cowboy skirts.

Sisters-in-law, actually. They married brothers, Luther and Duffy Barkley, both dead now. We're none of us at this table kin, but it's beginning to feel like a little family.

POOR MAMA. I hope she's okay. Back down in Florida now—she used up all her sick days to come up and stay with me; then she had to go on back to work. She's not a wealthy woman. Nowadays, she calls me up and says, "I dreamed you were in a burning house and you were screaming out the window for me to save you, and I couldn't. I couldn't get up there, Carrie. You were on the second floor. I didn't have a ladder."

I've had the exact same dream about Molly. You couldn't have a dream worse than that one, the one you love the most trapped and screaming for you, and you—well, it doesn't pay to dwell on things like that. My mother and I have a psychic connection, but I'd just as soon she didn't know about it. "I'm doing all right, Mama. Try not to worry about me."

"Oh, I wish you could be down here with me."

"They're taking real good care of me. I'll come down before long and let you wait on me hand and foot."

"That dream just made me so sad, Carrie. What kind of mother am I that I'm not with you now?"

"A good one. The best there is." I really mean it, some way, but the words sound hollow. I can't worry about Mama yet.

It's much better for me to be out here with Ona and Ruth. I can count on them, they don't need anything back from me. They parcel out the days for me, dinner at six, bed at ten. They draw down the western shades against the hot afternoon sun, sprinkle parsley on the potatoes for a touch of color. They pull this world up around me like a quilt, talking their slow, funny talk all the while. Ona sits me in her lap some nights and rocks me like she did that first night, when Cap brought me out here, and when the old sobs start, she says, "That's right, that's right, you have to, honey. Grieve it on out." She cares, but I don't have to worry that every pain that stabs through my own heart stabs through Ona's, too. With Mama, I have to watch what I think, because it will get into her head, and she'll think it, too. We've never gotten ourselves separated out right.

I feel grateful for this cool, dark house, up from the creek, this crazy old rambling place with its rooms you have to step up or down into, like everything in it but the first high log room was a spur-of-the-moment notion, its long hallways to nowhere in particular, its porches off of porches, its sheds nailed to wings. There's parts of this house I've never seen. We live mostly in the middle. It's as though everyone who ever lived here sat around after supper and said, "Why don't we . . ." and then they jumped up and knocked out a wall or nailed up some studs before they got it thought through good. A dozen or so rooms, connected by dog runs and arches and curtained doorways. Ona inherited it.

Sometimes I think I hear many voices, off in some distant part of the house, loud and cheerful and busy.

A braided rug beside the bed to put your feet down on first thing every morning, a nice patchwork quilt folded over the footboard, in case it should turn cool in the night. Somebody—Ona or Ona's mother, or grandmother—made the rugs and the quilts both, and every tablecloth, sheet, and curtain that's in the place. Even the dishcloths have crocheted lace edges on them, that seven-shades-of-purple kind. That's one way you could spend your life. You could keep busy making something nice out of scraps and then taking good care of it so you could hand it down. It would be a full, happy, busy life. I can see that it would.

I'm grateful to be here, with Ruth and her excited approach to the possibilities of life, with Ona and her old smart country ways you don't learn from a book, but from tending the same place forever. I hope to learn something from them.

Ona was born and raised right here; then she married Luther Barkley and they lived here together for their entire marriage, a good many years of it overlapping with her parents, plus whoever else might be on the premises at any given time—sisters, brothers, uncles, cousins. And then Ona and Luther's three girls, as well—I see them all sitting down together at the dinner table every night, privacy something none of them ever heard of, so wouldn't know to miss.

Cap is Ona's grandson. He was one of the ones at the table. Luther and Ona raised him from the age of six, when his mother—their eldest daughter—died. His father was sent to

Korea soon afterwards, and Cap stayed with Luther and Ona from then on.

A time came when the house gradually emptied out. The other two daughters married away from Oxford County. Cap grew up and moved to the little house that he and Luther built together, on the part of the farm that lies over on the other side of the Hawktown Road. Luther died soon afterwards.

Then Ona lived on here for eight or ten years, more or less by herself, until Ruth left the husband she married after Duffy, Luther's younger brother, died. Ruth came to visit Ona while she looked for a house to buy, and never got around to leaving. That was three, four years ago, I think.

And now here's the latest odd assortment at the kitchen table, Ona June Barkley and Ruth Ann Barkley McBride and me, Carrie Marie Mullins, slicing peaches together like we've been doing it forever. My little family, for now.

I picked a great time to flip out, the day before the band took off on the three-month tour that we'd been putting together for six months. It was supposed to be our turning point, when we got to be a headline act. They've been on the tour for a month now—I don't know what they're doing for a fiddler. They haven't been back, but some charge has gotten into the air around here. I feel Cap on the horizon. One of these days, he'll be standing right in front of me, with those eyes the color of a swimming pool at the deep end, asking, What's it going to be, Carrie? You can't blame him. They've held on and waited for me so patiently, so long, but sooner or later a band's got to know if it's got a fiddler. Sooner or later if you're a fiddler, you've got to go back to fiddling. Regardless.

I don't know whether I'm a fiddler or not. All I know is the music I used to play has fallen right out of my hands. I don't feel it, you know. I don't hear it, it doesn't rise up in me, the way it always did before.

OUT OF THE CORNERS of their eyes, Ruth and Ona are watching me use the small, sharp knife. I thrust the point in, slide the blade around, turning the peach in my hand, every move I make careful, like a child learning to tie her shoes. I'm hoping to pass the test. They think I'm attracted to things with sharp edges, because I broke the mirror that first night, when I temporarily went gazebo, as Mama would say, and unfortunately since then I haven't been able to get a good grip on anything, so we've been moving through the glassware at quite a clip.

Ona's put away the good china, with the gold rim around it, as though a bad two-year-old had come to visit. Every time I drop something and it breaks, I just stare at it. I can't seem to think of anything to say about it. I've about used up *I'm sorry*. I just put it on the payback list and get the broom. I can't hang on to things. My hand won't make a fist. Ona's stopped using anything but the Melmac. Once she saw I was determined to make it right, she got worried that I'd feel beholden beyond my means.

I'm beholden beyond my means no matter how you cut it. Nothing said she had to take me in, except Cap and maybe Jesus Christ. She just did it.

Anyway, they're afraid I might happen to get ahold of a little shard of glass, a little knife, when I'm in the wrong frame of mind one of these days. They're a little spooked by me. Who could blame them? *I'm* a little spooked by me, to tell you the truth.

My mind skidded out on me that one time, so I've lost my confidence. I thought I was doing exactly what I was supposed to be doing, what I needed to be doing. I thought I had everything under control. But maybe it's possible to do something, even the right thing, so hard you could go on out the other side without noticing. I do remember feeling it was a very small matter, a very thin line, between being alive and being dead. I got too close to the line; the closer you get, the less it seems like a line. I know that much now.

Cap, for one, seemed to think I'd gotten too close. That scared, serious look on his face when he found me, when he knelt down beside me, like he was about to start artificial respiration.

Artifical respiration, all right.

Oh yes, Cap's good, a good friend who gathers you up off the floor and holds on to you for dear life, loves you up one side and down the other, just what the doctor ordered, then puts you in his van, carries you out to the country, and dumps you. "Take care of her, Granny, take care of her, Aunt Ruth—I got a show to do."

He plunked me down in his grandma's lap and walked.

Cap's all heart. Cap's a true old buddy, he'll come running. Just don't look for him to stay. Put him on the list. Cap and Mama. The list for when it's time to pick up the pieces, tally the breakage. Right now, *I* have a show to do, too. Mine's all day every day. I can't say I see an end to it.

ONA PUTS SOME of the peaches in the kettle on the stove for jam and starts spooning the rest into freezer bags. "These will taste pretty good in a cobbler some cold January night."

For a minute the idea of it closes around me, comfortably—there we are, the three of us, snowed in, passing the dishes of cobbler to each other, under the lamplight, frost crawling up the windowpanes, but we don't care. We're passing each other the blue pitcher of cream.

I wonder when I'll wear out my welcome. I wonder when this life will begin to get old, when I'll start pawing the ground. I know it will happen. What will become of me? What's in store for me? January's a long way off.

We have finished this job. We have shaken every branch for the last peaches hidden like red-and-yellow jewels in among the droopy leaves. We have sliced up every one we could get our hands on, we have cut out all the rotten parts and thrown them on the compost heap. Now Ona and Ruth are standing at the sink, washing their hands, Ona short and round in her brown polyester burying pants with a baggy shiny seat, Ruth as tall as me but on a grander scale, tied up tight in her flowered red silk kimono. She probably makes quite a splash at the Ellenburg Country Club pool, where she goes to swim laps to keep her figure. Ona couldn't care less about *her* figure. She says, "I get plenty of exercise climbing up and down them stairs twenty times a day." But it's not enough, she's got the old Oxford County spread, belly to thigh, too much homemade sausage and corn on the cob.

Ruth dries her hands, looking at me with her head to one side. "Wouldn't you like me to braid your hair, Carrie? Wait and I'll get a comb." I don't even have to say yes or no. They treat me like I'm their baby girl. Ruth comes back and stands behind me, humming and combing. That good old Jim Croce song, "Operator." She leaves off humming and starts singing the words, sort of absentmindedly, about her best ol' ex-friend Ray. It makes me laugh out loud. Ruth laughs, too. "Isn't that the way they say it goes," I sing out, putting some English on the melody, "let's forget all that." It startles me. It's the first time I've heard my singing voice since—I don't know when. When I went back to the band, in those weeks between when the accident happened and when I flipped out, I'd play but not sing. I couldn't have stood to hear the voice that came out of me. The playing was a little different, something I *did*, not something I *was*.

If Ruth is surprised she doesn't show it. She just goes on combing. "If I had that voice of yours, Carrie," she says, when she's sure that's all the song I mean to sing, "I'd be long gone."

"I *am* long gone. This is where I went." I snap out the words. Then we all laugh at how neat that came out.

"Naw, this is just where you stopped along the way. You got a lot further to go. A lot further you *could* go, anyway. If you wanted to. If I had what you've got I'd go for the limit and I wouldn't stop till I got there."

"Gee, maybe you can be my manager when you retire, Ruth."

She gives a snort. "Don't say it if you don't mean it. I'd do a lot better than that little Joe Garvey, I'll tell you that."

Ruth will blend right in with those Arabs. She's got dark looks, a cross between Arab and Italian. She sure doesn't look like Oxford County, though she's supposed to be kin on one side or the other to half the people here. My guess is some circus passed through town back about sixty-five years ago and left its mark on one of the many fair Fister girls. Anyway, she's something else, something not from around here, leaning in on you with her long black hair caught back in a ponytail, and her big shiny dark eyes still looking for whatever's going down, even if it's just trouble, and her wide 1940s mouth over sharp strong gypsy teeth—she looks like she could take a good sharp bite out of the world. She likes scarves, big jewelry, long skirts. She could dance around the campfire any day of the week, just kick off her spike-heeled shoes. Or lay out the cards to read your future for you, but the only cards Ruth lays out are the bridge cards—I've seen her snap down that trump and gather up the trick with her quick flashy fingers. "The secret to living in a small town if you want to go your own way is, wear 'em out, break their spirit," she told me once. "You can get to the other side of their curiosity if you play right into it. When they ask why I want to travel so much, I say to pick up men."

Now she goes on with her pep talk. "What you *got* is star quality. You can see it a mile off." She stops, to concentrate on a tangle. "Such nice hair," she comments. "Needs a trim, though. The ends are splitting. You want to go into town with me?"

Yes or no.

"Couldn't you just do it sometime, Ruth? It's not hard at all. You just have to go straight across."

I haven't been back in Lexington since Cap brought me out here. I haven't looked at myself close since that first night, when I got up and broke Ona's mirror with the silver pitcher on the dresser. If my ends are splitting it's news to me, news from another planet.

That night Cap walked me up the brick path and I thought, *Ona's roses are doing very well—she must be watering them.* I thought, *This is the world. Here are Ona's roses, still blooming.* Then I don't know what, I came to a halt. I folded up onto the warm brick walk. It wasn't like fainting. I just folded up. And then I was getting rocked against something soft, someone was saying in a low, creamy voice, "There now, there. Why darlin', there, there." I put my arms around Ona's neck, and she gathered me up against her big soft front, which makes fatness a virtue, a gift to the world, as the sobs shook loose from me. I hadn't cried much till then, I don't think. I'd screamed but I don't remember crying. And finally, there in the dark, with Ona rocking me, I fell asleep.

What woke me up was getting lifted from something soft and comfortable to something tight, charged-up. Even with my eyes closed, coming out of sleep, I knew exactly where I was, back on full alert. Wired. Cap felt it, I'm sure. He carried me in the screened door and up the steps. He put me down on the guest bed. He sat down on the edge and took off my sandals, which he had also, earlier that evening, put *on* me. I pretended, even to myself, that I was dead to the world. I didn't want to see his worried eyes again that night. *All right,* I crooned to myself, still in Ona's voice. *All right, precious, all right.*

He leaned over me to fix the pillows, smooth my hair; I know he was looking at my face and willing me to open my eyes, so he could tell me something. Something about what had happened between us that afternoon. I kept my eyes closed so that nothing wrong would be said. I thought that someday we would both know what to say, but not yet. So then he unfolded the quilt and spread it over me. When he left I opened my eyes to the empty darkness pouring in.

I heard his car start up, go down the gravel drive fast, to get to Justice's in time for the first set. That's a sound I know all about—I grew up on my father scratching off on gravel, hustling down to the hardtop, smiling his blissed-out roadhouse smile, looking forward to another long night of music. But Cap was looking forward to more than that, a load of work between him and the next night, when the band had to go on at a bluegrass jamboree in Northern Ohio, with or without a fiddler. So maybe he wasn't smiling. Whatever he was doing, whatever he was thinking. . . .

I held on to him. The idea of him. I held on to the car's hum until it was nothing but a small hole in the night, and then the night's sound filled it, a buzz of peepers or crickets or something. The room smelled of roses and floor wax. I slept then, I think.

The next thing I knew, I was standing up. I'd gotten a light by the bed turned on. I watched my face crack and crack and fall to splinters. My cracked reflection was giggling with me as if we were each other's best friends, rolling our eyes around, making faces. Somebody a long way off was making some kind of deep bellowing racket, and I was saying to it, *Now young lady. Now you just. Now there.* And laughing. My face kept falling out of the mirror, though. I thought it was the funniest thing that ever happened. But then Ona was behind me, snatching the silver pitcher out of my hand. She said, low and sort of singing, "Now why did you want to go and break that mirror, Carrie?"

"I don't know," I said. *"I* don't know." A little quacky child's voice. Oh, flipped out, truly gone. Ona and Ruth, one in peach, the other in turquoise, carried the mirror frame out of the room with serious expressions on their faces. Two fairy godmothers, two old bosomy angels, I imagined them flying around the air above me in their waltz-length nylon nightgowns, plucking their—banjos! I howled with laughter at the idea, I laughed till I cried. Holding my stomach, gasping for breath.

I thought they wouldn't let me stay with them after that. I thought it was Eastern State Hospital for me. When Cap stopped to drop off my truck the next morning—Joyner and TJ were behind him, in the van—I heard him and Ona talking in the kitchen, underneath the room where I had just awakened. "We'll take it one day at a time," she told him. "We'll see if we can manage it. If we can't, we can't. Let's not get ahead of ourselves."

That sounded like good advice for me, too. But I don't know how this arrangement is going to turn out. I've got no crystal ball.

"THAT'LL BE COOLER for you," Ruth says. "I haven't done a French braid since Dawn was a little old girl. It looks nice, Carrie."

Sometimes I think I might have been all right if I could have stayed sitting against the wall of Molly's bedroom, where Cap found me, for a little longer. I was on to something. I was getting somewhere. I think if Cap had not broken in the door and come down the hall that night, I might have been all right by now. One way or the other.

I can feel him bearing down on me now, with that one big question on his mind: *Are you in this band or out of it?*

"Men shoot you full of holes," I announce, to Ona and Ruth, now. I've got no more idea than they have what's going to come out of my mouth next.

Ruth's got a raunchy old laugh she laughs sometimes. "Just one, darlin'." You can't talk dirtier than Ruth. She'll go right along with you till you back down. "That's enough right there, don't you reckon?"

She doesn't know what I mean.

Neither do I. "I mean—your life. I mean *full* of holes," I stammer, then laugh myself; I hear the laugh, high and sharp and surprised. "As full of holes as this colander here."

"Only if you stand still for it, honey child."

Ona's at the sink. She doesn't exactly mean to be heard, but I hear her. "If you don't want to be full of holes, don't ever love nothing."

I feel rage filling my head, throbbing against my eyeballs. I don't even know why. The certain way she says it, like I don't know anything about it and she knows everything. I don't need any lectures on love. *"That's* not what I mean, either," I say. "I'm not talking about love, I'm talking about men. I mean full of damn *holes."* When I say *holes,* I sound like a dog, its head thrown back, howling.

Ona turns, one hand still on the sink, and looks at me, hard. Then she gets the water jar out of the fridge and fills a glass and brings it to me. I grab hold of her shirttail. "I'm sorry," I say. "Everything pisses me off. I'm crazy half the time."

"No you're *not*! You're not one bit crazy." She presses my head against her belly and pats it. "You're trying to say the truth. Don't you be sorry."

Ona's been up since dawn. You have to get up early if you want to get anything done before the heat sets in to melt you down. If you want to stay ahead of the spiders, the ants, the roaches. The moths in the globes of the lamps, scorching. This house is full of insects. A wasp has come to the peaches. It lands on my hand. I shake it off, startled; Ona smacks it with the dish towel.

She watches me drink the water. I put both my hands around the glass to keep it steady. She bends to the cabinet beneath the sink and gets out some cloths and window cleaner, holds them out to me. "These kitchen windows haven't been washed since spring. You want to give 'em a lick?"

I stand up. "All right."

This is Ona's idea of how to get through things, how to come out the other side. Give yourself a little something to do. Idle hands are the devil's workshop, as everybody knows.

"The Devil's Workshop"—that would be a good name for a fiddle tune. There are those that used to think the fiddle was the devil's workshop. Idle hands reached for the fiddle, and went straight to hell, fiddling all the way.

IF YOU'D ASKED me what I wanted, that day twelve years ago when I turned the Riviera onto I-75 and headed north out of Lake Grace, Florida, I would have said, "Please God, let me play almost as good as Kenny Baker." Later, what I wanted got simpler. I wanted tone. I wanted to get deep into the core of every note I played with the strong fleshy part of my fingertip.

I can still play a decent guitar, the mandolin, too, in an emergency. To me, the guitar and the mandolin are happy everyday instruments. But it's the fiddle I've loved, the fiddle I've tried to be an artist of. That singing, better than any human voice, but kin to our own sweet, held notes, our most heedless soaring and sighing and crying. We bluegrass fiddlers call it sawin' and bangin', but we know better. We know where the fiddle can take us when the fiddler can go there.

All I want now is to go there. All I want is pure music. Pure free girl music, woman music. Christ, I don't even know what I mean.

Something's got to come to me.

I have always been pleased to think of myself as beholden to no one. But these days I keep thinking *rescue me*, like a damsel in distress.

Oh, my distress is real.

I've got to rescue myself.

I know I do, I know I do. But I don't know how. At first, after the accident, music was all I could hold on to. But then, I let it go. I just opened my hand and let it fall away from me. I've never since the age of sixteen gone a month or even a week without practicing. I think music will save me. But I can't remember it. And I don't have my fiddle with me here. I wish I did.

Not to play.

Not to play. Just to hold.

I SPRAY ON the window cleaner. I clean the first pane. Till dinnertime, I know, they'll be listening for the sound of breaking glass.

Lights, they call these little panes.

Light of lights, light at the heart of light: it's the pale yellow, nearly white old tomcat moving down the path out there, tail high. The same bastard that caught the squirrel yesterday evening. All three of us ran after him, screaming, till the yellow dog Willy got into the act, and ran the cat off, because he wanted that squirrel meat for himself and thought we were screaming to encourage him. But he dropped it, confused and sad, when we hit him. We held back the cat and Willy as the squirrel, crazy with terror, threw itself into the air, in the same place, over and over, clicking its teeth. Finally it found the hole at the base of the elm tree and went in, its leg all bloodied. We put some cat food and water in there for it, and then laid a board in front of the hole, to try to keep the cat away. The squirrel could knock it down and get out if it wanted to, Ona said. "It's not much chance but it's all we can do for him, honey. He's got himself in a mess."

The board is still in place over the hole. What does that mean?

Cat, stone path, bleached straw on the garden, all the same color.

I'm looking out through wavery panes on the wide, pale August weather. Two squirts for each light, then clean away the little film of grease and every insect speck, polish it with a paper towel. Into the corners and along the edges. *Am I a good girl?*

Oh don't, don't.

Fat uneven rims of glazing show through to the inside. Tiny air bubbles in the old glass. The women who've cleaned these long windows before me probably go all the way back into slave times. An unbroken line of women watching the same world I'm looking at waver every time they moved their heads. Oh, I wish I could see them now!

A long line of women, exactly right here, in the light, and gone, a long line of men and women and children, frogs, crickets, orioles, here and gone, trees, even, at last, here and gone, a steady wind blowing souls, little scraps of life, east to west, some lit up with the mica shine of consciousness, but going west all the same.

I used to raise my eyes to the stained glass window at the front of the church in Lake Grace, hoping for a way out. Is there a way out? I used to pray, Don't let Mama die, don't let Daddy die, don't let Dexter or Connie or me die.

Crank-handled pump over the cistern, rock path to the garden. Daylilies everywhere. The peach tree, its branches lifting back now.

I get the stepladder for the outside, because the house is set up on a three-foot-high rock foundation where the hill drops down beneath it. I set it up carefully among the bedraggled zinnias and nasturtiums and one last spindly delphinium. Now I'm looking in on Ona's kitchen, her deep world. Empty now—they're showing they trust me. Someone moves around upstairs, running water.

A little steam rises from the boiler of peaches. I'm from somewhere else, Mars. No. I'm a ghost, spooking around outside, looking in on something called the Land of the Living. Round cherrywood table, high-backed chairs with blue cushions tied in the seats. Woodstove, rocker in the bay. A bouquet on the mantel, from me. Those orange flowers I found growing in the North Fields.

"What's the name of that flower, Ona?" "That's butterfly weed, Carrie." Butterfly weed, okay. Once I knew the names of a lot of things. Then for a while my mind swept itself clean. Now I live in a different world, with all new names to learn. Boiler, root cellar. Butterfly weed, jewelweed, Araucana hen. I'm feeling my way, like a blind person, but it's not the way back.

The day's heavy. Something on the outskirts wants to move, but can't budge the heavy slabs of shadowless light.

This haze will gather together, make a gray cloud, late in the afternoon. The cloud will move over us. We'll hope for rain, but there won't be any. That's what drought looks like—like it might rain. Where the glare hurts your eyes the most is where the sun is. A dead leaf, caught in a cobweb, stirs in a one-leaf breeze.

And dead and gone come into me again, without warning. Dead. Gone. A big bell in my chest, a heavy clapper, gonging up, then down. *What you love isn't here anymore.* A terrible soundless striking. Gone, gone.

I WAS HANGING sheets on the line. There was a breeze. The sheets billowed and flapped around me, wings.

She rode the yellow-and-lavender trike on the sidewalk. Porch steps to driveway, driveway to porch steps. Doing what she was told, for once. I had her in my sight. I was off to the side of the house, at the clothesline. I wanted to get that last load hung out. I was always rushing to get through everything that had to be done, always trying to do two things at once. I could see her each time she got to the driveway and turned back, waiting for me to finish hanging the clothes, so I could walk with her while she pedaled the Big Wheel around the block on the sidewalk. She was talking to Bootsie, her sidekick from Arizona or Outer Space—whatever new place she had just heard about. I was hurrying, I was watching, but took my eyes off of her.

I took my eyes off of her.

If I had looked up even one second sooner and seen her coasting, legs held out from the pedals of her Big Wheel, down the sloping driveway, where she was never supposed to be, I would have screamed. She would have stopped. She would have minded me.

She just got carried away. She just forgot.

I remember myself at the clothesline. And then I remember running, as the dark green pickup truck did something, slid slowly into the dogwood tree. I remember the crazy calm voice in my head saying, "It won't happen. It won't." Even though by then it already had, and I had seen it.

The truck skidded. I ran, getting nowhere, still holding on to a foolish piece of laundry, a flowered pillowcase. The truck skidded into the tree. I ran, my body pulling itself inside out into an empty scream, *Molly*. The scream turned to glass, nothing in it. People say *I would give anything*. But nothing you've got will take you back to that moment behind the glassy instant of what happened. There's no way back to that time when you bent and grabbed another pillowcase, and straightened up and shook it out, thinking of something else.

I would give anything—arms, legs, eyes, breasts, voice, music, love, life itself—to have that moment back.

I would watch her every second. I would keep her safe.

TWO

One Main Sound

Two

In Florida, I had a fringed suede jacket I got at Second Chance and some cowboy boots. "Rodie-Odie," the boys at school called me then. Once, some chunky hood yelled across the parking lot, "Hey, ride me, Rodie, I buck rill good." I gave that boy the eye through my long brown hair. I told him to go buck him*self.*

My father gave me the boots for my fifteenth birthday; I bought the jacket to go with them and modeled the whole outfit for him, with my best jeans. He said, "Now you're cooking, Baby Blue."

I was a tall, loony loner, back then, trying to decide what I wanted to be when I grew up, a cowpuncher out on the prairie singing to my dogies or a motel mankiller. It was in my mind that if I played my cards right, I could manage both. But not in Lake Grace, Florida. *Not in Lake Grace, Florida,* was all I knew, for a while, about where I wanted to end up. The interstates are full of girls like me.

When I first got to Lexington, my waitress-and-pickup-band way of life, plus I guess a natural inability to sit still, put me in some danger of turning into what my mama calls a cheap tramp. Mama has cheap tramps on the brain because, according to her, that's what Daddy died of, in a motel room in Tampa, a few months after I showed him how good I looked in my jacket and boots.

He never got famous when he was alive, but afterwards, he was the rage for a while, till everyone in Lake Grace got the subject of him worn out. *Polk Jazzman Found Dead in Tampa Motel Room.* The police never managed to track down the lady in the story, but since everybody in town knew that my father lived from one day to the next on his bottom dollar, they all, Mama included, assumed that the other party was the cheapest of the cheap, that she'd gone with him for not much more than the quart bottle of Jim Beam found (empty) under his bed.

But I had my own idea about it. She loved his music, she'd gone with him for nothing. Under her own power. To please herself. She heard Daddy play at Dutch's Hutch and took him the bottle of Jim Beam as a token of her esteem. And Daddy drank it, as a token of his.

Mama nearly died of what she called the pure trashiness of the thing. But she's got a nice tight chin line from holding her head up. "Don't you ever forget you're a Shorter on one side—as good as any and better than most," she told Connie and Dexter and me.

As to the motel lady, we'll never have a final answer to the burning question, was she cheap or was she free. Either way, sight unseen, I said to myself at age fifteen, I'd rather be that one than Mama, in her baby-blue negligee and matching mules, eyes swollen from crying all night again, jamming in the basket of the Mr. Coffee, Daddy nowhere in sight for the fourth or fifth time that month, then, really and truly, forever and ever, flat gone.

I loved my jazzy daddy, I have to admit it. He was a hell of a case on the tenor sax, but like many musicians, he drank too much. He never was a mean drunk, just a gone drunk. You didn't want to depend on Daddy for anything at all, the honest truth for instance, or your next meal.

Our next meal was why Mama was working at True's Shoe Box from the time Connie was six and I was five and Dexter two or three. Now the shop's in the mall and she's the manager, but I'll tell you she's put in her share of time hunched over with somebody's damn foot in her lap.

Daddy wouldn't teach me the saxophone. He said girls couldn't play wind instruments and if they could they were perverts. You get the picture. If he'd lived, he and I would have gotten into it eventually, but I didn't know anything back then. Maybe he didn't either. He was still young. Maybe he would have changed. Anyway, once he saw I was determined to play something, even if it was just a plastic harmonica from McCrory's, he got me a small guitar and taught me the chords and a couple of ladylike strums. I was about ten. He'd lean around me, putting my fingers down—hard!—on the guitar strings. G major. C major. "My—*wife* and I lived *all* alone in a —*little* brown jug we —*called* our own. . . ." Oh sing it, sister! "That's my *girl*," he'd say. *"That's* the way! Good. Good! Hot damn, I think we got us a natural, Mama."

I think music was in my heart from early on because he was in my heart. He didn't have but about a half an hour a week to focus in on me, but when he did, I was the only thing on his mind. He'd come scratching up the gravel some weekday afternoon and in the door, yelling, "Get that guitar, Carrie Marie—let's you and me go off and jam a little." As if jamming with me was the thing he'd driven back eighty miles an hour for, and who's to say it wasn't? Oh, there was a load of heartache for all of us in being related to Daddy, but when he was there he was *all* there. I could understand why my mother fell for him, and stayed for him, and never could harden herself to kick him out, and never fell for another once he was gone. I'm sure when she got her half hour, it was even better than mine.

And if you woke some night, in that yellow concrete block house set down in the middle of a ten-acre cow pasture (given to Mama by my Grandpa Shorter, because after a year or two he saw she'd married a man who'd never be able to put a roof over her head), if you woke up in your ten-by-ten bedroom and heard music floating in the window, sweet and sort of drenched with sorrow, like that old Florida darkness, if you heard the lonely, deepgut, slow, lowdown sound of the tenor sax—and then, if you got out of bed and looked out the window and saw your daddy, who should have been playing at the Vanguard in New York City, sitting on top of a damned picnic table facing a drainage ditch that ran through, his tall skinny lonely back to you, if you heard what he was playing, "You Don't Know What Love Is," and how he was playing it . . . well, you'd know the meaning of the blues.

In the middle of a central Florida cow pasture and rattlesnake refuge. What a waste. In the middle of a county that thought jazz was what they played on WHEZ. Oh, my daddy was not easy listening.

I never blamed him for being mostly gone. I was grateful and flattered that he bothered to come back at all.

He put the Dave Mullins Trio together in the last couple of years of his life—he found Ned Agee, a bass player, right there in Tampa and Eugene Osborne in Gainesville, and they got the gig at Dutch's. It was just a place to play while they worked out their sound. I think they had a real shot. It could have happened. Dutch's was on the outer loop of the jazz circuit. It's conceivable that somebody could have happened by, heard them there, signed them up for a recording contract. My father was a great unknown tenor sax player. I'm his daughter, but I know. He didn't have a clue how to promote himself. Another of our great musicians, playing for drinks and fifty bucks a night.

Dutch's always sounded like the rough end of heaven to me. Someplace that would scare you, going in, but then you wouldn't want to leave. I've been looking for that place ever since—the place where the music gets real. Oh, I wish I could have gone there just once, to hear him with the whole trio. On my sixteenth birthday he was going to sneak me in, but he didn't make it that far. So all I got to hear was Daddy, bringing it home all by himself in the middle of the night, sitting on the picnic table. And a couple of demo tapes I still have that show how good the trio was—they'd just gotten to the point where they felt confident enough to make the tapes.

I don't believe they ever got them sent out before Daddy died. If they had, maybe he wouldn't have needed to take his mind off his troubles in that motel room.

At his funeral, the Dave Mullins Trio, minus Dave Mullins, played "Dancing in the Dark." They'd never heard *that* at the Teeter-Thompson Funeral Home before—Mama told them to play whatever they thought would be appropriate, and that's what it was. It sounded good, it made me cry, but it wasn't Daddy, it was just a piano accompanied by a bass.

I CAME TO THE FIDDLE after he died, all on my own. I was working at a record store after school, to earn enough for the last five payments on the Riviera. I found a Bill Monroe album in the marked-down bin, bought it on my employee discount, and took it home. Little did I know when I put it on the turntable that I was signing up for life. It didn't even say on the album jacket who the fiddler was—you'd think that would have told me something, wouldn't you. I learned later it was Kenny Baker.

"Jerusalem Ridge" was on that record. When I listened to

it for the first time, I found out what made life worth living—the pure headlong skidding joyfulness the musicians were feeling, making that old wild sound together. It seemed sweet and courtly, the way they brought each other into the breaks and took each other out again, the way the mandolin chunked along on the close chords in back of the banjo, urging him on, buddy I know you can do it. The fiddle standing back, making little runs of pleasure and approval around the guitar.

I was fifteen, I didn't hear the brag in it, I didn't hear anybody saying what I've heard said since that time: "I tried to kill him with my fiddle. I tried to kill him dead." I didn't understand till much later that a lot of the character of bluegrass came out of the old contests, one pitted against another for a ten-dollar prize—the big-ego strut: I'll knock your damn head off with *this* lick. No, I heard the opposite, the comradeship, the fun of it. Like baby colts, rising up on their back legs for joy. I heard a way to be happy in music—rolling-around delirious—a way that wasn't Daddy's way to take my own life in my own hands, to get from one lick to the next on my own inspiration, a way to know exactly what I was doing and see no end to how it could be done.

My first fiddle came out of a pawnshop in Lakeland, all scarred up, like it had gotten accustomed to being carried around in a croker sack. The purfling looked like the bumpers on an old Chevy truck. I gave the pawnshop fifteen dollars for it, plus the last guitar Daddy ever gave me. I turned it over to them, I let it go. I figured he'd have done the same.

I took the fiddle to Mr. Millard, my glee club director, who also played violin with the Central Florida Philharmonic, as it happened. He broke the news to me that I'd about got what I paid cash money for, and the guitar was something extra I threw in. He was mad at me. He said I should have consulted him. "What in the world was your hurry?" he asked me. "Did you think somebody was going to beat you to this sorry excuse?" But he had a friend who knew how to work on the pegs so they'd hold and fit a new bridge. That cost another sixty—I think Mr. Millard told him to go easy on me. Even so, I had to mow yards for a month to put that sum together. It turned out to be a nice beginner's instrument. It could take me digging with the bow, it sounded good to me high up on the E string.

Mr. Millard told me what to do: practice scales four hours a day for the next twenty years. He lent me a decent bow and showed me how to hold it and taught me the A major scale. Then there I was, sitting on the picnic table like my daddy before me, playing to the drainage ditch, plowing my uncertain bow up and down the strings, making a dreadful, untaught noise, hearing each clean note somewhere in the center of the blob of sound that my fingers came down on. After a few weeks, Mama came out one night and said, "Honey, you're breaking my heart. Why don't you call Mr. Millard and see what he charges?" She did without so much already, I don't know what those lessons came out of. Her lunch money, probably.

I was an eager student, I had a good strong flexible right arm and wrist and strong left fingers from playing the guitar, and I could trust myself to hear when I wasn't on the money with every note. I worked on up the higher scales like a mountain climber, one octave, then three, then arpeggios, staccato and legato, all the different bowings. I practiced my Kreutzer for Mr. Millard, but when I was done, I'd go off and try to play like Kenny Baker and Chubby Wise and Vassar Clements, for myself. I'd try to find the old 45's so I could slow them down to 33 1/3 and hear the notes. I was at it three, four hours every evening, till I fell across the bed, exhausted. I never did any homework—I don't know why they let me graduate. History, geometry, what are *they*?

At the graduation banquet, I was part of the entertainment—I played and sang for them, a sweet rendition of "Sorrow in the Wind," like I might miss one or two of them when I was gone. I already had the car packed up, the oil changed, and the tires rotated, good for another ten thousand miles. I figured that would be about far enough. Everybody clapped for more, so I came back and gave them a lowdown, growly girl version of "Salty Dog," then cut loose with the wildest fiddle playing at my command, mainly bluff and bluesy slurs, but they couldn't tell the difference and neither could I, back then. I thought I had some chops. They whistled and stomped, so I ended up with that great Hank Williams tune "That's All She Wrote—I Sent Your Saddle Home."

The next day, I was on the road to Lexington.

Three

Those years in Lexington, before Molly was born, I worked my day job, took fiddle lessons, practiced, played around Lexington with one patched-together group, then another, looking for my chance. I lived on the strung-out, hardscrabble edge of survival for a long time. I couldn't let down for a minute—maybe a pizza on the weekend if I had a coupon. The reason I wear my hair long and sort of unruly is I never could afford to get it seen to, and by the time I could, I'd gotten used to myself this way.

Sometimes my friend Martha would go with me to the Salvation Army and we'd stuff ourselves into their three-by-three dressing room with about forty items apiece and ten bucks between us, putting a look together. They hated to see us walk in the door.

After a year or so in Lexington, working as a waitress, putting something aside out of my tips, when it looked to me like I was thinking about staying, I used my little savings to go to Lexington Community College. I was working full-time and also playing most weekends—little grocery-store openings and county fairs and such—so it took me two years to get through the computer programming course. But I finished it, finally, with such flying colors that I got my picture in the paper and half a dozen job offers, just like that. I took the one at the University of Kentucky—I wanted to stay handy to the music in Lexington, and also, I thought they'd be the most flexible about letting me take time off, when and if, to pursue my opportunities as a musician. "Opportunities as a musician" was an optimistic way of putting it, back then, but you have to make your plans. I didn't want to hire on anyplace where they acted like what you did for them was what you did.

About six months later, when I felt I had the job nailed down, I started watching the ads for cheap houses. I kept an eye out for signs in yards. I was only about twenty-two, but I knew what I was up against. I knew I was going to be making my own way for a long time to come. At first the househunting was nothing but curiosity, a way to get inside places and see how the other half lived, but I got inside so many I began to feel that I'd recognize a bargain if one came my way. And then I started thinking I could pull off a deal.

I poked around for a good six months, on Sunday afternoons when I didn't have anything better to do, before I found the right property. I recognized it by the maple tree in the front yard and the room with French doors that was named "Music Room" on the old plans that the owner unrolled for me. I'd had in mind some modest frame bungalow, but what I found was a gone-to-hell two-story turn-of-the-century brick house in a neighborhood where a single woman had no business to be. The house had been cut up into three rental units, as the real estate agent called them, two upstairs and one down. The basic structure was sound, a friend in the construction trade told me, and the income I could get off the two upstairs apartments made the place possible for me to think about. That, and the owner being willing to hold the mortgage and not ask too many questions, if I didn't either.

The apartments had been rented to ignorant mean drunks who had punched holes in the Sheetrock and torn the fixtures loose from the walls and let the rain pour in the windows.

I wrote to Granddaddy Shorter and told him I didn't want to be throwing my money away on rent, that I'd rather be building up equity, a phrase I'd heard the real estate agent use. I explained, more or less, what shape the place was in, and what I thought I could do about it. It gave him a good impression of me. He told me to get a termite inspection and then loaned me ten thousand dollars for the down payment, and only asked five percent on it.

Then I commenced to work my butt off. Also the butt of Luke Rivers, a banjo-picker friend who lived in one of the units rent-free for a year or two in exchange for a fluctuating amount of labor. Luke had a good strong back and knew a little something about the essentials—wiring, roofing, plumbing. Just enough to be dangerous, some electrician later told me, but the price was right. Luke had a girlfriend he wanted to get to live with him, so we concentrated on his place first, and then moved on to the second apartment. When it was put back together, I rented it out for a couple of hundred a month to Irene Stevens, who'd had her own beauty shop in Mount Sterling, but moved to Lexington when she retired to be near her married children. Before she signed the lease, I felt it was only fair to warn her she might be hearing music late into the night. She tapped on her hearing aid, which I hadn't noticed till then, with a long French-manicured nail. "Honey, I wish it *would* get through to me a little—I like some life going on around me. If it was up to me, I'd just go on and live down at Rupp Arena." I told her I'd invite her down sometimes, to listen, or watch, or whatever. "I can hear it," she said, "if I can get up close enough to it."

Once the two upstairs apartments were occupied, I could

relax and begin to do something about my own place, down-stairs, besides getting it cleared out and doused with Lysol. I'd been sleeping during Phase One on an army cot in the kitchen, cooking on a hot plate, taking showers at the Y.

Little did I know I was on the cutting edge of historic pres-ervation. The whole neighborhood, ten years ago, was just in front of the bulldozers. That was why I got the place for a song, though nobody told *me*—the previous owner figured it was better to sell to me than to wait for the building to be condemned. Most of the houses that weren't actually boarded up and abandoned had been split up like mine into apart-ments for transients, with just a few that still had families hanging on in them, too poor to move. Then somebody got the neighborhood placed on the landmark list, and people who wanted something a little different from the south-end subdivisions started snapping up properties, putting back the gingerbread, painting four decorator colors on each house; now these houses go up in value every time one changes hands. I can't claim foresight—it was dumb luck. I was just barging ahead, as usual, buying where they'd take my money, trusting my untrustworthy hunches. It was a miracle I didn't lose Granddaddy's ten grand for him.

Fortunately, I was a girl who got a thrill out of dividing up the cash into little piles, this for telephone and electricity, this for gasoline, this for food. I liked to account for my paycheck. I had goals. I would write out the mortgage check and then one to Granddaddy Shorter first thing every month, without fail, and after that, have a look at the overall picture. I said prayers to the old boiler in the basement to last me.

I patched and sanded and painted drywall, refinished floors, retiled bathrooms. Luke took care of just about every-thing else, but lack of cash slowed us down. I couldn't carry any more debt than I already had. I kept my mind running on songs while I was pulling carpet tacks out of the nice oak floors—if I ever found a way to break into the Nashville market, I intended to be ready. I continued to play here and there around the local bluegrass circuit, on my own or with one of a series of bands held together with big ideas and wishful thinking—musicians in their early twenties have a hundred ways to wreck a plan. Anyway, if I had two gigs in a week, I could pick up another fifty, maybe even a hundred; it went straight to the building-supply store. At the University, I was getting fair wages, but my upward strivings—I had fiddle lessons to pay for too—took up just about my whole paycheck. I had to be thinking about money a lot. But, because the things I wanted were right there in front of me, making do had a nice solid feeling to it, watching for sales, buying two for one.

In addition to the upstairs apartments, I began to rent out the second bedroom of my own place, downstairs, plus kitchen privileges, sometimes, but only to somebody I knew real well. That's how Martha Wheeler came to live with me. And I began giving lessons on Saturdays to a few kids. I furnished my apartment mainly from yard sales or curb stuff. The overall effect was pretty funky, but walking in always gave me a thrill. "Mine," I'd say, like a two-year-old. I was managing to balance music and life a lot better than my daddy had, anyway.

It took me just two and a half years to pay off Grandpa Shorter's ten grand. He was tickled to death with how regular and responsible I was in my payments. "What's it going to be next, partner? That's my burying money you've got into," he said, "so make it snappy."

"You're my secret weapon, Granddaddy. I'm calling you Ace because you're my ace in the hole," I told him.

"In the hole is right," he said. "More ways than one."

The minute I paid him out, I got him to lend part of the

money right back to me, to buy the fiddle I had my heart set on, which was made very lovingly by a North Carolina luthier named Johnny Silver. "Look at it this way, Granddaddy," I said. "A lot of people spend twice as much on a car, which you'd have ten years before it rusted out on you or threw a rod. I'll have this fiddle forever."

The back was made from a piece of rock maple that had been a step at a mill for about a hundred years, and the belly out of a straight-grained spruce from high up a mountain that Johnny's father had cut down and stored away for just such a purpose years before. Everybody knows you can pick up a decent violin for a hundred bucks, if you know what you're doing. But I heard this instrument played once when I was out that way and thought that, whatever the cost, if I couldn't have it I'd die. It has a beautiful clear tone, just what I wanted, and it plays a little darker, more soulful, high up the D string, every year. I wouldn't take anything for it. In fifty years they say we'll know what it really sounds like. Somebody will. Not Johnny—he's already seventy. And probably not me, either. Whenever I'm around there, I go play it for him, to let him hear how it's coming along.

I knew what was important to me personally, music and a roof over my head, and that's what I invested in. I pushed forward, practicing every day, even if all I could put together was an hour before work in the morning. Afterwards, I'd race back home, do the laundry, throw some macaroni down me, then run off to rehearse or perform somewhere till midnight, or go hear somebody playing that I could learn something from. It was heaven, though on a tight schedule and a short leash.

I wasn't any damsel in distress back then, that's what I'm trying to show. I used my own wits and elbow grease and the wherewithal available to me to set things up so that I could spend the rest of my life making myself into a real musician. I'm bragging, I know, but it wasn't a small thing I pulled off. Starting where I started, I could right now be a thirty-one-year-old waitress, renting a room somewhere, playing my fiddle for myself, whenever I could fit it into my messy life. Or I could have found a man and hooked myself to his earning potential as so many girls before me have done—I won't say I wasn't tempted a time or two.

But I always kept my plan right in front of me. I had a realistic view of my assets. What I had going for me was a certain amount of talent, I didn't know how much yet, quick wits, bold good looks, and, for a while anyway, borrowing power up to ten grand. I figured it was only a matter of time till some established band picked me up. I'd already won prizes at a couple of old-time fiddlers' contests, up against some real pros.

And people were beginning to know my name.

THE YEAR MARTHA moved in with me—I was twenty-four, and she was about a year older—happened to be my wildest-of-the-wild period. I think now, though it didn't occur to me at the time, that I was doing my damnedest to knock the idea of Cap Dunlap out of my head.

I'd been loving him since the first time I saw him and heard him play and sing, a few months after I got to town. I was working as a waitress at Sweet's, the one bar in town that brought in a bluegrass band every once in a while. I'd been hearing about Cap Dunlap and Hawktown Road ever since I'd hit Lexington, so I was eager to hear how they sounded. The band had a following, and the bar was packed that night, though it was a bad tip night, because everybody was keyed up and concentrating on when the show started. I was ordinarily quite a snappy bar girl, racing around carrying four full steins, making change, hustling refills, squeezing between the chairs, keeping all the orders in my head. But once those boys came up on the stage and started setting up, I lost my powers of concentration.

One thing I need to make clear about myself is that, at eighteen years old, I didn't really know the meaning of *turned on.* It was an experience I'd more or less missed out on. I was too outward bound to notice anyone in Lake Grace, and I was still too worried about paying the rent to notice anyone in Lexington. So you could say a whole lifetime of noticing got unloaded on Cap Dunlap, the first moment my eyes fell on him. It truly seemed to me that I might blind myself by looking straight at him, roving that stage with his shirt cuffs turned back, kneeling to plug in a mike. Somebody spoke to him and he looked up quickly, with the spotlight falling on his smooth tight face, and grinned the kind of grin that is just short of tears. I guess you'd call it dazzling—the boy did shine. Before the first rousing chords of "Under the Double Eagle" rang out, I was—just gone. Struck to the heart and soul. And then he began to play, his face still and watchful, turned down to his hands, except when he raised it to glance at his buddies, to nod or give a little pleased, shy smile to Joyner. Or to lean in and sing, in that rich, reckless baritone. Well, I leaned against the wall, too weak-kneed to stand. I listened when I was supposed to be taking orders. I looked, because I wanted to know what hit me, and got fired for it. But it didn't matter—he looked back. At least that was my impression.

That's what Cap does, I've learned since. He looks back.

He was already divorced by then. It hadn't taken that Sheila long at all to get tired of lonely nights in the little house out on the Hawktown Road—she threw her wedding ring in Ona's pond, so I'm told. Since then, insofar as I've cared to notice, he's been dead set on not fishing it out. He's been through a pack of women. I could have been one of them, no doubt—we had our moments, over the years, here and there, but pride held me back.

So instead, I guess I was trying to lead the female version of the same life he led. The ones I liked, I liked a lot. I didn't care; if you weren't a little against the law, you couldn't play that fiddle. I'd go after men and I'd get them, but, sooner or later, I'd say, "Honey, I got to let you go." Old romance has always tended to turn stupid on me, some way, once I got in bed with it. Maybe that's what kept me on Cap's string all those years, come to think of it. Lack of follow-through.

Anyway, for more time than I like to think of—five or six years after that first night I heard him play—I kept my crush on Cap fueled up, with little to go on and nothing to show for it. He wasn't playing in Lexington as much as he once had; when he was, it was big news, especially among the ladies. By that year I'm talking about, when Martha started renting the spare room from me, I'd given up on him, I didn't see anything coming of it, but I couldn't help getting flutter-hearted when I saw him from a distance. He was still hanging out with local musicians when he was in town, and it wasn't unusual for him to show up at somebody's party, or at a jam session, or drop in at a bar where I was listening or playing. So I had my opportunities to keep looking at him, and getting him to look back.

I'd go to hear him if he was playing a festival anywhere within the range of the Riviera. I'd prowl around on the outskirts. I didn't want to be confused with those girls in tube tops waiting for him when he came off the stage. I told myself I was there to hear the band.

That was surely about fifty percent true.

I DON'T KNOW how I lived through that year of breaking loose—out dancing or playing fiddle every single night till midnight or later, getting up at six the next morning to practice, holding down a full-time job, drinking a gallon of coffee through the day to stay awake, and in my free time working my way through a good bit of tequila and my share of the eligible male population of Central Kentucky. I can hear Martha saying, *"Eligible!* For what? Parole?"

Here's what Martha and I had in common that made sharing my house with her work out. First, though we didn't meet for several years afterwards, we both came to Lexington the same year—I was straight out of high school, she'd worked as a cashier in Morehead for a year first. We were about the same age and degree of worldly-wise. Second, we each had a strong dream of what we wanted to do with our lives that gave us the energy we needed to keep going. Third, we both liked singing about as much as we liked breathing.

Martha has a beautiful, clear, sure voice. It can be as big and straight-ahead as you wish, a true bluegrass voice. Or high, slightly nasal and resonant, in that sweet Emmylou way. She comes by the old mountain music honest, she's the fast-disappearing real thing, a mountain girl who learned all the songs her mama and daddy knew, and they knew hundreds. We'd go up there to visit sometimes, in the small frame farmhouse at the head of a narrow bottom between two mountains, and Martha and Mrs. Wheeler and I would sit down on the porch steps before we ever even went into the house to put down our knapsacks, and we'd stay there all day long, visiting some and singing some, or I'd play the fiddle for them, or we'd go in and eat what Mrs. Wheeler'd fixed us for our dinner, and do the dishes and then go right back out and sing some more, until Mr. Wheeler got home from his job at the lumberyard, and then he'd sit down on the steps and sing, too, and Ardrie, Martha's kid brother, would appear from somewhere with his banjo, and on we'd go.

Martha played what I'd call a serviceable guitar—enough to accompany herself easily. But her heart was mainly in the singing, not the playing. She was born to make an audience sit up and listen. But she wouldn't perform. I've heard her sing at parties—that's how we met, singing together at somebody's house. But let there be paying customers and she froze. Once I foolishly persuaded her to come and sing with one of my flash-in-the-pan bands. She had a stomachache for two days before, and when it came time for her to sing, she shook so hard she could barely play her chords. When it was over, she said, "Not me, never again. Don't you *ever* come around again asking me to stand up and make a fool of myself."

All Martha liked about singing was *singing*. She liked winter nights when we'd both be half dead from the day we'd put in, until we got our second wind and built up the fire in the fireplace and piled up in our sweat clothes on the sofa to sing the rest of the night away. We were sort of addicts. We'd teach each other the tunes we knew and work them up. Other times, if one or two or three of our bluegrass buddies were passing through Lexington (and someone always was, bluegrass being a vagabondish way of life), why then there'd be music—we never felt we had to hold it down, since Luke, from upstairs, would be right in the middle of it with his banjo, and Mrs. Stevens, oftentimes, as well, making fudge for us in the kitchen, or if not, she'd be upstairs not hearing a thing. Then Martha would join in, gladly. Just don't say *audience* to her. She had to hide her light under a bushel, owing to nerves. To her, music was either private—behind the closed door of her room, the guitar so soft you could hardly hear it, her voice trilling quietly for itself—or it was sociable, another way of having a conversation. It wasn't ever *public*. She simply could not stand up on a stage and sing for strangers.

I didn't have that problem, myself. I was stagestruck from early on, standing in front of Mama's full-length mirror with a hairbrush for a mike, belting out "Nine-Pound Hammer" when nobody was home. Music was the main thing I had. Sharing it out, letting other people hear it, was the most I could know of happiness. Music represented the possibilities of life, for me. Also, I was a hopeless show-off.

What represented the possibilities of life for Martha was the French language. Who knows where people get their ideas, out hoeing weeds all summer in Rowan County, Kentucky? She worked at McAlpin's till she had the money for tuition and books, and could begin going to the University. It took her seven years to get her B.A. They gave her a full fellowship to get her master's degree, so she stayed on another year and did that. And then she went to Paris, where she is now, working for some American engineering firm. It ain't my idea of a dream coming true, but it's hers. She's got a nice apartment. And some money, for the first time in her life. And a Frenchman—some kind of teacher. She's bringing him over here at Christmastime for us all to meet. I can't wait to see *that* boy. His name is Alain. He's a big bluegrass fan. So I guess he can't wait to see *us*, either.

ONCE IN A WHILE, back in the days I'm talking about, Martha'd go out to a bar with me, if a band she liked was playing. "Chew 'em up and spit 'em out, Carrie," she'd say, rolling her big black eyes and picking at her beer label. "You just want their old bodies. You're as bad as they are." And we'd laugh. Then she'd take another swig and look around the River Rat or wherever we were to see if there was anybody worthwhile around. Right there was one big difference between Martha and me. She'd look around to see *if.* I'd gotten to where I wasn't so choosy. I'd look around to see *who.*

Martha wore her thick dark hair short and tidy. It brought out her wide, high cheekbones. Everything about her was tidy, which was a good antidote to me. I was trying to learn something from her about cleaning up as you go. She was the kind of girl to make her bed as she was rolling out of it, pulling the sheets up tight. I never made my bed at all. If worse came to worst, I'd sleep on a bare mattress with the spread wrapped around me—just any horizontal surface would do, a lot of the times, I was so exhausted from my life of pleasure.

Those desperate days, I did exactly what I felt like doing. And I felt like doing just about everything. Footloose and fancy, that's what Martha called me. "Sometimes you act like you don't have good sense," she said.

"Sometimes I don't have good sense," I said humbly. "Maybe I'll get some later."

"When you grow up."

"Yeah. When I grow up. The time is soon coming. . . ."

I didn't like making plans ahead—spur of the moment was my style. Love 'em and leave 'em, forget their names. Sometimes they got mad at me, but mostly they were free-range types themselves. Still, I look back and see some regular loving-hearted, cherishing, grown-up men among the numbers, men who really cared for me and treated me better than I treated them. Some would have made good partners. I liked them, I appreciated their attention and their kind souls and funny jokes, and occasionally, as Martha said, their old bodies, but I walked right over them. Regular wasn't what I wanted. I couldn't keep my mind on regular. I wanted something gorgeous and out of reach. Something exactly like Cap Dunlap.

A psychiatrist would say exactly like Daddy, don't think I don't know.

Since I couldn't have Cap, I took it out on what was handy. That's the truth about my younger days.

Four

Well, it was a phase.

Getting pregnant ended it.

I got pregnant on purpose, I suppose. I just didn't let myself in on the plan till the last possible instant. What happened was, I ran out of patience with myself at exactly the same moment I ran out of optimism about what was going to become of me, one night at a party that Cap passed through like our own bright meteor.

He gave me a little generic hug—put an arm around me, sideways, and pulled my left shoulder toward his chest. "Well, hey, Carrie," he said. "Some of us are going over to Denny's later and jam some. Why don't you come along?"

I smiled and said, "Yeah, maybe I will. Thanks." I looked straight into his love-for-all-humankind smile and thought, *You're looking at a true dead end, sister.* This wasn't the moment I'm talking about yet, though. So far, nothing new. I'd seen this far into my situation a hundred times before.

I don't know if he was even remotely aware of how much I'd always appreciated every little move he made—he had so many women reaching out and grabbing at him that I doubt he would have noticed a bashful, polite, silent crush such as mine, especially since in most other ways I was what they call outgoing. If anyone had asked us, we would both have said we were some kind of friends, that we'd been knowing each other for a long time, jamming together once in a while at parties or back among the RVs at festivals, in the early days. I'd had my little chances, but I never took them. With Cap, it's not a question of refusing to go out with him. It's more refusing to ask him to go out with *you*. He's not one to run after the ladies. He never learned how, since from the time he was about twelve and a half, I reckon, they were running after *him*.

By then, I knew that Cap had a house out on the Hawktown Road in Oxford County—everybody knew that—and that he stayed out there as much as he could between road trips. And that he didn't take women out there. The common wisdom was that that's what his apartment in town was for— well, not so much for taking them to as for giving them a place where they could *find* him. When he was out on the farm, he kept himself to himself. That made him know what to do, back in the world. And, oh, he did it. Life of service to others, to a certain point. His way of being has always attracted people. Especially women—women who sense they can get something they need from him. Something they need for their lives. And what can a bighearted boy do?

At first glance, Cap looks like a fellow who's never met a stranger. He's America's sweetheart, a pleasant grin under a cowboy hat and an autograph for all who ask at the record table, a few helpful hints for the pickers who seek him out. But just beyond that grin is a boundary, a mountain range, and on the other side of that, a world cut out for only one. A certain type of woman wants to find a way in, a pass. The more she doesn't find it, the better she thinks the place it leads to will be when she *does* find it. She's looking for a place to call home. What she gets, instead, is high mountain scenery, then back down the same way she came up. With a nice-mannered escort to show her the way.

I knew all that. I did not want to be such a woman. But I was helplessly interested, anyway.

That particular night, I dared myself to give it one serious, honest-to-God try. To give both of us a chance to get real. I distracted myself for a half an hour or so with my everyday pals and a couple of glasses of mountain white. Then I ambled into the dining room, honed to a sharp edge. Cap was at the back of the dark room, literally cornered, a young, plumpish, gentle-looking blond girl leaning toward him, both her hands cupped around a beer can, as though offering it up to him, some kind of holy chalice. He smiled over her head at me, just a faint, brief, serious kind of smile, and almost invisibly lifted his shoulders. That was the moment, right there, that shrug, like, "You're looking at my life, girl." I don't know. My own life, for all its jigs and its hornpipes, seemed suddenly like a small room with no air in it. I think I might actually have gasped. I know I turned and headed for the door, propelled by an absolutely physical need to break out, to change my life. To have a crush on something that knew I existed, for a change. I didn't know what I meant, exactly, only that I felt determined and dangerous. I see, looking back, that I must have meant a baby.

And on the stoop, I ran straight into a sturdy, fair-haired stranger in rimless glasses. His face cracked into a wide, delighted grin as he righted me.

I said, "Oh, sorry. I didn't see you—where'd you *come* from?"

"Georgia," he said promptly.

"Oh!"

"I'm just passing through," he explained.

"Oh," I said again, cocking my head, holding his gaze. I grinned, then, myself. *"Well* then."

I nabbed him. I chose him for his good humor and his genes. He claimed some kind of kin with old Fiddlin' John Carson. He was a fine-looking boy in a rough, cheerful way, and he liked to have a good time. We had a merry forty-eight hours together, but I wouldn't like to have pushed it. He was headed for Colorado, "I don't see why you don't just come along and drive it with me," he said, looking down at me, jiggling my elbows encouragingly. "We could go to all the honky-tonks between here and there, and camp out under the stars. Don't tell me it wouldn't be fun."

I laughed out loud, and he did, too, then. "I wouldn't dream of telling you it wouldn't be fun," I said, giving him a great big hug.

"Well, then you better come on and go with me."

Maybe if I had, things would have turned out better.

But I didn't. "I'd love to," I told him. My sincere sad eyes. "You know I would. But there's no way I can get off work right now." (Actually I had ten sick days piled up.) (But it turned out I'd need them, in the next couple of months.) "We're running behind on a big project right now."

That made two lies that I told him in the time I was with him.

So he went on his way. He said he'd drop me a line, but I knew he wasn't the long-distance type.

When the time came, I took the blue test. Afterwards, I kept my arms folded over my stomach, hugging my secret future to myself, for a couple of weeks more, until one of the rare evenings when Martha and I were in the kitchen at the same time. She was fixing her favorite, frozen broccoli cooked in some kind of Cheez Whiz sauce—the people in Paris would love *that.* I was feeling none too happy about it myself.

"Want some?" she asked generously.

I shook my head, trying to concentrate on my Cream of Wheat. Then I said, "Would you stir this for me for a minute, Martha?" And, head lowered, walking fast and light on my bare feet, I went down the hall to the bathroom to throw up as quietly as possible. When I came back, Martha looked across the room at me, alert as a bird dog, then let her thoughtful gaze drift down to my belly.

I put my hand on it, smoothed it, as if comforting it.

"You're kidding," she said.

"It's a planned pregnancy," I said brightly.

"When did you plan it?" she came back in a pleasant tone of voice. "Just before or during?"

Old Martha. She could really cut through to the heart of an issue. I guess I'd been carrying the notion of a baby around for quite a while, because about two weeks before the actual conception, I'd gone to the head of my division and asked her about the possibility of my going on three-quarters time, say eight to half-past one, without a lunch break. And she'd told me we could probably work something out, if that's what I really wanted. I told her to let me think about it.

Now I gave Martha a hurt look and didn't reply. I carefully stirred some brown sugar into the Cream of Wheat and took it into the music room, to get away from the broccoli. I slid down on the couch with my feet on the hassock and the nice warm pot on my belly.

Martha came in behind me, sat on the arm of the other end of the sofa, playing with a dish towel, staring at me. I didn't look back. Finally she asked: "Does the man know, Carrie?"

"No. I told him it was an okay time." I spooned up some of the Cream of Wheat and stuck it in my mouth, out of embarrassment. I swallowed with difficulty. "It was okay for me," I added, glancing at her.

She slid her eyes upward. Then she opened her mouth—to ask who he was, I figured—but thought better of it, in case I couldn't answer that question. She twisted the dish towel and looked worried instead.

"It's nobody you know," I volunteered. "Nobody *I* know, when you get right down to it. He was just a nice feller, passing through."

"Carrie! You did it with somebody who was just passing *through?*"

"His papers were all in order, Captain."

"It was that big toothy blond guy from Georgia, wasn't it. Dudley or Duncan or something like that."

I gave a modest little shrug and tried to stir the Cream of Wheat around. It was stiff enough now to cut in slabs and fry. I set the pot on the floor and clasped my hands in my lap.

"Carrie, honey, listen," she said, reaching over and shaking my shoulder. "You're crazy."

"I've got it worked out," I said, hoping to make her understand. "I think I can manage. I really do." I explained about my plan to work three-quarters time. "I can keep my health insurance. And I have the two rents, and yours. I'll give more lessons—that's something I can do at home. I think I can hire Mrs. Stevens to baby-sit while I'm at work. And maybe sometimes at night? If I had someplace to play? If you weren't doing anything, you could baby-sit and we'd take it off your rent."

"That's me, honey. Born to baby-sit."

"Or I'll work it out some other way," I said hastily. "I'll do what I have to do. I'm positive I can handle it."

"Oh, you're always positive you can handle everything! Do you have any idea at all how much space a little child wants to take up? It's a big job, Carrie, if you mean to do it right."

"Lots of people that have *way* less going for them than I do manage to put it together."

"But look how they *live* and what kind of lives their kids have, parked in front of the TV or who knows what, these days." She scraped her fingers up through her black hair, dramatically. "Between your job and your music, what will you have to offer a child? About three hours a day? You can't raise a child on three hours a day!" I had turned to face her. I listened to her carefully, studying her narrow face, her huge black eyes, her worried forehead. "How far along are you, anyway?"

"Seven weeks."

She touched her soft lips together cautiously and glanced at me. "Uh huh." I spread my hands over my stomach and waited for her to work through her thought processes, which took a minute or two. "Listen, Carrie—give it two more years. Things may be a whole lot clearer by then. About—you know. Everything. I believe I know why you're doing this. And it doesn't make any sense. At all." When she said this, my blood flooded up to my face. Martha was always the soul of tact—Cap's name never passed her lips. "If you thought your life was a mess before, just wait till this baby's sick all night and you have to get up anyway and get to work at eight. Wait till you don't have time to practice because it's cutting teeth."

"I'm going to have this child, Martha." I remember the way these words resounded in the silence, how extreme and peculiar they sounded, even to me. "My mind's made up."

"I feel like crying," she said then. Her eyes in fact filled with tears.

"Me too," I said. "I'm crying for joy. I think this is going to be good. What are you crying for?"

"For *you,* you headstrong girl. Everything was just lining

up right for you. You're so good and you've worked so damn hard to get where you are now, and you're just about ready to make your big move, and now you're going to screw everything up."

"I've got it all figured out," I told her again.

"The hell you do. You haven't got one blessed thing figured out," she said, punching my arm, not all that playfully.

I gave with the punch and rubbed my arm. "So—you're telling me you don't want to be its auntie?"

"Oh, I'll *be* its friggin' auntie." She stood up, wiping her eyes. "I ought to just let you get on any way you can. But I'll pitch in. Only keep in mind, if this kid turns out to be a wailer, I'm *gone*. I'm serious, Carrie. I have to be able to do my studies."

PREGNANCY TURNED OUT to be a lot like an awful disease, at least the first trimester did; I threw up at six o'clock every morning, then went about my business. If I was lucky I'd only be sick a couple more times that day before I fell in bed at nine, exhausted. "Well, you wanted to change," I told myself. "So now you're changing." My Upheaval, I wittily called it, just before another wave of nausea caught up with me. As if to say: *Wipe that smile off your face. This is serious. Pay attention.* I had my nights of lying on my back, terrified, staring into the dark, feeling my aloneness settle densely in my belly. But the next day I'd pull myself together around my favorite saying—*Oh well, it will probably be all right.*

And then, in fact, after the third month, it did seem all right. My changing self took my mind off my problems, that high, tight, blue-veined fullness of life, the thumps and bumps that showed that what I was full of was full of itself. And I began to feel ready for it, ready to move on, into whatever the future held. I loved the word *quickened.* The baby I carried was taken by life and I was taken by its life inside me. I stayed home nights, practicing, feeling heavier and heavier in my straight-backed chair, as the winter months went by. I wasn't even scared. By then I felt calm, concentrated, right as rain.

Before that, sometime during the summer, I went down to Florida to break the news to Mama. She was surprisingly calm about it—in her experience, there were worse things than being a single mother.

Granddaddy Shorter was another matter, though. He turned his back on me, wouldn't talk to me when I went to see him—he'd gotten the news from Mama by then. He just told me through the screen door that I was his greatest disappointment. I wasn't far enough gone that anybody could tell who didn't know, but he told me I was an abomination to his eyesight. "Come down here parading around like you're proud of yourself."

"I'm not parading around and I'm not proud of myself. But I'm not ashamed of myself, either."

"I'm ashamed enough for the both of us," he said.

"I'm sorry you feel that way," I told him, in such a self-righteous voice I'm surprised he didn't keel over right then, from sheer irritation. "This child could use some kind of daddy, even a great-granddaddy."

"The child's *got* a daddy, I reckon," he told me. "If the world still runs like it used to. You go speak to him about it. If you know who it is."

Mama tried to patch it up, but he just accused her of marrying way beneath her and raising me wrong. He sent my checks for the fiddle back, after that—I still sent one, every month, and every month he'd return it, in its unopened envelope, inside a new one, addressed to "Miss or Mrs. Carrie

Marie Mullins" in his old-fashioned scrawl.

Granddaddy Shorter died in the April after Molly was born in January. I'm afraid I speeded him on his way. In his will, he forgave the loan he'd made me for the fiddle. But he never forgave *me*. I thought he'd prefer for me and Molly not to abominate his funeral, but on the day of it, I had a date set up to play for Art à la Carte. I dedicated "On Heaven's Bright Shore" to him and hoped the words were true.

When people ask me how I came by such a fine instrument, I tell them my granddaddy gave it to me.

AFTER I GOT too pregnant to play in public anymore, it happened, in a gradual sort of way, that some women I knew took to getting together to play music once in a while, in the evenings, at my place. Ordinarily I wouldn't have had the time.

At first, we were just trying to have a little bright spot in our overburdened lives, a way to goof off. One would bring her mandolin and one would bring her guitar and one would bring her kids or her beeper or her envelopes to address, five bucks a hundred. We'd trade songs and have a beer or a diet-something and sit around telling stories and laughing our heads off and bouncing kids up and down on our knees. Some were friends of Martha's and some were friends of mine. It was a fluctuating bunch, as many as a dozen, but finally down to Stony on bass, Jess on a pretty basic rhythm guitar, Kathy on mandolin, and me on fiddle. Other people came and went, but we were the core. Martha'd sing with us, when she wasn't at work or at school—or bring in her guitar to help Jess out, teach her what she knew.

What we mainly had in common was a love of the old mountain music and nothing better to do. I was the only more or less professional-level musician among us, but it didn't matter to me. Sometimes you come to a period in life when there's something to be said for performing beneath your level. I could work it into my life. I could take the whole deal for granted. It wasn't serious—it was just fun, in a strictly temporary, undemanding sort of way.

Martha was there when I went into labor, timing contractions at three a.m., saying, "You've done it now, buddy honey." Martha was the one who got me to the hospital in her ancient VW Bug and stayed with me as long as they let her and called Mama and said, "It's a girl." Martha was the one who set up the crib and the bathinette and put bunny decals on the white chest of drawers that we filled with blankets and layettes and buntings. She was the one who brought me a pot of forced hyacinths and Molly a nice little stuffed raccoon we named Rackity, the one who took us home through a snowstorm to pink balloons.

Then there I was, with my baby girl. I'd nurse her, I'd rock her till she fell asleep. I'd lie on the sofa, wanting nothing else, holding her against me, feeling fixed to the center of the earth by her small warm weight, compact but buoyant, on my breast, my one hand cupped under the swell of her perfect skull, a fragile, fragile globe containing all her possibilities, my other hand memorizing, as the snow fell, as the bare branches thrashed against the storm windows, her tiny complicated wrist, her curly long pink fingers, her soft earlobe, each particular miracle of her actuality.

I didn't have a thought in my head, just a full, accomplished peacefulness all through me. For the first time in my life, I wanted nothing. I wanted exactly what I had. If I never moved off that sofa, it would have been okay with me. I'd turn off the lamp and leave the blinds open so that the last of the blue winter light would come back, after it seemed to be gone. Sometimes, there with her on my chest, I'd sing myself and her to sleep—*Come and go come and go, Molly Snow,* my voice rising softly and questioningly through the notes like a moth going up through leaves.

When I put her down, it was only to pick up my fiddle. During that time, milk and music formed our whole world, Molly's and mine, day after snowed-in day. She seemed about as tuned in to the one as to the other, right from the start. If you sang a sad song to her—"Go Tell Auntie Rhodie" or "Over the Sea to Skye"—she'd get tears in her eyes. I'd never heard of such a thing. From when she was newborn, from when she could fit into the crook of my arm. Lie there with tears pooling up in her other-world eyes, as if the music made her remember her old home. Her eyes had no particular color you could name, at first—they were the color of a lake in Florida when the sun's coming up. Later they turned a deep definite blue, with black around the edges. Irish blue, dangerous blue. If she was crying and I played my fiddle, she'd stop crying to listen, with her eyes fixed on me, as though she remembered me from before. As though she were seeing me through some puzzling new element, but recognized me all the same. Then, when the music stopped, she'd start crying again. Did you ever hear of anything like that?

I had no doubts, no thoughts, no wants, those first months. I was living in a dream. With a baby and a fiddle and two months of snow.

Stony and Jess and Kathy would bust in on Tuesday and Friday evenings, then disappear just as suddenly, taking their jokes and big hair and five little kids in parkas and boots and their instruments and book bags and what was left of their six-packs with them. And peace and quiet would float back in like sea fog. Martha would come and go in her orderly, purposeful way, but Molly and I would be there alone a lot of the time. I barely stuck my nose out the door. Each day seemed like a complete universe, its weather separate and permanent.

I'd settle into it as if it were my new home, with my small hearthside companion.

But February passed and my charmed life came to an end. I entered the uncharmed life of the working mother. I had my Salvation Army wardrobe down to about a half a dozen outfits, any of which I could throw on in five minutes. At ten to eight, I'd take Molly upstairs and give her to Mrs. Stevens, leave her the bottles I'd pumped the night before, and then get myself to work, where I'd put in my six and a half hours. Afterwards, I'd run by the grocery, get back home by two. Sometimes Mrs. Stevens made me a sandwich and we'd eat lunch together in her philodendron-entwined kitchen. Then I'd carry Molly downstairs and nurse her and play with her. When she dropped off to sleep, I'd put her down and reach for my fiddle.

I worried a little that my interests were getting too narrow. I was wholly absorbed—I guess every mother is—by my baby's fits of brilliant vigorous kicking, her drooly grins, the fistfuls of air she'd grab hold of and bring down to her mouth, the serious round careful sounds she made, eyebrows lifted.

"I think she's singing," Martha said.

Her first word was *Mama*. She called everybody Mama. She had three, counting Mrs. Stevens, six, counting Jess and Stony and Kathy. And five brothers and sisters under the age of six, all wanting to hug her, tug her, nuzzle her belly. "Now y'all be sweet," Jess would croon. "Be sweet, nothing, you wild children," I'd yell. "Back off! You're going to cut off her *oxygen*." I don't know how she lived through all the pushing and pulling. She'd just lie there curling her fingers and toes, bright-eyed, eager as a puppy. By the time she could crawl, she was wanting whatever *they* had—popsicles, crayons, gumbies. Wanting to be in the middle of things.

All she didn't have was a daddy. The only men in her life,

her first ten months, were Luke, who'd pop in some nights on his way up to his own apartment, and Ardrie, who'd followed Martha to Lexington and now lived down the block.

Those were the only men in *my* life, also, come to think of it, except the guys I worked with. I can't say I didn't get a lust attack every once in a while, but it was more or less without an object. I guess I thought there'd be time for all that again later. The last man I'd what you could call *noticed* was Molly's father.

I rarely laid eyes on Cap—except that when he was playing a nearby festival, I'd go listen from far back among the lawn chairs. He was in D.C. a lot of the time—that's what I heard. What I'd wanted to happen had happened: I'd changed. I moved around now with an untroubled mind. I had no time for what I'd formerly called a social life, meaning whatever I ran into at the River Rat. My wild times appeared to be over, and who cared? My wild times had been a nervous habit.

The only thing I actively missed was playing for an audience—I had my job, I had my baby, I had my arrangements.

I had my all-girl band.

"Well, to me that sounded hot," said Kathy. "Maybe I don't know anything, but if I was at some festival and heard that number, I'd say, now what's the *name* of that band?"

"What *is* the name of this band?" Stony asked.

"Sad to say, it doesn't have a name," Jess said. "It doesn't have a name because it's not a band. It's got a long row to hoe, a very long row, chums, before it can have a *name.*"

"Well, what do you all say?" Stony said. "What do *you* say, Carrie? Are we any good at all?" She laughed, but went on, "Couldn't we make ourselves good enough?"

"I don't know," I said, wanting to be honest. "It depends on whether you all have time to practice about a hundred hours a week. Maybe not a hundred. But a lot. If you put a name on us, it means you want to get up in front of people."

"Maybe if we gave ourselves a name, we'd take ourselves serious," Stony said, creasing her earnest brow.

"Yeah, we'd think we existed," said Kathy.

Ardrie happened to be there, seeing what we had in our re-frigerator. "Name yourself after my mama," he yelled in from the kitchen. "She taught Carrie all those songs you're singing, anyway."

"That's the truth," I said.

"Mrs. Wheeler's Dealers?" Kathy suggested.

"Or something about Pearl. That's her first name," I said.

"Hey, Pearl's Girls!" said Stony.

Pearl's Girls suited me fine. It was going to be a year *at least* before I'd be at all of a mind to try again for fast-lane bluegrass. I had a baby to raise. I figured if I could help them lift up their level while I maintained my own, there'd be no harm in it. It might work out for all of us. I thought, well, why not see what might come of a band of girls like ourselves, with all this enthusiasm and interest in bluegrass music and real good voices. "But I want this to be a hard-driving blue-grass band. I want a hard, traditional sound," I said. "If we can't find a good banjo player, we might as well hang it up. I'll ask Dinah Potter if she'll come sit in with us. She's be-tween bands, I know. If she'd play with us, I believe we'd have us a sound."

So there were two of us that could step up to the mike and knock their hats in the creek. Stony and Kathy and Jess could play backup, till they were ready to go after it.

I don't know, maybe we were just kidding ourselves. We were all trying to fit the idea of a band in around the rough edges of our lives. Stony practiced so hard through the spring, learning chords and rhythm patterns on the bass, that she kept a blister on her thumb. Kathy had real talent on the mandolin, and you could begin to see it, after three or four months. I gave Jess my guitar-playing videotape, and she practiced whenever she could, but it wasn't all that much, between her kids and her day-care babies.

I wish we could have had Martha to sing and play with us. But forget it—even if she hadn't been scared, she was all taken up with this French business. French movies, French magazines, French-speaking exchange students for friends. All her energy went into those papers she was always writing on Rousseau or whatever. She'd read them aloud to me. They'd make my eyes cross.

Sometimes Jess and Kathy sang duets; sometimes I made it a trio. Mostly, we could just improvise the harmony.

I still remember the first songs we worked up: "Tom Bigbee's Waltz" and "Sim's Boogie," "Angelina Baker" and "Old Joe Clark," "Limerock," "Grey Eagle," "Hold What You Got," and "Why Did You Wander."

"You start seeing if you can't get us a date somewhere, Carrie," Kathy said, along about June of that year. "I believe we're about ready to play at somebody's wedding reception."

"If the guests get into the champagne good before we show up," Dinah said. Dinah was a rangy girl with a big laugh that actually went yuk yuk yuk.

Dinah and I worked out the arrangements and chose the tunes. I was the one with the connections to the local bluegrass scene, so I was supposed to get us bookings. By accident, sometime that summer, we were booked into a club in Richmond, when some other band canceled at the last minute. It was murder just to get all five of us there each night; we didn't have the time we needed to get ready—we had to put our faith in our close harmonies and cute looks. Ardrie babysat for us; he made as much per hour as the whole band made playing, so it was hard to see how this was going to turn into a money-making proposition. But it was a good dress rehearsal, and showed us how far we still had to go.

We were unruly girls, all five of us. Half of the reason for the band was to have something to laugh about and somebody to laugh with. We had to tamp down our natural high spirits to get down to business, so I don't know what kind of a future we had. By the time we'd been playing together for six months, we were a lot better than when we'd started out. We'd stuck together, which is more than you could say for many a band I'd played with by then.

That fall we started playing, every chance we got, around town, and when we did, sometimes people would listen to us and come up afterwards and wish us good luck. We didn't know how to take that.

In November, we worked a few nights at the club where I had gotten fired for listening to Cap when I first came to town. And on the last night of this run, in the middle of our last set, who do you suppose turned up in the door? I'd thought Cap was still in Washington, insofar as I'd thought about him at all. But I saw him the minute he came in, and my heart leapt up. I was amazed to find my radar still set on him. I told myself, well, old habits die hard.

He got himself settled at a table at the back, by himself, turned his chair around, and leaned his arms on the top of it. He had on a baby-blue cable-knit sweater, I remember, with the sleeves pushed up. His hair—which had grown long since last I saw him—was caught at the nape of his neck in a pony-tail. The waitress brought him a Corona; he upended it and took a swallow, then held it in front of him while he listened.

Listened to me. I played right to him, for him, around him, what else could I do? When it was time for my solo, I chose the song I'd just written, with its lovely minor change, called "Birds Sing After the Rain." I sang it in the low, suggesting voice I'd just discovered was within my range of possibilities. When Jess and Kathy came in, one then the other, then all three of us on the chorus, it brought tears to my eyes. There's no music that gets to me like my own.

We went on then to our set pieces, a nice version of "Cumberland Gap," "In the Hills of Shiloh," and a couple of old jigs. And he never took his eyes off me, I swear. Be still my heart, as Mama used to say. I thought it was love at hundred-and-first sight. I thought he was looking back this time for keeps, I thought he'd changed, too, in the year and a half since I'd last spoken to him. I thought he'd done made up his mind, that's how he looked.

And it was true. He'd made up his mind about a fiddler for his band. Stony, who was usually too shy to talk onstage, wandered over to the mike, as if I'd paid her ten bucks to do it, as if she knew exactly what was going on, and said, in her husky voice, "We're going to close out the evening with a tune called 'Lowdown Hoedown Showdown,' written by our own great fiddler Carrie Marie Mullins."

It was a real nice impulse, but I could have strangled her for calling me a great fiddler, which was a laugh—and also for picking that tune. I'd written it as a crowd-pleaser, a sort of parody of "Dueling Banjos," full of cheap tricks and showy licks, but I saw it on through, trying to make an honest woman of myself with every little bit of my technique, and Dinah answered me brag for brag on the banjo, grinning the whole time, throwing her hair around. There was a lot of applause and shouting afterwards. We brought down the house, such as it was. It's a good thing I didn't know anything was riding on it then. I couldn't have stood the tackiness.

At the end of the set, I saw Cap threading through the tables toward me, and felt my knees get weak, just as they had eight years before, when I was a baby girl that didn't know anything, and I said to myself, "Oh damn it, Carrie." I really had counted on being beyond such foolishness. I really had thought I would be safe now.

I had never wanted to be the next item on his life list. I'd always had my defenses up, whenever I was around him—I had never liked feeling defenseless. And now, especially, when I'd gone to such a lot of trouble to rescue myself, to get my life rolling past him—I was damned if I was going to make a fool of myself, even to myself.

"I heard you'd had a baby," he said, taking me by the shoulder and looking at me as if he didn't believe it but just the idea by itself was enough to make him laugh out loud.

"Don't laugh," I said, laughing too. "It's the truth."

"I didn't even know you were pregnant."

"You're the *only* one who didn't know. It's been a regular little scandal. Name that dad."

"Don't look at me—I've been in D.C." I didn't tell him that, in point of fact, the last time I'd talked to him was the very night I'd gotten pregnant—either that night or the next.

"I'll look at you if I want to, darlin'. But if you were a serious candidate, I'm sure I'd remember."

"I can't believe it," he said then. "I missed the whole show."

"Don't feel bad—if you were going to miss something, that was what to miss." We smiled at each other in an old-friends way. I felt real good about the even keel I was keeping myself on. "Her name's Molly Snow Mullins," I volunteered. "She's ten months old now." He studied me for a long, serious, tender moment, rubbing his chin with his knuckle. Looking back, I believe he was just calculating whether I'd be able to play the dates they had in front of them. "She's wonderful," I added shyly.

"Where is she now?" he asked, in an interested, light voice, rocking up on his toes and looking around as if I might be carrying her in my fiddle case. And I *might* have been, except that I didn't want her around all that cigarette smoke.

"At home asleep, of course. I've got an arrangement—if Martha can't stay with Molly, her little brother fills in."

"How's Martha?"

"Martha's terrific."

He shook his head and came back around. "It's hard to take in, Care—I thought you was the wild woman of bluegrass music. What you doing with a baby?"

"Just living." I was looking into Cap's turquoise-blue eyes, sort of swaying in his direction in spite of myself. "Living and breathing."

He nodded. "Well. Congratulations."

"Thanks."

He put his hands on his hips then and looked casually behind himself to see if anybody was in earshot. Then he said in a low voice, "This band can't play with you, Carrie."

I felt an actual pang, that he should say something so cold about my buddies. "I think we do pretty good," I said. "Dinah can flat bang a tune out of a banjo. I think we can make something out of us—it's just hard to get the time to practice. They know a lot about bluegrass."

"Knowing bluegrass and playing it, that's two different propositions." Said with a smile, shy and tender, breaking the news.

I had to blink to keep the tears from springing to my eyes. "Did you come over here especially to put us down?" I asked. I gave him back that smile, with a little spin on it.

"No. I came over here especially to listen to you—I mean, to *you*. See if you're sounding as good as people say you are."

"And, well?" I said, hard-edged and wary now, torn between the praise of me and the insult to my friends. *This man's just teasing you along,* I warned myself. *Cutting you out of the herd.*

"I'd say you're coming along pretty decent."

"Thanks." *Who needs it,* I asked myself, suddenly just real tired, ready to get on home. Some man, I don't care what color his eyes are, coming along passing judgment, giving you an update from Mount Olympus on how you're doing, wanting you to lick his hand in exchange for a word of encouragement. *Well, good then,* I told myself. *This time he'll be easy to forget.* I turned away to stow my fiddle in its case, feeling like I was putting my*self* in there, kneeling, snapping down the clasps.

Knowing what I know now, I wish that that had been the way our conversation turned out. "Thanks," and me picking up my fiddle case and walking out the door, leaving him standing there. If I could pick out one moment and unravel my life back to it, if I could say, "I will do it again from right here," that would be the moment I'd pick. Out the door and into the night, by myself. I would have gone on to whatever the future held in store for me and Molly that didn't have Cap Dunlap and Hawktown Road written all over it.

Instead, Cap stood behind me and said, "So what I'm wondering is, would you like to come sit in with Hawktown for a few weeks? Andy's going to be in Nashville."

My heart banged. I looked back over my shoulder at him. "With Hawktown? Are you kidding?"

"No."

"With *Hawktown?*"

He nodded, shrugging modestly.

"Well, of course I would." Then I thought I'd better re-mind him—"But, hey, I'm a girl."

"I was figuring that in," he said, finally letting the full power of that world-famous Dunlap grin loose on me.

I had that chance, and I took it. When I told Martha, she said, "Here we go." When I told the band, they were surprised and excited for me, but we all thought it would just be for a couple of weeks. Nobody could believe that Hawktown would let a woman sit in with them.

Andy had gone off to Nashville to play behind Jez Jordan. I'd noticed that he was getting into some fairly uptown progressions in the past year, and I'd known, just from hear-ing him, that sooner or later he'd be gone. It was a big blow to Cap, I know—he and Andy go way back, practically to the start of Hawktown, and they were like brothers. Andy told them he was leaving on Tuesday, and he was gone on Wednesday. Hawktown had a booking the following week-end at a local club, a couple more dates after that, and then a big festival in the Florida Panhandle.

I was the handiest thing around to plug up the hole left by Andy when he went off to plug up the hole left by somebody else. These hell-prone fiddlers, they'll leave you in the lurch. They're every one of them a losing proposition. Somewhere in the world at this very minute, some fiddler has cut out on some band. And some other fiddler, like Carrie Marie Mul-lins, is getting her big chance because of it.

Five

The next day found me on the Hawktown Road itself, headed for Cap's house, to practice.

It had happened so fast that a merciful dreamlike state had set in. I was so far out the other side of thrilled that I'd bent back around to regular. Perfectly willing, perfectly open, stepping over all my modest hopes and dreams into *whatever comes next.* Once in a while, life moves out ahead of your imagination and leaves you following behind without a thought in your head. Stunned, I guess you'd call it.

I left Molly with Martha, feeling as though I were starting out on a long ocean voyage. Martha held her up at the front window, moving her arm up and down to wave me goodbye, both of them smiling. It was a bitter late-November afternoon, the dark clouds sailing south out of some cold city already knee-deep in dirty snow. I got in my car, turned on my headlights, and headed north on the Newtown Pike. I didn't know what the future held now. But I was driving toward it, and I guess I knew it, down there somewhere, as you do sometimes.

I had the directions written on the back of a napkin, from the night before, for getting to Cap's place—left off 62, right off Double Culvert, bear right at Mount Hope Church onto

the Hawktown Road. Two miles past the bridge, third drive
on left. I could have made a few bucks selling those directions—the address he doesn't give out, though I imagine a lot
of determined girls have got as far as the Hawktown Road.
Just the road itself, the fact known from his songs that it's
where he grew up and rode his bike and his horse Moonshine
and the schoolbus and his big old Dodge Polara (a lot of Cap's
songs are lovesick odes to modes of transportation), would
make the trip worthwhile. They probably drive up and down
it looking for the van—I would have done the same, back
when I first heard the band, if I'd known there really was
such a place as the Hawktown Road. He was safe, though—
you can't see the house from the road, and there's never been
a name on the battered mailbox.

And the Hawktown Road is seven miles long, so good luck,
girls.

I turned into the gravel farm road, drove past a field and
over a little wooden bridge, then uphill into a deep cedar
wood. The house was almost invisible, even when you'd gotten there—a long, low cabin, built out of grayed-out barn sid-
ing, with a green tin roof. Protective coloration. The cedar
trees grew right up to the long shed porch across the front.

I drew my car up beside Louis Brody's battered van. I got
my fiddle off the seat beside me and sat for a minute, taking
deep breaths to ward off nervousness. Then I opened the car
door and walked up the stepping-stone path that threaded
through the trees, into voices singing, *a cappella,* one of those
smooth, full-sounding gospel trios, I believe it was "Jesus
Made the Wine." I stood on the covered porch, my back to the
door, listening, trying to decide what to do. The countryside
looked—how can I say the deep sense I had of it?—as if it had
been living a quiet full life of its own, for a long long time,

without me seeing it, and now, for a moment, I was seeing it:
the black-green cedars with patches of snow frozen in them
and, through a clearing off to the side, a field, then another
woods, bare ghosty limbs crisscrossing, running up the next
ridge, an intricate weaving that drew you into it.

Now TJ gave them the lead-in with the bass and they all
took off, oh that sweet music—all it needed was a beautiful
fiddle part rising high up above it to lift it to heaven.

Finally, I didn't knock. I just put my hand on the doorknob
and turned it and let myself quietly into Cap's house.

I saw, right away, that on the Hawktown Road, he was a
pilgrim and a stranger, a lonely piecemeal farmer, living like
a monk. It was the high lonesome, out here, like the sound of
bluegrass music, not the low lonesome, which was my daddy
and the tenor sax and whatever else the low lonesome needed
to keep itself going.

It looked to me like the high lonesome didn't need a thing.

The front room was almost dark, the kitchen opening to
one side of it, like a stage. Louis, Joyner, and Cap sat around a
wood table back there, with TJ standing behind them. An
overhead light shone down on them. They didn't even look
up. The only furnishing in the front room seemed to be a sin-
gle-width mattress on the floor, with a quilt thrown over it. I
didn't want to sit on it, in case it was Cap's bed. I thought that
would be way too much of *whatever comes next* for me. So I
sat on the cold floor and leaned against the wall, with the rollicking, many-noted music tumbling down around me, Louis
chunking his mandolin two-forty, egging them on, all their
heads together, like they knew how to keep a secret.

They knew I was there. They were letting me know what
kind of company I'd landed in. I think they were giving me
fair warning, in case I wanted to quietly disappear. In case

Cap had made a mistake on me. Cap smiled at TJ, as TJ hollowed out a little well in the middle of their playing and then Joyner poured some notes down into it, while Louis stood back, biding his time.

It speaks for the kind of bands I'd always played with that I was almost always the best musician they had. I was always in the position to teach, not learn. And now I'd landed in the same room with four of the best individual musicians I knew of, playing together like they were blood brothers. Bluegrass is full of claims, you know—every player is always the all-time best this or that, but, for my money, Hawktown really was right up there, as fine a group as you're going to hear—a dazzling, inventive Dobro and mandolin player rolled up in one, a genius, really, that's Louis; a hard-driving, wild-hearted banjo-picker who can play Scruggs-style or old-time clawhammer, that's Joyner—he could have had his choice of any job in Nashville, if he hadn't wanted to stay with Hawktown; a solid bass player you could lean on in a hurricane, TJ, with nothing between his ears but music; and, well, the best all-around honest-to-the-bone lead guitar in the business, period, who happened also to sing so good you wanted to eat the sound with a spoon.

And here *I* was, sitting on the floor, my fiddle case in my lap, in the same house with them and practically nothing else ·
to divert my attention—a couple of straight-backed chairs, an old electric range so clean it looked like it hadn't ever been used for anything but boiling water, a woodstove giving off a blast of heat on one side of me in the dark front room, and a draft of cold air coming in under the door on the other side. I don't impress easy, but my heart was racing at the idea that any minute now I was going to have to get up and play my best for this band, which had also, I forgot to mention, until a couple of days before, claimed a brilliant fiddler, with a beau-

tiful confident sound and many jazzy licks, whose shoes Cap was hoping I could temporarily fill.

When they came to the end of that number, I got up and took my fiddle case into the kitchen, shyly. *"Here* she is," Cap announced—his voice had about the same degree of light friendliness as it would have had for a lost sock he found under the bed. The barest paring of a grin, so that I got the idea I wasn't quite as warmly received as I was expecting to be, under the circumstances.

"That sure sounded good to me," I allowed.

Cap shrugged. "We were just warming up a little, waiting on you."

"Well, I'd hate to hear you play that tune when you're hot, then." Silence, Joyner scratching his neck and studying up on the corner of the kitchen ceiling. "I'm not late, am I?"

"Naw—the boys just came out a little while ago. We were ironing out some details. You know all these folks, don't you, Carrie?"

I nodded, they nodded, then silence threatened once again to fall over us. "Yeah!" said TJ, a beat too late. "Carrie and me, we played together once, remember that, Care? At Johnny Dell's place, one summer."

"Yeah, I remember—that was some kind of pickup band, wasn't it!"

"Somebody made a tape of it. Old Jenkins Ballard, remember him? He was playing mandolin. He's dead now. I forget who was on banjo."

"Pete Simpson, wasn't it?"

"Yeah, it's coming back to me."

Which was the end of all small talk. I knelt on the floor to unclasp my fiddle case. I felt like saying, "You still need to warm up a little bit more, boys. I'm feeling a definite chill," but I lifted out my fiddle and my bow and tuned with them, so they would see I was just as bent on business as they were.

"Well, let's try 'Keep on the Sunny Side,' " Cap said. "If you're ready, Carrie."

That was music to my ears—I thought he'd heard me play the great improvisation I could deliver on this tune, and wanted to show me off, to give the rest of them confidence that I was up to the job. Cap told me the key, and then I noodled around politely on the edges, listening to their wonderful licks, watching Cap for my cues, my heart in my throat, thinking any minute I'd get the nod to take my break, but I could have spared myself the uproar—they forgot to give it to me. They leaned in and sang their up-tempo, syncopated, close-harmony version of the song, and then, without warning, the number was over. I almost said, "Hey, don't stop yet, listen to this!" but they were already taking off on something else, leaving me scrambling to catch up, nobody even looking at me. I got the message, through my confusion—it only took a few minutes—that I was supposed to be the all but invisible fiddler, seen but not so you'd notice and surely not much heard. Their hot-damn smiles were all for themselves. Their true loves were each other. I might as well have been over at the sink washing the coffee cups.

Their feelings flew back and forth through the music. I worked in some little doodad where I could, while they leaned in together in a way you could only describe as closing ranks. I stood off to one side, amazed, doing lonely little runs.

By this time, my big thrill had deflated and was drifting like a sad balloon back down to earth. When the next tune came and went without anything in it for me, I had a good mind to get my coat and my fiddle case and tiptoe out while they were appreciating each other so good and shut the door real soft and when they came to their senses they'd look around and I wouldn't be there. I wondered how long they'd play on before they noticed they'd lost their new fiddler. I'd be back home, with my baby girl settled against me, on the telephone to my girl picker friends. We might not have been great musicians yet, but at least we were kind.

But I decided not to give up without a fight, so I said, "Hey, guys! You *got* me here, you might as well see if I can play." They all looked at me with serious, grieved expressions on their faces, like they wished I knew how to be a lady and not embarrass them. Then Cap ducked down his head and started tuning. "I can play," I went on. "You want to hear? What's next? What about 'Billy in the Low Ground'? I've heard how Andy does that one." It didn't seem such a big thing to ask. They couldn't expect to keep me feeling grateful if all they let me do was bang along on the outskirts of all their fun.

Louis looked at Joyner with a small masked smile, like I'd just confirmed his worst predictions, Joyner raised his eyebrows and looked at Cap, then they all looked at their sneakers. I was beginning to think Cap hadn't done such a hot job of preparing them for me or me for them, and he didn't get any points for hospitality, either. He didn't seem to think it was his responsibility to make things easier for me.

Cap took his time finishing tuning while we all waited stony-faced. When he got his strap adjusted, he looked around at us as if he'd just woken up from a nice nap and smiled a little. I put my fiddle under my chin, raised my bow, and waited, looking fiercely at the strings. I was overjoyed when what I heard was a lead-in to "Billy in the Low Ground." And off we went. If I didn't get a break this time, I was going to leave, I'd made up my mind, but at last Cap raised his eyebrows for me to step up front, and I did, I took off, rose above myself, tearing along that sweet old melody line, to let them know they weren't dealing with just any old crumb-bum fiddler off the streets. I was so mad I took it out on my fiddle, and then I lost my irritation in the sound.

I couldn't stop smiling as I played. We clicked solid on that tune, and I felt like we all knew we did. When it was over, the air felt clearer. TJ accidentally said, "All *right*!" and Joyner cleared his throat and gave me a nod and a gentlemanly, kind-hearted, Christian smile. Cap said, "Great, Carrie."

Flustered and pleased, I muttered something smart about wanting to take advantage of my opportunities.

Louis gave me his honey-eyed long-lashed look that was supposed to melt the hardest of hearts and said, in a light, cooled-out voice, "And we know you know how, sweetheart." I could hardly believe what I'd heard. Me and Louis had already had a run-in or two over the years; I must confess I always found him a real jerk, but I forgave him, on account of his music. There are plenty who get by on that—they don't have to act human if they're boy wonders.

"Piss off, Louis," I shot back, not taking the time to think of anything special, just operating on my fast reflexes—a girl would be dead in this business without them. I paused afterwards—you can't pause beforehand, timing is all—to see how the other ones were taking what Louis had said. They all looked sort of frozen. Cap's face went careful and blank, his lips snapped shut. But I saw it was at me, not Louis! They weren't used to plainspoken girls—all these boys had a lot to learn about the world and only me to teach them, looked like. If I'd been one of them, I would have come to my defense, but since they didn't, I just shrugged my shoulders and said, "What's next?"

Because when it came time to play, I was in their groove. They had to know it. It was inspirational. They knocked my socks off, even old Sleazeface did, once he let that Dobro do the talking. I thought, *This is gonna be good.* And in the next couple of numbers, I did my very best to let them know they hadn't made a mistake on me. I stepped forward and took my breaks when I thought it was time for them, whether anybody asked me to or not. I came in over the top of them. I pried open their previous arrangements to make a place for myself, just out of high-spiritedness. I thought we'd gotten that settled. Nobody said much in between, but that's how bluegrass musicians are, mostly. They hide what they feel about the music. They're the silent type, a lot of them. The most they'll say is "Mighty fine."

Mighty fine was how I felt. And I thought it was how they felt too, judging by the music coming out of us. It was how TJ felt, I know, out in the middle of an ocean with no land in sight, hanging on to his bass like it was his life raft. Looking back on it, I think Louis and Joyner couldn't help themselves. They were in control of their opinions but not their fingers. It was kind of comical, I see now. They kept making up their minds to boycott me, but their fingers just didn't have the heart and played along in spite of them. If they were sulking between numbers, it was lost on me.

As for Cap, who knew? He was making himself scarce, psychologically speaking. Shades down. Eyes on his fingers.

We stopped for a breather, and Joyner lay back on the mattress in the front room and fumbled a smoke out of his breast pocket. Louis got himself a beer out of Cap's ancient refrigerator, which was painted John Deere green. He held it up to me and raised his eyebrows without smiling—a peace offering, I suppose. I shook my head. After a minute, I went to get a cup of water from the tap. TJ squatted in the corner, cracking his knuckles behind his head. Nobody talked much to me, but then they didn't talk much to each other, either—I guess they were self-conscious, with me around. A strange lady in the living room tends to shut down a group of old buddies. They tried to act natural, cracked jokes, five words long, some kind of code, but they didn't laugh; they'd give a snort through their nose but keep their face straight.

It was a lot different from Pearl's Girls—we were giddy and irrepressible, that was our *problem;* sometimes we couldn't get through a song for cracking up. The Wise Crackers—I always thought that would have been a good name for us.

I leaned against the wall and drank the tap water. It tasted cold and full of iron. My eyes followed Cap's moves helplessly—here I was, looking in on the everyday life of my hero, how he lived and breathed, why hadn't I brought my camcorder? He went out to the porch and came back in with an armload of stovewood. He squatted and opened the door of the stove and loaded it carefully, while I gazed at his long, serious back. I wished I could look inside the refrigerator and see what he kept on hand. I wanted to know what happened here after dark—did he fry himself a pork chop? Did he go out? Did he walk across the road to his granny's? I didn't know yet that he *had* a granny. At the same time, as much as I enjoyed watching him, I hoped we'd get started again, because I needed to get back to Molly.

Cap banged the door of the stove shut and hung up the poker on its nail. He was the neat and methodical type, I could see. He turned toward me, then, smiling and full of purpose, and took the fiddle out of my hands. "Carrie and me are going out for a little hit of oxygen," he said.

"Yeah, right," said Louis, looking me over, leery and jeery, and it came to me that he thought he knew how I'd gotten asked in. Even after all our wonderful playing together, even after I'd worked so hard to prove I had it in me. . . .

Cap put his hand on my arm and guided me out the door and down the wooden steps into the bitter weather, no coats, either one of us. He didn't waste any time. The minute we got to the path, he looked down at me, heaved a sigh that made me think, *Uhoh,* and said, "Do me a favor, Carrie."

"Here it comes," I said, out loud, going down the path ahead of him.

He caught up and walked beside me. "Don't push too hard. We got a situation here. You understand? Let them get adjusted to you."

"Oh shit," I said.

"I know I'm asking a lot of you, but I'm asking a lot of *them,* too. They've got ears, they'll come around. But don't ask them to do it all this afternoon, okay? Don't keep, you know—"

I went on walking, looking at our two pairs of Reeboks, while I took in the whole message. Then I said, "Come around when? Are we talking about three weeks? Is Andy coming back?"

"If I had to guess, I'd say we done lost Andy."

He meant don't push too hard on *him,* either. I hugged my arms around me. The wind whipped my hair into my face. The branches of the cedars rose and fell. "Because you can say what you want to about Pearl's Girls, they like for me to do what I can do. We're all in there trying, all for one and one for all. I can't play and hold my fire at the same time, Cap—why should I?"

He rubbed his eye with a flat finger and smiled at the sky.

"I can't figure out what's going on here," I said, truly aggravated. "If I were you and Joyner and TJ and Louis, I'd be out of my mind with how good we all sound together, with the possibilities opening up here. If you want my opinion, I think my sound goes better with this band than Andy's has for some time. I lift you up instead of just setting myself off. But nobody's saying one word. Where do *you* stand?"

He took my arm and gave it a little shake. "I stand by you," he said, in a husky, deliberate, meaningful voice, but with a smile I would become accustomed to, that separated him a little from the words he was saying. He looked at me, while my arm warmed under his hand and the comfort of it washed upward, and also the certainty that this was a man who knew what to do for a woman, so that I had to make a real effort not to lean in toward him. He started walking me down the road. "I *am* out of my mind with the possibilities opening up here," he went on at last.

"You could have fooled me." In spite of the wave of heat spreading out from my arm, the rest of me was shaking with the cold or what-have-you, and I wished he would put his arm around me and pull me close, just for bodily warmth, if nothing else. Instead I felt it my duty to point out, "You wouldn't tell a man fiddler not to push too hard. He wouldn't have to *push*, for one thing."

"Well, look here, Carrie, that's exactly what I'm talking about. If Joyner and Louis thought you were anything but the emergency fill-in, they'd walk. At least, as of about two hours ago, that was the story—what you wandered into here was a fight. Don't take it personal. They've just got their minds set on how our band should look. You're a shock to them. I want you to give them a little time to get won over—if anyone can do it, you can. They've got a lot on their minds right now."

"Well, honey, so do I. Where does that leave *me?*" Stamping along down the gravel drive now, out in the serious wind.

"It leaves you playing with us for three weeks, like I said last night. And then we'll take a reading. We'll see for sure if Andy's gone. And then we'll see if they can stand the thought of you."

"If I can stand the thought of them." I meant it—this was beginning to seem like a real bad idea.

"There you go. Just don't get up in their faces too much. Use some tact."

"Tact."

"Right." We were facing each other. My teeth were chattering. A big purple cloud with snow in it was fixing to unload. All I wanted now was to get back home ahead of it. A safety light by a barn across the road had come on. "That's why we're standing out here in the wind-chill factor. I'm trying to coach you."

It was true, Joyner and Louis both had pitched a fit about my coming in for Andy, I found out later—Joyner's the one who told me. But Cap had insisted that they try me out. "Three weeks ain't going to kill you" is how he put it. TJ didn't express an opinion. I don't think TJ's mind has ever been messed up by an opinion. For Joyner, it was just that he didn't see how anything could ever be the same about the music if you put a woman in the mix, and he sure had a point there. Louis was the only common SOB in the band, one of those guys who didn't know how to quit insulting women, couldn't get insults out of his vocabulary, much less his head, couldn't quit talking about this one's this and that one's that, though his eyes could get all shined up with sentiment from time to time.

"I was thinking, Carrie," Cap said, when we went in to start rehearsing again. "We don't have time to work up anything special for you for tomorrow—what about if you sang that pretty tune you did last night. You know?"

" 'Birds Sing After the Rain'?"

"Right. What if you just came up to the center mike and sang it? It would be a showstopper. I thought last night that it would sound wonderful unaccompanied. That melody just needs the voice. *Your* voice, anyway. Just stand up there and sing it. And when you finish the singing, you could end up with a little turn on the fiddle. Why don't you try it?"

So I stood up in Cap's kitchen and sang my song, all by my-self, as if I had a sign on me saying, "Not a Regular Member of This Band," my arms hanging down by my sides, fiddle in one hand, bow in the other. It did sound good, though. My voice sometimes has a way of seeming like it's coming out of a vault, out from underground, and with that minor turn, it was a beautiful, hair-raising effect. When it came to the chorus, where the three voices are supposed to come in one at a time—"And birds sing—birds sing—birds sing—And birds sing after the rain," Cap and Joyner stepped in close, on either side of me, and finished out the chorus with me, their voices tender and true, as if they'd always been hearing that har-mony. Then I settled my fiddle on my collarbone and played a sad little finishing riff, exactly three measures long. I aim to please. Cap said, "That's perfect. That'll get their attention. It'll be a good introduction to you."

Joyner said, "That's a good un, Carrie."

I bowed my head and said, "Thank you."

But any old girl can sing.

Six

"Carrie Mullins from Lexington, Kentucky, over there on the fiddle—give her a big old North Florida welcome, folks."

I was the emergency fill-in, the holding operation.

I fell in with the plan. I hung back, reined myself in, so tactful I wanted to puke. As with most bluegrass bands, it was Hawktown's practice to stand stock-still up there, not even tapping a toe, looking at their flying fingers with deep puzzled interest as though they'd never seen them before in their lives and couldn't say what they might do next. I tried to hold still too. I took my one break per set and made what I could out of it. I didn't push for more.

See, I secretly agreed with Cap. I felt he'd given me good advice, to hold back. He took a risk when he let me in—these audiences sometimes don't like women to play the way men do, at least when they're playing with men. If there's a woman in the band, oftentimes she's sister or mama to the high man, back there in her church dress, beating on a tambourine or joining in on the chorus. Or some sweet number in a plaid shirt, goes with the Dobro player, plays a nice mandolin herself but strictly backup, and when she's introduced they go, "Ain't she purty, folks?" One of those old sirs—you know the one I mean—used to have a woman bass player he'd introduce by saying, "She can't do no good, but she's getting old so I let her thump along." He'd hold his nose when she took her break, to be funny. And she was *fine*! I'd have broke my bass over that guy's head, but I guess it was her only chance to play.

Bluegrass music is mainly man music, and the men who make it aren't in the general habit of considering women their picking buddies. Mountain music is another story—you feel a lot of those traditional songs came out of women's hearts, women's lives. But the music changes in bluegrass, gets that drive, that sharpness. A hell-for-leather pace that everything else is secondary to. There was a time when you had to be a good tough belt-'em-out woman or else someone's dear daughter to play in a bluegrass band. There's a lot of pure male thrust to it, if you ask *me*. I've heard women who could pick circles around some famous men. But even when they've got the speed, there's some kind of edge that gets by many of them. Maybe they can't work up enough appetite for showing off—they're used to going back behind the music, to the thing it came out of. Some men play that way, too, of course, but if they do, they're likely playing old-time music, where you almost never hear anybody stepping up to play a solo. I don't want to throw a lot of wild generalizations around. I'm just saying what I've noticed in my own experience, that it's mainly men who have that hard-driving, in-your-face bluegrass sound.

Look around, at the festivals, and see who's jamming of an evening. See how many are women. I used to wander around with my fiddle case, back in the campgrounds, just begging to be invited to open it up and show what I could do. They'd all lean in a little tighter and sort of get their backs to me. But once in a while they'd let me in out of chivalry, because I was young and kind of lost-looking. I'd stand there and my fiddle would tell who I really was. I'd get carried away by the joy of being able to do it, which was still new to me in those days, till it was contagious, I guess.

But by and large, if you're a hot-lick technician, if you want to step up there and show you can cut it, you'd do well to stay with your all-girl band, or start a band of your own, and hand-pick your male players. Because most bluegrass men think it's better if the balance isn't disturbed by a woman in a black spandex miniskirt, wanting to take her riff.

I'm not saying that a lot of bluegrass musicians aren't the sweetest men you'd ever want to meet—friendly, good-hearted, smiling like angels up there, nice-looking, some of them, liking to sing the good old gospel tunes, raised up to like and respect their mamas. I'm just saying, if you want to pick with them, watch out.

Cap put himself out on a limb. He let me in, looked around for the best fiddler he could find on short notice, regardless of race, creed, sex—there's not many in this business who would have done that. Maybe it was just desperation, but ordinarily bluegrass band leaders don't get that desperate. If I hadn't already loved him, I would have loved him for that. He had enough sense not to put it to them, did they want me to stay on or not. I think the way he handled it was to keep on not finding exactly the right fellow to take Andy's place, until it finally sort of slipped all of their minds that they were looking.

He said we'd take a reading in three weeks, but if one was taken, he was too subtle to mention it to *me*. Somehow he communicated to me that the best thing to do, for the present, was keep a low profile and play along. I played along, and listened. I'd been in friendlier bands in my life, but never in a better one. Nowhere close. Nobody mentioned Andy, or much of anything else except what key we were going to play the next set of numbers in.

At the end of the three weeks, Dinah and Jess and Stony and Kathy and Martha and I got together at my house. It was nearly Christmas—it felt like a year since I'd seen them. We had little Dollar Store presents for the kids, and for each other. Somehow the instruments, though they brought them, all ended up propped in the hall. I'd made cookies and spiked the eggnog with a heavy hand, feeling I needed all the help I could get. We sat around eating and sipping and joking about what Christmas was doing to our thighs while we waited for me to get up my courage. One thing nobody said was, "Let's play some."

Finally I took a deep breath and said, "No sign of Andy. I guess I'll be sitting in with those guys a little longer."

"You *guess*? Jesus, what are you, Carrie, a piece of furniture?" said Kathy. "Can't you ask?"

"It's hard to explain, but I can't."

She looked at me, truly perplexed. Kathy's the kind of Kentucky girl that doesn't smile if she doesn't feel like it, and talks fast, flat, and grim, right at you. "If he doesn't come back, if they ask you, will you sign on with them?"

"Yes, I think so," I said. "If they ask me. It would be a big chance for me."

"Of *course* she will," Martha said, poking up the fire. "What do you think she is, crazy?"

There was a moment then when nobody looked at each other. Then Jess put her plate down on the floor. "Oh, heck, Carrie. Just when I was starting to play decent."

"I know," I said miserably.

"We were sounding good," Kathy said. "Think where we were last year this time. She wouldn't have to be crazy to want to stay playing with us," she said to Martha.

"Kathy, you all can still have the band," I said. "We'll just have to find another fiddle player."

"Right. Look behind the couch there, will you?"

"I'll help. There was a young girl I heard last week in Berea, she had just a beautiful sound, and she could play good short-bow . . . ," I said. I could tell it was falling on deaf ears.

"I think we all got too dependent on you," Jess said. "Who'll tell us what lazy-ass goof-offs we are? Who'll get on the phone?"

We were having this conversation while the kids were running in and out, in that general sugared-up Christmas hysteria they get into, hanging on the back of our chairs, wanting to open their presents. Molly careened over, taking a smiling, daredevil step all on her own between Jess's knees and mine, and I swung her into my lap, where she quickly stuck her whole hand in my eggnog and spread it all over her new Santa Claus sweatshirt. I welcomed the diversion, got busy wiping her off.

"I'd go with Hawktown, if it was me," Stony put in then. She was curled up in a quilt in the morris chair, still in her court-stenographer suit. "I surely would. But I don't see what difference it makes *what* we'd do. Hawktown isn't asking *us.*"

"They've got an unfair advantage over us. We got no cute studs to offer her. Stay with us, Carrie. We'll get a cute stud for you." This was Jess, sitting on the floor. She reached out a booted foot to nudge my leg.

"They've got an unfair advantage over us, that's for sure," Stony said, laughing. She polished off her eggnog. "This stuff sneaks up on you. I'd better watch it."

"But they haven't committed," Dinah said now, from over in her corner, lounging back under her cowboy hat.

"No."

"So any day they could say, 'Hey, thanks for helping us out,

Carrie, it's been great, but we've found a permanent replace-
ment for Andy now.' "

"I suppose so. But I don't think that's going to happen. I
think, if Andy doesn't come back, I'll be their fiddle player."

"*So . . .*" said Kathy.

"So let's find another fiddler for Pearl's Girls," I said. We
all looked at each other. "I'll practice with you as much as I
can, till we find someone."

But they didn't do it. They just folded. Dinah went on to
play with another girl band that's had real success and isn't
just a sideshow. The rest of them took up their other business,
as they probably would have done eventually anyway. Stony's
the one I feel worst about. She worked at it harder than any of
us, with less time.

I guess I did the right thing. We'll never know now. I
didn't mention it, but Cap had to know what I'd done. I felt
he admired me for not making a big deal out of it.

MARTHA AND MOLLY and I drove to Florida behind Hawktown's van, for that first festival date. And that was the way it
was, from then on. If it was a festival date or a county fair or
something like that, I tried to take Molly with me, and if
Martha could work it in, she'd come too. If it was a night gig
at a bar or roadhouse, I'd leave Molly with Martha or Ardrie
or Mrs. Stevens and drive there alone, trying to get used to
this version of hog heaven—the boys in the shiny new dark
blue van with "Hawktown Road" painted on the spare-tire
cover, the girl fiddler following at a respectful distance in her
fourteen-year-old Riviera.

I babied that car along for ten of those fourteen years, from
the time I got my license and Mama signed it over to me until
it finally, permanently, conked out on me. I hated to give it
up, mainly because it was the last connection I had with

Daddy, but also because it had gotten me everywhere I'd been in my life—which wasn't all that far, to be sure, until I joined Hawktown. Hawktown was too much for it. I put the last fifteen thousand miles on it the first year I was with them. Then I bought a late-model Nissan truck with a pop top, so that Molly and I could camp out when we went to the festivals.

That's what it came down to—I played with Hawktown, but I never rode with them, not when they were all together. And there were only a couple of times, in the thousands of miles I traveled with them, when one of them rode with me. If I hadn't had my own wheels, I don't think we could have made it. The van was *their* world, I could dig it. I left it to them, so Louis could tell them, without leaving anything out, about scoring with the lady of whatever house he was painting then, how the bedroom was painted black with red sponged all over, and then white, with red woodwork. I'd heard enough about his stippling or mottling or whatever it was called to last me. "I'd *kill* for a bedroom like that," he'd told me, white teeth glinting. "But at least I got to break it in good."

I didn't doubt it. I was glad he wasn't stippling *my* bedroom. Louis, like Cap, had no shortage of women throwing themselves at him—he was pretty adorable in his painter's overalls torn at the knee and butt. The Butt Brothers, I sometimes called them, to myself.

I was just as happy to follow behind, by myself, or with Molly crooning in her cozy companionable way beside me, or counting her fingers, or telling herself jokes, throwing her head back to laugh, well pleased with herself. I didn't need to be making a social effort any more than those boys did. My teeth were already banging together from my new proximity to Cap.

When I think how loaded down I was in those days, I really

don't see how I managed. "Stamina" is a word I don't relate to much lately, but I sure had some eighteen-hour days in me back then. Life was a mess of laundry and mashed bananas on the floor and runny noses and alarm clocks going off just when you were getting to sleep, but we kept it going, day to day. I got to where I could really hear music, all by myself on some highway, those boys burning up the road somewhere ahead of me, me doing forty going uphill, when I still had the Riviera, pedal to the metal, shoving in the cassettes.

When I took Molly to the festivals, even without Martha, I didn't have to worry. Some family I'd known for years would like as not be on the front row, happy to look after her while we played. She never got far from the music, anyway. When Kelly and Joyner brought along Mary Emma, who was just a little older than Molly, the two girls would sometimes dance together over in the grass, imitating the people buck-dancing on boards off to the sides. But mainly Molly was content to sit still in somebody's lap with her face raised up, listening, or singing along with a serious expression on her face—she knew a lot of songs, from her life on the couch in front of the fire with Martha and me and whoever else. What had held her as an infant never wore off.

For her birthday when she was three, Cap bought her a tiny guitar. He taught her to play some chords on it, too. Does that sound familiar? He'd hold her in his lap sometimes and put her fingers on the strings. I'd just have to turn around and leave the room.

IN THOSE FIRST heady weeks, I would say aloud to myself sometimes, "I'm playing tonight with Hawktown Road!" Like, pinch me, I'm dreaming, because Hawktown was *it*, in my book. But they didn't change overnight into men a girl likes to be around. In fact, each of them besides TJ was a sticky situation, for different reasons. Joyner, once he accepted the fact that I was there to stay, wanted to give me advice. He set a lot of store by being a man who knew how to take care of women, how to tell them what-all to do. Many of us girls cannot do without a man like Joyner, because we don't yet know enough ourselves about our mortgage points and crankshafts. But at least he had a kindly spirit.

Louis had an unkindly spirit. What he liked best was taking me down, one way or another—it was all the same to him, *se*duction or *re*duction. "That's supposed to be a C-*sharp*, Carrie. You're sliding in pretty close to C-natural for a girl that's rumored to have such good—*intonation.*" War, misery, and hatefulness. I think now, looking back, that his only true, pure pleasure in life, the only time he could let himself down into his true self, was when he was jamming with his buddies; I messed that up for him, and he couldn't forgive me.

At first he couldn't hear me. Didn't have any way to listen to my music, too busy listening for my mistakes. If I made one that was obvious to everybody, so that he didn't have to point it out, that's what he liked best. He'd just stop picking then and say in a patient, cooled-out voice, "Let's try that again, how about." Not looking at me. Saint Louis. Nobody held *his* feet to the fire that way. When *he* messed up, everybody just laughed, including him. Including me. "Hey, I'm only human." "So you keep telling us," Joyner would come back. "We're waiting on confirmation."

It was Louis I couldn't handle. Or rather, I could have handled him fine if it hadn't been for Cap. I've been dealing with old boys like Louis all my life, with one hand tied behind my back. But not *both* hands.

I like to go head to head. That's what I know how to do.

I've got quick wits and a biological urge to say what's on my mind, sooner rather than later, before it accumulates into permanent hard feelings.

But Cap didn't want me to make trouble. So my natural ability to take care of myself was messed up. It was like setting me down with a shin-kicker and making it against the rules for me to kick back. He called it trying to get along.

"Why don't you tell Louis to try to get along?" I asked him.

"Well, Louis is a lost cause, darlin'."

Cap's style was more to ease us all on ahead of him in the general direction he'd picked out, like a swift, smart Border collie, now he's here now he's there, nipping at our heels so light and expert we thought getting back in line was our own idea.

So, before I knew it, I'd given my responsibility for myself over to him. Old Mr. Leave-It-to-Me. Lounging out of the kitchen with a cup of instant coffee. "You done, Louis? Let's try this new song of Carrie's."

"Another new song of Carrie's? Don't that girl ever take a break?"

"Hear it, man."

Why did I put up with this Louis situation, I ask myself, looking back.

Because in the middle of a set, when our five instruments lifted up whatever melody we were given, when we filled it up with our many notes, well, I would not have asked to be any other place. You play "Wheel Horse" right, it carries you away to a better place, lets you leave your body behind, your irritations and your sorrows, finally even your fingers behind, still picking out the notes, while your joy ascends to the rosy banks of clouds around the pearly gates.

When the audience loved me, Louis could abide me, feel simple friendliness toward me. You'd think it couldn't help but carry over into everyday life. But after the show, we all took off, Cap and Louis with whoever was courting them, Joyner with Kelly—or *to* Kelly, if she wasn't able to come with him—or else off with TJ and his drinking buddies. Me, most often, to collect Molly from whoever was watching her for me, or, if Molly hadn't come with me, to drive back home, as fast as I could, alone.

It was a hard, lonely life I'd bought into. I was a woman with a baby in a man's world. Sometimes I wished I was back trying to make music with Stony and them, babies squabbling around the edges, wandering into the middle of our doings with their popsicles dripping on the rug.

Cap didn't help me. I thought his prescription of tact and restraint was just temporary, but it was beginning to look like the whole deal.

I hung on the way I started out, just this side of invisible, for a couple of months. I played my one break per set and then stepped back into the scenery. I kept waiting (patiently—patience was my middle name for a while there) for Cap to start bringing me forward a little. But he was too skillful in his negotiations. It never occurred to me to wonder if I was getting the same cut Andy had gotten, the same cut the guys were getting (I wasn't), oh no no no, I was too high-minded for that.

Well, finally something got me going, but it wasn't money. I got tired of waiting to be appreciated—patience I could stand to learn, but I was fundamentally opposed to humility. I know what I am. So I made a decision to bring my own self forward. I figured if *I* couldn't make them give me my due I'd make the *audience* make them. I went over their heads, you might say. I set myself to do a little show-stealing—just enough to get the crowd's attention. Just enough to where people would yell out for me. I didn't want to be the star. I just wanted my equal share of time up front.

So I used what I had. I can play wild and I can play mean, when I let myself go; I can wring every chromatic scale out of my strings, double-stop till the cows come home, steal a note with my little finger and scramble back down. I let myself go—but not near as much as I could have. Cap's not the only one who can walk a fine line. I knew a few little tricks for swinging my long hair to one side while I adjusted the mike, for nestling the fiddle under my chin. And I didn't wear no plaid shirts or church dresses, I'll tell you that. I wanted to look like a regular twentieth-century woman; if I erred, I wanted it to be on the dangerous side. I had a few songs I could stop the show with; I could jump into the music and give it such an excited bright edge that the audience would stand up and yell for more.

I gave up trying to hold absolutely still all the time. It was against my nature anyway.

It worked. Before long, the band began to realize the positive side of me. For instance, we got a reputable recording studio to agree to bring out an album, not the fly-by-nighters the band had recorded with the first couple of times. And we started getting more and more bookings. I'm not claiming all that action was on account of me—they'd been getting a bigger following every year, with Andy, and they deserved it. But I have to say I didn't hold them back any; I made the audiences sit up and take notice and call my name and yell out that they loved me.

Our first song to get on the charts was the lullaby I sang to Molly when she was first born, "Come and Go, Molly Snow." I got roses thrown up on the stage and fan mail, and very soon an article about us came out in *Bluegrass Unlimited.* So I wasn't a disaster, anyway. I pulled my weight. "Let that *gal* sing," somebody would shout out. Or, "Come on, Carrie Marie, play that fiddle." So that's how I got myself up front. I didn't push too hard, I worked up the audience to do it for me. If you want to talk about subtle.

Seven

I can't remember exactly how Cap and I started singing duets together. It happened gradually. By the time I noticed, it was as though I'd never sung any other way.

The difference between Louis and Joyner and Cap singing and me and Cap singing was this: I made him mean the words. The way I look at it, that's about the worst thing you can do to a bluegrass man.

Bluegrass music, you know, doesn't like to show its feelings, not like Daddy and Ned Agee and Eugene Osborne, reaching way in for what they didn't know they knew. Bluegrass has that little sternness and distance in it, like the dancing you do to it, stiff from the waist up, feet flying. That's one of the reasons I took it up, I have to say. It has a kind of manners, a code. The music sort of takes the personal sorrows of life for granted and comes out the other side, cookin'. *Step aside, heartbreak, you're nothing new. What's new is this bass run I'm about to lay on you. If you think I can't play this thing, watch out.*

What's left then, at least when it's the kind I like, is fairly flat-out old-time music, pick-up-and-dance music, no matter what it's about, even if it's about a little walk with Jesus or somebody solid gone. Eight/four or swingtime, it don't have much truck with whatever had my daddy sitting all by himself back there on the picnic table at three a.m., going deep down, coming back with his private heart, offering it up to the starry night, for free.

A lot of people describe bluegrass as heartfelt, but I've heard heartfelt, and bluegrass ain't exactly it. It's got no private heart. It's sociable, from all those years of front-porch picking with your family or buddies in it, all that white country church. You feel sorrow and loss in bluegrass—hell, it's three-fourths *about* loss—of the cabin on the hill, the yellow-haired child, the mama and daddy, the old-time ways. But the music seems to be speaking for a whole bunch of people, not just for itself.

For myself, I've always liked that little distance. I'd never been in favor of grief. Grief was too personal. My father had gone way down to the bottom of his jazzy, blues-heavy heart, and his heart had failed him. Coitus permanently interruptus. I just couldn't, wouldn't, take in how sad his life had been.

In bluegrass, there's sad songs to sing, but somebody makes fun of them beforehand. "We do this one real pitiful." To protect themselves, in case you accidentally thought they had some feelings. It's mainly white men who sing bluegrass. They're not like black singers, who used the one chance they got to say exactly how their lives felt to them. White men's whole raising is to keep the lid on, to live public, to keep their feelings to themselves. The only thing bluegrass bands have feelings about, by and large, is how good the music sounds. Good-sounding music suited me fine. I just wanted to get going on "Windy City" or "Ridin' the Midnight Train."

Only when Cap and I sang in harmony, something happened. Our two voices—well, they sounded good together. They slid together trustfully, they were of one mind. The harmony was all instinct, his voice just found the right place for itself against mine, through every last little edgy turn. Harmony's all there is or needs to be, when it's right. It was like dancing. Or worse.

Old footstomper. I gave him something to stomp his foot *about.*

I began to think of Cap pretty near all the time, my unmentionable disease, no matter what else I was doing. Molly was the melody at the top. But Cap was the drone, the ground bass, at the bottom.

Hopeless, is what it was—I didn't want anyone but him; he seemed to want everyone but me, a situation that took up all my nervous energy.

I tried to stop; we both kept it under control, but our eyes were like children or dogs that wouldn't always mind. There was that time, about six months after I started with Hawktown, when we were setting up for a gig in some high school auditorium down in Western Kentucky. We backed into each other, and turned at the same moment—these accidents will happen—and his intent glance touched me like a hand. It might as well have been on bare skin. I felt myself getting ready for liftoff. He met my eyes then, blushing hard, not denying anything, smiling down at me with his deep-end desperate blue eyes. Then he reached out, sort of in spite of himself, to put his right hand in my wild hair, and pulled me toward his shoulder. "Oh good God, Carrie," he said, in a low, unwilling voice.

God knows what would have happened next, right there among the folding chairs, except Joyner came marching bowlegged into the auditorium and yelled out, "Break it up, old buddies." Never dreaming, you know, that anything serious was going on. Cap turned then and started slamming the chairs open with his foot. But during the break he caught up with me in the hall, where I was leaning over a water fountain. When I raised up, wiping water from my mouth, he cupped my face in his hands as if he were going to kiss me. He looked and looked at me, and God, I looked back.

"You know it and I know it, Carrie," he said at last, in a low, hurried, hard-pressed voice. His hands dropped and gripped my shoulders through whatever clingy little number I'd chosen to deck myself out in that night. "But there's nothing we can do about it. I'm not a faithful man. I don't trust myself. This ain't a faithful line of work."

What would you have done? I laughed.

"I'd end up breaking both our hearts for us. I'm sorry." I guess he thought he owed me an explanation.

I thought—I don't know whether I was doing him an injustice or not—that he might have been willing to risk our hearts, but he sure as hell wasn't going to risk his fiddler. "Hey, don't apologize," I said then. "You're the one that's got to live it, not me."

"You telling *me* I've got to live it?" He leaned in toward me with a fierce look. "I'm *living* it!"

I looked back at him the same way he looked at me. Then I pulled myself free and said, "Ignore it, honey. Maybe it'll go away." I pushed my hair out of my eyes with both hands and stomped out the back door to smoke a cigarette on my own time.

I didn't mean for him to take my advice, but he did.

Our playing and singing together was as close as I thought we were going to get after that night. Closer than you might think. Music makes you lean toward each other, pay a close loving attention to each other. We both knew what the other could do. Our minds were on nothing but the music when we were in it, but the music was everything there was. He bent toward me. We gave it back and forth, sliding along each other's voice. I got to where I couldn't tell music from bodies, oh me.

Cap's face is from early times, the flat thrifty way it's made, with nothing extra, the spare lips, the sharp nose that has the slight break to it just below the bridge, like the line of one of these ridges out here, the brow not high but from temple to temple broad, the bleached eyebrows, the long lines in the cheeks that come from a hard life, too much weather.

All his muscles are economical and well developed, even in his lower arms and hands, from his strong playing on that old Dreadnaught. Veins run near the surface through his fingers and up his arms. I'll tell you, there have been times when I have just wanted to lick the path they took.

There have been times when love sat in my throat, right where you swallow. I couldn't eat. But I could still sing. We sang hot songs—might as well put all that misery to good use. He lifted my voice, brought it out. And it was as if he wanted to be invisible then, to everyone but me.

I've heard that the monks of old weren't supposed to sing their chants in harmony because harmony was too sexy. Somebody sure had a point there. Maybe Cap made a mistake on me. What was he doing letting in a steamy woman with long legs and dangly earrings who didn't even believe what most of the songs were about, heaven and all that? I didn't know how strange I was.

Joyner was right in thinking I'd change the nature of the band. Imagine a woman coming in to play with Seldom Scene or Doyle Lawson or any of those Brothers and Boys and Gentlemen, and you'll understand what a shock to the system I was. If a person had a talent for self-effacement, it might be different.

But then they saw I could leap in there and play as full of

invention as any man they could name, almost.

They saw I would go home alone, always alone. I would walk out fast, carrying my fiddle case, trying to get out before I saw who was taking Cap home with her that night. I would park close to the exit wherever we played, so I could slip away before one of my own mainly drunk admirers started leaning in on me.

At home, I would move Molly over gently so I could get in our double bed. She would put her hand on my arm, I'd lift her tangled damp hair away from her cheek. Sometimes she would wake up and whisper to me, little sleepy urgent whispers blowing warmly in my ear, rambling indecipherable stories like dreams, monologues interrupted by chuckles, her hands lifted, clasped, until she fell off again into sleep, and then I would lie there with my eyes open, in our little house full of stuff from yard sales and the Goodwill—cushions covered in tie silk and lace tablecloths and hooked rugs with roses in them—I would lie there with my lips against Molly's round warm head, trying to be as deep and lost in sleep as she was, saying to myself, *Oh this is enough this is heaven take it let it be enough don't want anything else.* But then I would be dreaming again, awake, about Cap's sweet voice, his sweet body that was an authority on many subjects, that knew exactly what to do with itself, except when it came to me, his old buddy Carrie Marie.

As for me, my body had turned into an authority on the subject of wanting. I had it bad, I guess. A sickness, a fever, they're right. Makes every part of you hurt, even your elbows and knees. What had the women knocking on his door all hours was the message he gave out when he sang: "Everybody talks about it but I know how it's done. Easy."

I could have found out if he knew how it was done. It was up to me, I guess.

Our bodies moved closer together when we sang, that was all. But he was the man in my head.

By then I'd learned Cap's story: how he had dropped out of the University of Kentucky, where he was an ag major, when his granddaddy got diagnosed with cancer; how, that winter, they built Cap's house together, working as hard as they could every day, racing against the time when Luther wouldn't be able to get up out of bed anymore. Then Cap married Sheila—"As soon as the varnish on the floor was dry," Ruth said. She told me she thought all that domestic activity was Cap's way of promising Luther he meant to live there on the Hawktown Road forever. "A nice idea that needed to be thought through a little more," Ruth said. "But I guess he thought he'd think it through later, when his granddaddy was gone." He and Sheila married in the spring; Luther was dead six weeks later. The marriage lasted a little over a year.

Sheila cleaned him out when she left, and cleaned out is how he seemed to intend to stay. When we went to practice at Cap's house, it really was a lot like practicing in a bare studio.

Usually, I took Molly with me. She'd lie on her stomach on Cap's mattress, coloring, or sometimes she'd join in our singing, leaning against me. *"There's* what the world needs," Louis said. "Another one just like the other one." But at least he couldn't keep from laughing after he said it, scratching her head like she was his good little hound dog. They were all nice to Molly.

In summer, Ona might cook dinner for the ones who hung around after practice. Afterwards, Molly liked to get Cap to swing her up on his shoulders and take her to see the calves or the chickens, or walk her out to the pond. The Hawktown Road was heaven to her. To me, too.

I'd help Ruth and Ona clean up when Cap went back to his farm work, and sometimes we'd go sit out on the porch afterwards, to cool off, while I put off the moment of gathering up my fiddle and my girl and hitting the road. One hot day, a couple of summers ago, Ruth and I sat on the back porch, drinking iced tea and watching Cap out in the field throwing bales of hay on the wagon. "A man like that would give you pause, wouldn't he," Ruth said, folding her arms across her chest in speculation. She flashed me a grin. "What every woman always wants and never gets." Like she knew my dreadful secret, and was giving me a little advice. "Too good to be true, as the old saying goes."

When he came into a room, the air perked up. When he came in, with his brown-and-gold hair blown around, his quick keyed-up body, his alert eyes.

Well, so what.

Finally, after a couple of years, I learned to live with it. I somehow stamped my desire down into friendliness. With my cute cowboy boots.

AND THAT LEFT me free, or so I thought, to find a peaceful self-sufficient life like the one I'd known in Molly's first month on earth, when I didn't want anything I didn't have. It was never so peaceful as that again, of course—by now Molly was in the process of fixing herself, no one else, to the earth's center. Her strong will had already put starch in her back-bone, as they say, caused her to wiggle and squirm and push away, to stand upright, to take a few wobbly determined steps toward what she wanted, and then a few more. To run. To say the magic words that would get results. To say "No, no" to what she didn't want. To shout and stamp her foot.

To want her way. To want things.

One of the things she wanted was a father. Though she'd been in and out of Joyner and Kelly's house all her life, when she was about four, she put it together that Joyner lived in the same house with Mary Emma. She started calling him Daddy, because Mary Emma did, until Mary Emma broke the news to her: "He's not *your* daddy, Molly, just mine." Later, Joyner reported this to me. "I told her I was her honorary daddy. But I believe you better explain the facts of life to her, before she has a chance to get confused. The facts of *her* life, anyway."

But it was Molly who brought up the subject, one afternoon a few days later, after her nap, when we were sitting in the morris chair, reading *Uncle Wiggly* after her nap. She was squeezed in beside me, sucking her thumb, her head against my arm, looking at a drawing of Uncle Wiggly and Curly yelling to Floppy Twisty Tail, who was stuck inside a hollow log. As I turned the page, she took her thumb out of her mouth. "Joyner is Mary Emma's real daddy," she informed me, softly and carefully, looking up at me. Her eyes were solemn, attentive.

"That's right," I said, holding my breath.

"Which one is *my* real daddy? Cap?"

"Well, in one way," I said, deciding on a matter-of-fact tone, "you and Mary Emma are a little bit different. Mary Emma has a daddy that lives with her. Not every child has that kind. What you have are friend-daddies." I'd been preparing myself, and hoped to God I could do this right. "You have a real daddy, too, of course—everybody does. But yours isn't like Joyner. Yours went away before you were even born. He never got to see your little nose with the freckles on it." I touched her nose lightly. She touched it too, thoughtfully, gravely. "I feel sorry for him, don't you?"

She studied her knees for a spell, then asked, "Doesn't he like me?"

I winced, and hugged her up tight against me. "Oh, Molly, he would if he knew you were in the world. But he never even knew you were on your way. I'm sorry, honey—when you were born, he was far away over the mountains."

Enough people had told me by then that it was unfair of me not to try to find him, not to let him know he had a daughter. The little I knew about him made me feel he wouldn't have been all that interested—he didn't impress me as having a very long attention span. But I could have been wrong.

"I thought you'd be fine, anyway, because from when you were a tiny baby, you had so many friends," I hurried on. "I don't know one child who has so many grown-ups that love her. I'm your real mama and I love you, and Martha's your friend-mama." Molly looked at me, concentrating. "And you've got Grandma Janette in Florida and Aunt Connie and Mrs. Stevens and a whole lot of others. And then, see, you have friend-*daddies*, too. Cap and Joyner, Uncle Dexter, Luke and Ardrie and TJ. Even old Louis likes you and gives you presents—and *he* doesn't like *any*body, hardly."

She flashed a quick, guarded look up at me from under her bangs. It stabbed right through me. I saw that time was taking her into her own separate life. I saw that I would have to let it. That I would have to start to let her go.

"Mary Emma has a real mama and a real daddy that live with her," I continued chattily. "You have a real mama and a friend-mama that live with you. And a lot of friend-daddies and friend-mamas who live in their own houses. That's just the way it is, for you. It's different for every child. But in my opinion, you're a real lucky girl—luckier than most."

Molly sat quietly, curling her hand on top of Uncle Wiggly's picture. I rested my chin against the top of her head. She didn't say anything more, so I started reading to her again. " '*Oh, Floppy, what are you doing in there?' called Uncle Wiggly.*

" '*I'm not doing anything!' grunted Floppy. 'I can't do any-thing! I'm stuck!'*

" '*How did you get in there?' asked the bunny.*

" '*I—I crawled in,' squealed Floppy in answer, and his voice sounded as if he might be down in a cellar. 'I just crawled in.' "*

I was throwing myself into it, trying to sound like a stuck rabbit. Molly interrupted me, in her shy, undeflectable quack. "Where is he, then?"

"Your real daddy? Honey, I don't know. He's out there in the wide world someplace." I really didn't have any idea. I didn't know exactly where he'd come from—out of the swamps around Waycross, was what he said—or exactly where he'd been headed, back then, five years before—just Colorado. All I knew for sure was his name and his age and the make of the pickup truck he'd been driving back then. The rest was all jokes and music and frolic.

"Could we find him?"

"It would be very, very hard. When you get older we might try, if you still think it would be a good idea. But if we *did* find him, you have to understand he wouldn't be like Joyner, who lives with Kelly and Mary Emma. He'd be more like Uncle Dexter, because he would live far away and only visit you sometimes."

"I think it would be a good idea," Molly told me, with great dignity, pressing her head back against me—I couldn't tell whether she was trying to push me back or press her will on me or just deal with her general embarrassment.

"Well, let's keep thinking about it, and talking it over. When you're a bigger girl, if you still want to, we'll give it a try.

"Hey, Molly," I said then, flipping a cushion at her that she caught and crammed down in her lap, hanging on to a spaced-out look, but thinking about smiling. "Let's walk up to the corner and get a slushie. Want to? What did you do with your flip-flops?"

"I gave them to old Floppy Twisty Tail," Molly said, falling down laughing at her joke.

"*You're* Floppy Twisty Tail. Hold still, girl."

I SOMETIMES WONDER what happened to that grinny Georgia boy. He's still on the face of the earth, I'm pretty sure. I used to think he'd come back through Lexington again someday. Or recognize my name and come to hear Hawktown, out at some Colorado hoedown, turn up backstage when I least expected him. I thought that someday our paths would cross again, and that maybe I'd tell him then about Molly. Now, if I saw him, I guess I'd just say, "Hi, how've you been? We had a good time together, didn't we, back there in the dark ages." It would be too late to tell him about that quick, flashing girl, that jolly explorer of the universe, hopping down the street ahead of me, on her way to buy a grape slushie, squatting to examine every bug and leaf and cigarette wrapper.

Eight

I took out the little policy on Molly at the same time I took out the big one on me. The guy talked me into it. Accidental death, double indemnity. The big one's still got Molly as the beneficiary. Maybe I should put my mother's name on it; she could surely use the money, if I should kick off.

Mama stayed with me for about a week after the funeral. The evening after I put her on the plane back to Florida, I came home and sat down at the kitchen table to fill out the form on Molly's policy. I sat up straight at the kitchen table, all business, both feet on the floor, like a good student. I folded the papers and put them with the death certificate in an envelope. It was the first time I'd been alone in the house since it happened.

After I licked the envelope and put a stamp on it, I stuck it between two cannisters on top of the refrigerator and went into the living room. I knelt at the window, looking out past the maple tree we used to hug and put our cheeks against. To face it. To get all my business taken care of.

This was about a week after it happened.

The dogwood tree was gone. My brother, Dexter, had borrowed Cap's chain saw and taken out what was left of it when he got here.

As I knelt at the window that night of my mother's departure, I heard the refrigerator motor click off in the room behind me. The sudden silence filled the house, opening out into—nothing. It was like the sky opening and everything we know as the world falling upwards into it, a long way.

Against this panicky, weightless sense, I had a single thought: of drawing my bow down, hard, across the strings. Of making one rough, honest sound.

That sound might have lasted me a long time. I might have gone way down into it. That's what I really wanted, I know now, one sound, but force of habit made me think I meant music. The strong fingers of my left hand started feeling how they would move along the fingerboard.

I pushed myself up off my knees, went into the bathroom, pulled my hair all to one side. I shoved in the combs. I leaned into the mirror and made up my eyes real dark. I buttoned up my satin jacket, pulled on my black boots with the crimson roses stitched in. It felt like dressing a manikin in a store window, making its stiff white limbs go this way and that. My fingers were ice-cold. I closed my fiddle into its case, got in my car, and headed out.

I drove through the dark, gulping like a drowning fish. I opened the window. I thought, *I'll be okay, I'll be okay.* I headed toward music as though it were something to breathe.

The parking lot of Justice's was filled up with cars, the band's name on a yellow plastic marquee—*Cap Dunlap and Hawktown Road.* We'd been playing there all spring, whenever we weren't on the road—packing them in, if I do say so, paying off Kenny Justice's mortgage for him. I pulled around to the kitchen entrance by the Dumpster. Empty dark cars in lines, nobody out there but one couple, under a security light. The woman leaned back against the door of a pickup truck, the guy faced her, one hand propped on either side of her. He looked down at her, then lowered his head so that his brow rested against hers. They'd be in bed together in fifteen minutes, they were going to miss our whole show.

Doc Watson came over the jukebox from inside, singing *Don't let your deal go down, pretty mama.* Cars passed on the dark highway.

Sometimes *still here* seems stranger to me than *gone.*

I got my fiddle case out of the backseat. I figured if I was going to stay in the world, I'd better be playing my fiddle. I'd play it curly and light and fast, like Curley Ray Cline.

"Well," Cap said, into the mike. He ducked his head, strummed his guitar a little bit, checking it sideways with TJ's bass. Then he turned and leaned the mike toward his mouth a little. "We got Carrie back." He let go of the mike and looked over at me without smiling and let everyone clap and whistle while I finished tuning. We have our regulars at Justice's now. I guess they knew the story. I tucked my fiddle under my chin. He nodded and, my heart thudding, I arched up my shoulders and brought us into the rousing melody of "Brown County Breakdown."

The fingers of my left hand flew through the patterns; they didn't have to think. That one rough note I'd wanted to crawl deep inside of would have been eternity. Two notes together, that's time. My bow would pause, then plunge forward over the strings, ducking and dancing, bright sixteenths to take a person's mind off how music rushes ahead, weaving and rollicking, through the ticks and tocks of the time there is in this world. I waited, all wired up, for my turn to leap in there. I sent my bow singing up the strings, over the melody, reaching high and beautiful, or I was down underneath it, in the serious ranges. I wove little arpeggios in around the words Cap and Joyner and Louis sang.

There were nights during this time when I had the feeling

I was the bow, my whole body sliding sideways, just this side of a faint.

They were always right behind me. They watched out for me. They were careful what they played, no "Six More Miles to the Graveyard," no "Strand from a Yellow Curl." Not that it mattered—I couldn't hold words in my mind, they fell right through.

Louis sang up over Cap and Joyner, in his old-time yelling voice. They sang like brothers. Like three brothers in business together. Like three brothers going over a bill of lading. It was a relief in some ways, more like bluegrass is supposed to sound, without some old loose cannon on the deck.

"I want to play, but I'm not singing, Cap," I told him, that first night back.

He nodded. "Ever what you want."

One main sound, somebody said. We were sitting at a long table between sets, drinking beer. This was a few weeks later. If somebody said something funny, everybody's eyes would slide sideways to see if I was laughing. I laughed, Lord. I couldn't talk, but my smile felt hooked over my ears. A woman I hadn't seen before sat with her arm around Louis's shoulders. She blew out smoke and said, "If you concentrate, you can kind of hear it." She was down at the other end of the table. I strained to hear what she was saying. "And pretty soon you hear it all the time, underneath everything." Everyone got real quiet, trying to hear it under George Jones on the jukebox. "One main sound. So they say."

That night I went home and sat against the wall.

I tried to hear it. I heard a high tingling buzz. I wondered if that's what she meant.

Nine

One main sound. It made sense, it figured. There's one main light in the world; everything we call color is a splitting apart of this light. So I thought there might be one great chord, too, like the light of the sun, that separates into the notes of the world. Creation would be the splitting apart of this chord. Music would come out of it, every note, every harmony. Music would also try to get back to it.

It was just an idea, but the idea excited me. I seemed to know what it meant; it drew me. It comforted me.

I didn't hear the sound, not that night. The next night I did—just for a moment, but I was sure of what I heard. A way-off steady chord, a full, low G major, I'd say. Resonant and harmonic.

Then that was what I did. It was my work. Listening. I latched onto the idea of it.

I would come home from Justice's, or wherever, at night. I would undress in the dark and put on my bathrobe and sit against the cool plaster, listening, till the light came.

When the accident happened, I'd just been granted a leave without pay, for half of June, July, and August, so that I could go on the tour. After the funeral, my boss offered to put my vacation time on the front end, to let me off right away.

So I didn't have to be anywhere at all until it was time to go play again, in the evening. I'd get myself something to eat, unplug the phone, and go to bed. I'd sleep, on and off—never a really deep sleep, but I figured it was easier on me to come awake not screaming in the daylight than in the dark. I told everyone that I was sleeping a lot, and not to call me or come by before two or three.

I'd get up in the afternoon and practice for a couple of hours. There was a place I could still get to where I could stay alive. Then somebody would show up—Mrs. Stevens or Luke or Kelly and Joyner or Ardrie or TJ or Stony or one of my friends from work (they had the job divvied up by days of the week, I guess)—to bring me something to eat, and eat with me. Then I'd get myself dressed and go play at Justice's. We'd play our three sets. Then I'd come home.

And sit against the wall again, trying to hear the one sound. That was the work I was doing then.

It went on for several weeks. Mrs. Stevens sat across from me at the kitchen table one night and said, "Carrie? I don't like how you're doing. You ought not to be in the bed so much. Don't you reckon you ought to try to get back to normal? Wouldn't that be a help?"

"It takes me a long time to unwind at night, after I get home from playing. I seem to want to sleep in the daytime, to make up for it."

"You shouldn't be staying here all by yourself."

"No! I want to be!" I said.

"I wish Martha hadn't gone off. Why doesn't your sister come stay with you?"

"That's all I need, old Connie bossing me around. *You're* bad enough." We both laughed. She squeezed my hand.

The sound did finally seem to encompass everything. The names did finally fall away from things. I don't know, I guess

I was hallucinating by then. When I looked at the thing we call *table,* I couldn't remember the word for it, didn't even want to—its name seemed to have nothing to do with the density of matter the name stood for. What was important was the sound this density gave off, a solid, steady, particular sound in the one ongoing chord.

I'm just trying to reach back and say what it was like. I can't make myself hear it now, though I hear it every once in a while in spite of me.

Everything was within that chord, myself and my dead child and every breath ever breather ever breathed.

I guess I needed to hear it.

Cars would go by on the street, a siren far off. Down the block, a party would swing into gear, with loud music. Wind blew through the maple tree, carrying the heavy backbeat with it. A branch would brush the roof, or somebody on the street would call out.

These separate incidental sounds of the world going on seemed like rocks that the river of the one main sound separated itself to flow around. Or like flashes of light thrown off of that river.

I began to think of it as a river. I was on its banks. On its banks. The ground under my feet was this: there was no way in the world out of what had happened; it was final. I would never see her again.

I would hear it. Then I would go and play my fiddle with Cap and Joyner and Louis and TJ. One night, right in the middle of "Sallie Goodin," I heard the sound. Playing was like bidding the notes to rise up out of it, one at a time, flash and shake themselves, then go back.

So I heard the music a new way. This hearing gave my playing a definiteness, a clean certainty, a brilliance it hadn't had before. Playing took a lot of concentration. I had to keep the one sound in my mind the whole time I was calling the separate notes out of it.

I was further from singing than I'd ever been.

I kept my mouth shut and played to save my soul. They gave me room, they cleared out a place in the music for me and let me have my head. They didn't look at me after I finished a riff. I'd sort of drift back and disappear. Joyner would step up quick to his mike through the applause and quiet it with that wild-horses clawhammer banjo-picking he could do, to take everybody's minds off what they'd just heard. Or poker-faced Louis would crawl inside his shiny white Dobro and break it loose. Then we'd all be in the melody again, and Cap and Joyner and Louis would sing one last chorus. After that, we'd all step back and finally take quick sidelong glances at each other, fall to tuning or adjusting capos or taking care of busted strings, getting ready for the next number, Cap chatting the audience up while we did it, joking with Joyner as though nothing unusual at all was happening. "Might ought to tune this thing," he'd say, and Joyner would laugh and say, "Why mess with it now? We was all just about to get adjusted."

I smiled and joked around, I smiled and drank my beer, and all the time, I swear, that sound was looming underneath everything. Vast, harmonic, taking in everything. I smiled, sliding sideways, the big glissando, like a leaf sliding on the wind, down and down and down, while Cap and Joyner put their heads together and sang, *See that freight train, coming round the bend, See that freight train, coming round the bend—*

And then I'd go home and listen again. If I could have sat there a little longer. If Cap hadn't come after me that night.

Sometimes I lost it, of course. I had to sit perfectly still for a long time sometimes. So when I got it, I would try to hang on to it. It held on to *me*. It folded around me, it gave me peace.

This business of being alive or being dead didn't matter so much then. When I could keep hearing the sound for a long enough time, it would lift me up out of my grief-struck body. I would feel myself not just connected to but somehow part of the same thing Molly was part of. And I would be light.

But Cap came and rescued me.

I don't try to hear that sound anymore. I understand the danger, for me. But sometimes when I'm tired, it will come over me, the way an uncatchable rush of a dream from the night before will come over me when I turn down the covers to get back into bed.

I sat against the wall. Then I slept, or tried to. Then I practiced, first the precise lonely singing of the scales, then the figures. I would break them apart, studying the bowing. Some of these old jig figures, slow them down and they'll break your heart. I would fill the little house with sounds of my own making.

Then I would go meet the band. We were all playing beyond our abilities. It was a miracle, and we all knew it, though nobody mentioned it, except to say, once in a while, "Damn, that sounded good to me."

Then I'd go home alone and lean against the wall. That listening was the hardest work I've ever done. Tougher than learning the fiddle, even. Nothing dreamy or absentminded about it.

The darkness was full of high hums, buzzes, cracks, flutters, roars. Then these fell away, or were overcome. Toward the end, the sound of my own breathing was incidental, detached from me, far off.

A deep rushing. I wanted it. The image of lowering myself into it came to me. I began to think I had a choice in the matter. Thinking I had a choice helped me, made it possible for me to sleep. I'd sleep then, a dreamless dark sleep. And when

I woke, there would be at first some momentous relief, elation, as though Molly and I were together. No separation, she
was with me.

The grief would come upon me later, as I picked up my fiddle, as I drew the bow over the strings. The low grieving
sound of the violin. But I would discipline it to the scales, to
the figures of the jig and hornpipe, to a grave, full tone.

So I gave my life over, not to music, but to the sound music
came out of.

A roar, a low powerful continuous rushing noise—a river,
unstoppable, steady, swift.

There came a time about a month after I went back to play
with the band when I didn't want to practice after I woke. I
pressed my face into her clothes, still hanging in the closet.

I slid down the wall next to her closet, to try to hear the
sound. It was a thirst, an addiction. Need entered in. I needed
to enter that current.

If somebody showed up at my door with food, flowers,
tapes, I would put water on for tea. I would listen hard to
words. I would nod, smile fast, say some words myself. I
wasn't able to let the words into my understanding.

Martha called almost every day, from Paris. "Talk to me,
Carrie," she'd plead.

"I'm all right."

"Like hell you are."

"No, really."

"Listen—I've asked for some time off work. I want to come
back to stay with you for a week or so. I can be on a plane
tomorrow. Would that be all right?"

"Oh, Martha, don't worry, honey. There's no reason for you
to do that. Really. I'm working through it. It's better for me to
be alone right now. I'm all right. Honest."

I thought I was all right. I got myself over to Justice's on the nights we played there. Afterwards, I drove home, fast, as soon as I could leave, with the radio turned off. I knew what I wanted.

Better to want the melodies. The clever progressions, temporal arrangements. Since we have to live in time. Can't live outside of it. I know that now.

The deep swift current. It was just a matter of getting up the courage. A serious, ongoing sound by then, a roar. It would get quieter when it went through the rocks to where Molly was. It would be as quiet then again as the heart of music.

If I could get out into the middle of it, I understood, it would take me to my girl. It would carry me beyond the pale. Beyond the curb, into the street, where I had found her, and beyond that place, too. I prayed to be taken to where she was.

The one most dark full sound. If I could be inside it, not just listening to it, but part of it. . . .

The sound of blood, coursing through the universe. All I needed to do was to leave the bank. On the surface it would be still, but swift underneath. The other river, underneath.

I got dressed in my jeans and red silk blouse, my brown boots. I put on my earrings. I tried to put on my stage makeup, looking at my faraway face in the mirror. I didn't stop, exactly. I just couldn't make myself hurry up, even though it was getting late.

I'll just sit down by her closet for a minute, I'll just sit down on the floor for a minute. I'll just lean back against the wall for a minute, and listen. It didn't matter if I was late, none of that mattered. *I'll just close my eyes for a minute.*

I got out into the middle of it. It was easy. I let the current take me. I didn't breathe, the sound breathed for me, it was partly made of breath.

I don't know what happened. Time stopped. Time dissolved.

The sound had to separate and flow around some rocks. Six. Then, when I thought I was past that place, six more. And I thought, this is the rocky place I have to go through to get to her.

Loud sounds I thought I should see about. But they didn't matter. Loud definite sounds from the place I couldn't remember, like: *no! no! no! no!*

THEN HARD SOUNDS coming through the rooms of the house. I saw the sharp U-shape of each one come down. Cap leaned toward me with a look on his face as though he'd found me lying in a pool of blood.

My red silk blouse.

Pool of silence.

Ten

He knelt on the floor beside me. He said my name. I still remembered it was mine.

What would have happened if he hadn't come? Would I have died there? Of what? Would I have literally opened a vein? I don't know. I can't see me doing that. I don't know.

Maybe I would have just sat there on the floor for a little longer, gotten up when I'd come to the end of it, and lived my life in a normal, regular, quiet way. Maybe I just needed to sit there a little longer.

He knelt beside me, talking to me, sounding the way you do when you try to sweet-talk a cat out from under a bed.

He put his hand on my bare arm, flat at first, and then he grasped it around with his fingers. I drew back, I jerked my arm back. "Leave me *alone*," I said, but he held on. He wanted me to get up. He didn't know what he was doing. He was where he had no business to be.

I heard his calm voice: "Come on, honey, you need to get up from there." He didn't have a clue what I needed. I shut my eyes tight. I didn't want him in my sight. I was shaking with rage. I felt in my fingers how I would choke him for interrupting me, for saying my name. I was way past the field of gravity of his take-charge voice and his sexy eyes and black cowboy jacket. "I want you to leave me alone, Cap," I said. "I want you to back off." My voice felt chiseled.

His fear was in his hand tighter than he would have wanted on my arm.

"All right, Carrie," he said. "But I'm staying. If you need me, I'm right here." I didn't need him. He went somewhere a little way off, took the bad-memory smell of bar smoke and beer with him. I heard him breathing, then that sound was gone, too. I was so close, so close. . . .

But then it was first light and he was sitting on the edge of Molly's bed putting his boots on. I saw him from far back, a distant memory. I could hardly place him. "How long has it been since you ate?" he asked.

It seemed to me then that my only hope was to get up off the floor and act natural, so he would leave. I found my legs, I stood up shakily. I took a shower and put on my bathrobe. He was in the kitchen, fresh as a daisy, when I came out. The man I'd always most wanted to eat breakfast with. His jeans still had a crease in them. I wanted to ask, "Does your grandma iron them for you or do you send them to the laundry?" He put a plate of scrambled eggs in front of me. I ate them to get rid of them. I said, "I'm fine now. Thank you. You go on now, Cap."

He sat down in the chair across from me and leaned across the table, put a hand on my hand. "Carrie, listen to me. This is important. Are you going to be able to make this tour? You know we're onstage in Dayton tomorrow night and we ain't offstage again hardly till September. I don't want to push you. But you've got to tell me. I can still get somebody to fill in for you, but I've got to know now."

I heard him from my wayback place, where *onstage* looked like small lights you see from an airplane. "Oh," I said. A deep gasp, a real pain, under the rib cage. I had forgotten about the tour. It wasn't anyplace in my mind. It frightened me that I could have forgotten something so important to my everyday life. "Oh God! Look at the time! I have a million things to do to get ready to leave, a *million.* I've got to get on my horse."

I pushed myself up, but something heavy pushed me back down. Cap sat on the other side of the table, looking at me, his eyes glazed with fear for me. "Oh, pardon me," I said. I held on to the edge of the table with my fingernails. I took some breaths. "I had a list," I said then, scanning the kitchen hopefully. "I'll have to find it."

"Sit still, honey." Calm, offhanded voice. "You don't need no list. I'm going to call around and get somebody to take your place. Just till you feel like you can come on and join us. Believe me, you're not supposed to go on this trip tomorrow."

"Oh yes. I have to."

"You're not up to it."

"Yes I am. I'm up to it."

"You need a rest. You really do."

"Oh hell, I'll rest on the tour. It'll be good for me. Get me away from—*here.*" I waved my hand at all my pots and pans and jars of stuff, the pictures from nursery school still on the fridge. "Get me out of myself. Besides, I wouldn't quit you at a time like this, Cap. Jesus. What do you think? I have to go get on my clothes, pardon me. I'm losing my marbles. Knock-knock-knock," I said, knocking my knuckles against my forehead.

He had a kind of horrified, askance look on his face.

"I wouldn't miss it for anything." I got myself up from the table, to show him I was in control now.

He still sat there, holding his cup, looking up at me. "You sure? Because I can still get on the horn and find somebody else."

"No. Trust me. You don't need to be worrying about me. You got enough to do. I'm all right."

He rose then. He picked up my hands, ran his thumbs gently back and forth over my knuckles. His eyes moved over my face like he was checking to see if I had a rash.

"Oh come on, Cap."

"I'll be by this afternoon, then. I wish you'd go crawl in the sack."

"Cap, nothing personal, but could you get on out of here? I got things to do. Thanks for coming over. Thanks for the eggs."

I stood on the kitchen stoop in my white bathrobe waving goodbye goodbye as he climbed into the van and backed it down the driveway. And then I turned to go to my bedroom to get dressed, but walked straight into Molly's room instead, slid down the wall again, thinking, *Irresponsible, neglectful, crazy. Making trouble for everybody. Send her to the loony bin.* But the words fell away, I dropped right back into the stream, the river. The river flowing. No problem, no problem anymore.

A loud, serious, working sound, like machinery now. I was getting somewhere. Then, to my joy and amazement, I began to think I could hear something else, beyond the clanking roar—a perfect sweet silence. I can't tell you the quality of it. It was like—a wide expanse of still, pure water. A wide lake that the river emptied into, at last. I think now you must hear this sound right before you die. Or right afterwards. I tell you, I could see the rocks I had to go through to get to her. I could see through them, a little, to some *beyond.* A radiance. A sweet, loving shine. I was on my way, I really think I was. Gathering momentum—I was into the rapids already.

As close as I'll ever get and live to tell the tale.

I don't know what was in store for me. I don't know what would have happened, what I would have done. I'm only remembering as well as I can the feeling of what I was moving toward. Freedom, peace. Still, silvery water, golden light. I forgot everything, except that there was plenty of time, that I would know what to do, that there would be time to do it. That the way to do it would be clear to me.

Then there was Cap again. I hadn't heard him, I didn't know he was there, until he was standing above me. He knelt swiftly to lift me. *Too soon!* was all I could think, bitterly. A trick. I don't have any idea what time it might have been. Four-thirty. Or ten-fifteen. He didn't talk, this time. He just knelt, fast, to lift me. But I was fast, too. All instinct, fighting for my life. I grabbed his arms, we grappled together. I slapped him, scratched at him, desperately. I had come so far, it had been so hard, I'd had so much to learn. I was almost there, dear God! And here comes Cap, taking it upon himself to pull me back, out of the deep, sacred current of that river. "Who in the hell do you think you are?" I screamed at him.

He held me off. He warded off my slaps and kicks and struggled this way and that till holding me off turned into holding.

Until this dead-serious wrestling turned into what I'd always wanted from him, but not then. And then I wanted it then.

I tried to stay in the current, even as I fought with him, even as he lifted me away from it. Tears running down his face. They stopped me. Tears. I let go of it. Of the chance to go through to my girl. I let go. Like fingers forced open.

He held me then, cradled me, rocked me. My muscles were all so tight. They'd been clenched ever since she died. His hands moved then, knowing how to help me. To help my poor old body. He put me on the bed to help me. Everything happened then, I wanted it to. The old thing with Cap, flashing out, leaping out of the darkness I had made. Grief and lust ringing against each other, like I'd swallowed a set of church bells.

Going down, sliding down. Our bodies giving in to it, at last. Easy, the pure release of it, like I'd been holding my breath for years, and then I breathed. Necessary. No keeping from it. I turned away from that radiance and entered something else, a darkness, like the dark at the center of a plant. It closed around the two of us. The realest thing that ever happened to me, happening almost in sight of Molly, of her everlastingness. How will I ever straighten that out? Grief and lust, sorrow and love. As if there's one deep place that every real thing comes out of, and when we're in that place's charge, there aren't any rules, it's just being swept along without any will whatsoever.

I couldn't help it, I sank down into the mattress. Molly's mattress. I guess the thought crossed my mind. Molly and I had slept together there many a night, when I fell asleep reading to her, with her curled up against me. It couldn't be helped. I couldn't help it. I was pulling him down then, into that sliding place that doesn't know anything but wanting and not having and having.

His serious face yielding, those lines around his mouth. His neat hard brown hands, bringing me, bringing me.

Back to life.

Come back, come back, each side called out. Each side said the other side was death. Love was on both sides. I had to choose. I chose to go back to the side I knew about.

Oh little screamer, cheeks all flushed out. Bright Eyes, coming back for more, shrieking and swinging that feather pillow around your head, blond tangled hair flying.

I feel I've failed her twice. I didn't look, the one time when

I should have been looking. I took my eyes off of her and down the driveway she went, her legs held out from the pedals, coasting, free.

And afterwards, when I almost had her in my sight, when I felt her right there waiting for me, I chose to turn back. I missed my chance.

Passed it up.

Those tears running down his face. Crying for everything, I guess. For poor dear life. I held him. I didn't cry then. I didn't cry till Ona rocked me in her lap on her front porch.

I HEARD WHAT he said on the phone. "I'm bringing her out, Granny. Somebody who knows how has got to take over for a while. You're the one, sweetheart. She's in a bad way." I didn't care what he said about me. I had no pride, by then. I gave myself up, withdrew my claim.

I slept, and woke to his voice on the phone again. Talking to Andy, probably. "There's a flight that'll get you into Cincinnati at nine-thirty tomorrow morning. We'll meet you. You and me and Louis, we'll drive up to Dayton together, go over the tabs on the way. Joyner and TJ can get up to the motel at four. Yeah. So we'd have a few hours before we go on. Okay, yeah, okay." He gave a little laugh. "Yeah, well— that's the way it sometimes usually goes."

OH THE WORLD had slipped away from me so fast, so fast. Or I had slipped away from it. My life. What I used to do.

He was packing things up in my knapsack, rummaging through my dresser—looking for underwear, I guess. *Good luck*, I thought, drifting in and out of a luxurious calm sleep. I watched him coming and going. He fixed the lock on the front door that he'd broken the night before. He washed the dishes from the morning, made me some tea and toast, and brought them to me. He stroked my hair, propped pillows up behind me. While I drank the tea, he put out some clothes for me. "Don't I take good care of you?"

I laughed, from way down. It felt good. "You're like a mother to me," I said.

He brushed my hair. I put on the flowered dress he'd laid out. I sat on the bed. He knelt and buckled my sandals. I leaned forward and kissed his forehead. He had some kind of miserable, blind, sorrowful look on his face. I saw what it was. He was scared. He'd come here to patch me up, get me on my feet. And look where we'd ended up. He was afraid he'd sent me round the bend. Well, he'd kept me from going round one bend and sent me round another.

He washed my cup. He picked up the knapsack and took me by the arm. He walked me through the rooms of my little house, its arrangements of patchwork quilts and funny pictures from old magazines. I stood on the porch with my hands long and empty at my sides while he tried the new lock. He put his hand at the small of my back, to guide me out to the van. He opened the door and I stepped up.

He drove with one hand, his eyes wide open in the wind, looking straight ahead. All I heard was the tires on the road, something singing in the fields, crickets, I guess. I closed my eyes and nearly slept again. It was her smallness I remembered then. Death made her so little.

I opened my eyes and saw what was left. Mackerel clouds, converging to a point in the east. White cows with the last long light of the clear day making them glow against green fields, as though lit from underneath. The beginning pink of the sunset, over on the other side.

THREE

Star

Quality

Eleven

The blue bottle of window cleaner, the cloths, the roll of paper towels. I have left them spilled across the grass behind me. The stepladder, knocked onto its side. I didn't stop to right it. I just took off running, away from the job Ona gave me.

When I get to the wagon road, I slow down to a fast walk, through the stalled light. I can't hear anything now but the whirring song of the cicadas and leafhoppers, coming in waves, rising and falling like the electricity that runs the world. The hot glare of the sky hits the baked fields and bounces back. Sweat rolls down my forehead into my eyes. Even the straw color is baked out of the grass. These hills, ghosty with dried weeds and grasses, the bleached fescue waving in the low wind, like a spirit hovering a foot above the earth, matching its configuration, but stirring in the wind— earth's breath. The only color comes from the redtop, great bays of it, in with the other grasses. Redtop takes over and spreads itself in bad years, Ona told me.

I don't love the world anymore, not like I did. If I knew I could be with Molly, I'd go right now, without one backward glance. I can't think of a thing that would have the power to hold me back—no person, for all the love I've gotten, no place, for all the ones I've held dear. Out into the woods with something sharp. Oh, all the old songs I've sung in my day, all the times I've sent my fiddle flying above the old words, *death is only a dream,* the old words, full of assurance. *On the opposite shore she'll be waiting for me.*

I never paid much attention. It was always more the music that got into my heart, not the words. I don't know what the ones at Justice's think. The ones at the festivals, sitting in plastic-webbed lawn chairs, passing beers around out of their coolers like the loaves and the fishes. Some have stickers on their RVs testifying, "No End to What Jesus Can Do." But some wear black baseball caps that say, "Shit Happens."

I don't much care anymore about this life or even about God. I just want to know what comes next. I want to know if the circle will be unbroken. I thought I knew more or less what that question was about, singing it. Now I know that love is a circle and either death breaks it or it doesn't and no one knows. It could be either way. Maybe the circle will be unbroken, but not in any way I can imagine.

What if it turns out that death is just the end of this tiny flame of consciousness, and then the body goes back to nature?

Then it's better to stay alive, so that I can remember her. Carry her memory inside me as long as I'm alive, the way I carried *her.* Keep her safe, preserve her. I wasn't able to keep her safe in her real life. I let her out into the real world. I thought I was giving her life, but it wasn't enough to shake a stick at. I gave her death.

Not your fault, they always rush to say. *Not your fault, you must not blame yourself.* "Something terrible could happen to every one of us a hundred times a day," Ona told me. "The miracle is that mostly it don't."

"You can't watch them every second," my mother said.

"You've got to trust to luck, a little." But you can't. You can't trust to luck.

Maybe the accident was—pure accident, one of the many things that just come down out of the sky and happen to people for no reason at all, except they were walking past the building when the bomb went off, sitting on the plane, looking at the clouds, when the engines failed.

That's not how it feels, though.

"SOMETIMES I THINK I'm a horse." That tie-dyed cap she loved, too big for her, so that it fell down over her eyes. Somebody gave it to her, TJ I think.

"You're a little old painted pony, is what you are."

"No, I'm *not* no pony. I'm a high horse, that can run."

AT THE END of the wagon road, I go through the gate onto the ridge, and then along the mown path, eyes down. *God of the days help me, God of the daylight help me.* There isn't any God. Not one who can help me. If there is a God all I have to say to him is *Give her back, you bastard.* The grasshoppers spray out before me. I can barely raise my eyes above my feet. It feels like lifting weights to drag my eyes up to the horizon.

Maybe God is a tree or a mountain or the whole earth that just *is,* no questions asked.

The world grieves till the hole that our absence from it makes closes over. Sometimes it takes no time at all. To *cease*—what a word, like the breath going out of everything. Stone stays, but wears down, dissolves. Water goes up and comes down over and over. Maybe water is eternal.

Light comes and goes. Maybe light is God.

Pain rises in my eyes and turns to light. Emptiness rises upward, out of the dried-up pale grass.

I plunge into the seeded redtop, waist-high, wading

through it, down the steep side of the ridge toward the woods. The long grass, the poison ivy, the ticks waiting, hoping for something to come their way. I pick one off my bare leg. Little flat hard moving seed of life, wanting to take hold—who knows how long it's waited for its chance.

I have a map of these woods in my mind by now. The line fence makes a dogleg up the side of the hill, then runs south again, through deep cedar woods, before dropping steeply to the creek bed.

Cooler here, deep in shade. I walk the dry bed stone to stone. There's still a little mud, though, moisture caught under stones. I kneel and touch it. I put a little on my face, I try some on my tongue. It's all right, just leaves and long-gone dead things, dissolving rocks. Just topsoil, earth—they named this planet for what covers it, which is made of things that used to be alive right here.

A thin coat of earth. Then rock and rock and rock.

I come upon the rock I want in the middle of the creek of stones. It would stand up out of the water, if there were water. I crawl onto it and lie down. I look up at the sycamore leaves above me, stirring a little, like breath. I find a smooth pebble lodged in a crack in the stone, work it out, hold it in my hand. Stone woman. Stone and bone woman. I imagine water running all around me.

Molly left her rocks behind, her small gravels. She would squat and pick up one, then another, and examine it. She liked the shiners, the ones with little mica flakes in them. Every one of her pockets had a rock in it.

Maybe I could spend the night out here. Maybe something would come here. A deer or a fox. But Ona and Ruth would be setting the table for supper, waiting, while watching the news, for me to come back. If I didn't show up by the end of the news, they would come up along the darkening ridge, calling, "Carrie? Carrie?" They wouldn't know where to look for me.

I need to get up. The deer and the fox don't come here anymore, anyway. They've had to scout out another place to get a drink. I need to start back, but instead I turn in the opposite direction. I want to. I follow the streambed to the line fence. Where the streambed dips, I can crawl under the bottom wire of the fence. On the other side, a long field stretches down the bottom, but it hasn't been mown for a few years, and now ragweed and goldenrod have taken over.

Whose land am I on now? The creek bottom zigzags back for a half mile or so. I find an old cowpath; even so, it's a job to get through the tangle of rose thorns and brambles. Finally the valley forks. I take the right fork and go on.

The land lifts slightly, until the creek loops around the base of a wooded hill, and up against it there, almost hidden in a grove of oak trees, a small log house stands, with a board barn built against it. They lean together, hold each other up. A fancy scalloped wire fence, such as you might see in town, not enough to keep a cow out, runs along the front, with a little waist-high wrought-iron gate set in. I push it open and slip through. A short stone path runs from the gate to the sagging front porch. I step up on it and look into the house through a cracked glass window.

A long time ago, the window frame and the ceiling of the porch were painted a soft greenish blue. A pretty place. Somebody must have thought so, to paint the trim and put up that gate. Through the window I can see a stone hearth, and scraps of wallpaper pasted right to the logs. I try the front door, but it's locked. I step across the porch, joist to joist, to look through another long window into the attached barn. A big stone fireplace rises right in the middle of it. So it was built as an addition to the house—where the children slept, maybe. But it's been used as a barn since then. Someone's torn the puncheon floors out—I can see the notches they rested in. A ladder goes to the loft, a few old bales of hay forgotten up there, along with a shrimp-pink dresser without any drawers.

I press my forehead against the glass. With my hands up to shut out the reflection of myself, I look through the window, singing: *Oh the moon shines tonight on pretty Redwing.* Just the one line—the sound surprises me and I shut up. The door to this part of the house stands slightly ajar, opening inward, sagging toward the dirt. I push at it and set off a sudden commotion inside. Something flutters and flaps above me out the big chimney—a barn owl in disheveled, startled flight, into the highest branch of a dead locust tree nearby. I step back, startled myself, and stare up at it. It doesn't look at me, but coolly turns its head to survey the hillside, as if to say: Don't think I was bothered by anything as trifling as *you.*

Careless and gay—the words come into my mind. Are they from some song? I hear them with a little upturned melody, a high thin child's voice, and something behind it, coming in, fading, coming in again, some sound like laughter, like distant knee-slapping laughter, all around, above me, rowdy hilarity, as though on an out-of-range radio station, tuned way down. Then the sound is gone. The leaves give a sharp little flash in the breeze. The owl still sits right there in the dead locust tree, looking elsewhere. As if I didn't exist, never had and never would. Then, as I watch, it lifts off negligently, to disappear in the woods.

An empty string bag hangs from a nail out here on the porch.

I turn, not running, exactly, but walking fast, tearing through the brambles, back to the line fence, back to where I came from. Then straight up the ridge through the redtop.

Climbing calms me down. Now I walk along the crest of

the ridge, toward the pond, my passing a sort of shining, far off, to myself. As if I'm looking *back* at myself, pushing through the shining red grass, from some time long after the day when I saw the owl come banging out of the old stone chimney.

WATER THE COLOR of an old nickel glints down there in the hollow, under the glaring gray sky. I go down the hill toward it, and then around the edge, over the dam, to the far side, where I can stand on the rocks someone has piled out past the cattails. I go in, in my clothes and thongs, and strike out for the middle to get away from the gray ooze. Big, breathing clouds of algae stir near the edges, underwater. But out toward the middle the water is clear. A layer of warm; cold underneath.

That time Cap gave her the cane pole and brought her out here to the pond was the last time Molly was on the farm. He helped her catch a dozen little bass, big enough to eat. She was thrilled and bossy, telling who could have each one. Cap gutted them in the kitchen sink and broiled them with lemon. And they were good.

I turn and float, my back to the far-down bottom of the pond. I look up through the thick light. I feel absence, dense as a stone, on my chest. It could sink me, sure as a hand pressing me down.

The water would close over my face, closing out most of the light, my eyes would still be open, I'd see what was left, the tipped surface, a window of light. The weight I couldn't get rid of would sink me, I would come to rest, ten feet down. The clay would billow up around me, the panicky moment would soon arrive, when I would have to have air, and couldn't get it. Couldn't rise. I would be heavy. The clay would get into my nose, and then my mouth.

I couldn't drown if I wanted to.

I don't want to. In spite of everything, I don't want to sink and drown.

Swallows slice their little curves through the air above the pond. I've wanted to die, but it has come this way: a stab of pain through me, a howling, *Let me die, too! Let me die instead!* It's easy in those times to imagine driving a knife into your breast. The misery I'm in right now is different. It's just looking at these old blackish-green cedar trees, some small, some large, standing on the hillsides.

I see a long life ahead of me. Forty or fifty more years, and Molly, no matter what I do, farther gone from me every day.

The refrain of the first song I wrote went like this: *Never asked much but to know I'm alive/Doing 75 on I-75.*

I know I'm alive now, buddy.

I float on my back on my breath. My heavy body, my space and time occupier, held up by breath on the surface, ten feet above the bottom of the pond. I choose not to drown. What do I choose instead? Breath. I choose to keep breathing, for forty or fifty more years.

I turn and swim through the tepid olive-green water, the clouds of algae here and there, the sudden cool springs beneath layers of warm, through herds of grasshoppers, living and dead. I rescue one or two, picking them up and throwing them as hard as I can toward the shore. But, as my daddy used to say, we can't save the world, cousin.

Some earthly creatures can live here, but grasshoppers can't. Humans can't. It's a border, an edge. I crawl carefully over the slippery rocks, my shirt bellied out with water, which spills out from it now. I stand up on the bank and walk around the pond and up the steep hill, sliding backwards in my muddy thongs at every step, until I gain the wagon road again, at the top, and start back toward the house.

And there's Cap, holding a foot under the spigot by the back door.

He's been in the garden, running the big old tiller for Ona, plowing under the whole sad mess, I guess. I want to turn the other way and run, but he looks up and sees me, a long way off still, as if his eyes knew just where to go. He pulls on his laceless running shoes and comes up the road to meet me. Chapped lips, bleached eyebrows. Old Angel Eyes. Here I come, dripping wet, my legs covered to the calves in clay, my hair still up in Ruth's French braid, smelling like swamp ooze. A serious, shining look tightens his skin. He stops before me, arm's length away, smiles, reaches out his hand and brushes my face. I make my eyes meet his—against my better judgment. I want him to know he doesn't have to explain anything about what happened. I want him to know it's all right, but that I can't stop now.

I fish into my watch pocket for that little smooth pebble I dug out of the crack in the rock in the creek bed. I hold my left hand out to him. He holds out his, thinking to take mine. In a friendly way, I give him the pebble. I should stop and explain that it's a gift from the heart, my most precious possession, but my throat closes up and all I can do is nod once, as if that pebble settled something between us, and let him draw me up to him through his bright blue eyes for a second; now I tear myself away, now I walk on past him. "Carrie, for Christ's sake!"

I walk on past him. It's cruel, it's not brave, but I walk by the thought of his body smooth and sharp inside that T-shirt and those old pale jeans with oil stains on them. I have to. I'm not in that frame of mind anymore. I've got a long row to hoe.

I can't keep him from coming here, but I don't aim to think about him. I have to think about what I'm going to do, but I don't have to think about *him.* I don't have to think about what happened. I break into a run. I can't help it. I feel him, all in back of me. I run as fast as I can, like a spooked child, down the road to the house.

In the kitchen, I chew a cold biscuit from breakfast, wash it down with a drink of water, standing at the sink. Ona comes behind me; I don't turn around. "I only did one, Ona. It got so hot. I went for a walk."

"A swim, too, looks like." She turns me around and takes my chin in her hand. She laughs. "Honey, you threw mud all over your face." She rubs at it with her thumb. The creek mud I smeared there. "I want you to go up and take a bath. Out there bare-legged, banging around in the poison ivy. You scrub those feet and legs good, or you're going to be broke out terrible. Use soap and hot water. Then you can either get dressed or try to sleep for a while. But if you go to bed, I want you to put on your nightgown." She means I shouldn't let the bed reach out and grab me the way I sometimes do. She means it's got to be my idea. "Are you hungry?"

"No. I had a biscuit."

"Oh, them stale things."

"Did you know Cap was coming back today?" I ask her.

"Nobody knows what *that* boy's up to," she says, sailing past my mean, accusing tone like a big peaceful sailboat. "You know that. We're real glad when he walks in the door—but we don't look for him."

"That's Cap's arrangement with the whole world," I comment grimly.

"Well, he's sure of his welcome most places, don't you reckon?"

"Oh, absolutely." She looks at me hard, as though she's never heard bitterness before and is trying to translate it into her native tongue. Grandma to the sex bandit, but she'd be the kind to sit there on the couch with the cameras rolling and say, "I know my boy didn't do it. He was always a good boy." I don't think sex ever crossed Ona's mind. As far as she's concerned, I'm just another stray cat big-hearted Cap's brought home for you-know-who to feed and fall in love with.

I take out the stupid braid, sink down into the water, wash my hair, scrub my scratched-up legs. Nothing else I can do. I go back to my room, Ona's spare bedroom, with the blue morning-glory wallpaper, and put on my nightgown, turn back the sheet, and slide in, lay my wet head on the feather pillow.

"Cap brought out your mail," Ona says, coming in to sit on the edge of the bed. "Did you see it? There on the bed table. Look yonder at that stack of cards, Carrie—it's from all over the country. I never saw such a thing. You got a raft of people that cares about you. One of these days you're going to want to play for them again." Her eyes land on my legs. "I hate to think about the chigger bites you're going to have," she says sadly.

I open one of the cards. It says, "May the dear Lord hold you in the palm of his hand and bring you back to the music, love from your admiring fan Estelle J. Wright." I hold it against my chest, then put it down. Next to the stack of sympathy cards, Ona's arranged the regular mail, from my house. It looks like the payout on Molly's insurance has come.

A couple of weeks ago, during one of those weepy TV commercials about life insurance, Ruth gave me her sharp Senior Trust Officer look and said, "Carrie Marie, did you have a policy on Molly?"

I didn't know how to tell her the claim was still stuck between the flour and sugar jars on top of the fridge, where I'd put it that night three months ago. It wasn't exactly that I forgot about it; I just gave it a wide berth. I couldn't look at it or touch it, much less take it to the post office and send it off by

certified mail. Money getting mixed up with Molly's death—
it felt like betrayal. I think I had the idea that if I sent in that
claim, her death would be final. She would disappear even
from my memory.

And later, the claim really did fall out of my mind, along
with almost everything else.

"You did, didn't you?" she said.

So I told her where the envelope was, and she went by my
house and collected it and mailed it in for me.

And now the check has come. I open the envelope and pull
it out. Pale blue. I raise it up to show Ona. She glances at it
quickly, not wanting to be nosy, and nods.

"That's a good start on something," she says.

"I don't know what to do," I whisper.

"Not a thing in the world. Just rest. That's all you got to do
right now."

"But then what? I can't just stay here forever, Ona. I'm
going to wear out my welcome."

"I'm *glad* for you to be here. When the time comes for you
to do something different, you'll know." She's sitting on the
bed, looking at me. "You'll be wanting to get back to your
music one of these days. But even when you do, you can stay
here if it suits you. It don't bother me any. You can stay here
till kingdom come. You won't want to, but if you did it would
suit me fine. The three of us get along pretty good, *I* think."
She hikes herself off the bed, crosses the room to pull down
the shade and turn on the fan.

"At least now, if I stayed, I could pay my keep."

"Don't you be worrying about that. Your keep ain't nothing but what you eat and you don't eat nothing. It costs me
more to keep a chicken. You just rest now."

"I don't want to be the star of the band, Ona. I don't even
know whether I want to be in the band at all. I can't see me

anymore, standing up there, playing the old way."

She shakes her head and smiles. "You don't have to be in no band to play your fiddle, darling girl."

"I won't tell Cap you said that."

She regards me with her calm, open-eyed look.

"I don't think he'd be too crazy about me staying out here with you, if I quit the band," I explain.

"I believe that's a bridge we don't have to cross just yet," she tells me, to calm me down and let me sleep.

I curl on my side, knees up. I'm bleached, sweet-smelling, like the sheets. Wrung out, hung on the line to dry.

I press the pillow tight against my belly, pretending it's Molly, sound asleep in my curve.

Twelve

Let her sleep, I wake and hear someone say. I fall back. A drone, far off. Then closer. Then gone again.

Where he is.

I try to rise toward it, as it comes near. It's as if the heel of a hand against my forehead shoves me back. Then I have to do it all again.

I climb a steep bank, the high slick side of a question. *My life now.* It looks like a cliff to me, pale blue.

I wake in the heat. I lie under the sheet with the electric fan blowing over me.

Is this evening, or rain coming on? How long have I been asleep in this flowered room? Not long enough, if the first thing I know about the waking world is that Cap's down there in it somewhere. And then, the second thing, that Molly isn't, my stomach cramping down on its main fact again. I get my fingers dug into my belly. The shade slaps once, twice, against the windowsill: *Get up! Get up!* Thunder in the distance, rolling around like empty barrels. What time is it, anyway? The shade that Ona pulled down for me is as brown now as an old cut apple.

And there's the blue insurance check, still propped against

the lamp, to greet me. Twenty grand, and a little over, where once there was a child.

Maybe I'll invest the round number and save back the extra to buy some Jack, sip it slow. Stay up here in this sweet room for the rest of my life, rocking and sipping, telling myself jokes. Ona'd leave my dinner outside the door if I asked her to.

Wallpaper morning glories twine upwards. I have a vision, slipping backwards again towards sleep, of morning glories growing all over me, Heavenly Blues. The white muslin curtains blow out, edged with cotton lace from something previous, you can tell from how it's pieced together, if you look closely. I see Ona ripping lace carefully from a child's skirt, some long-ago evening, winding it on a card.

A few weeks ago, when I was still going to the grocery store, I read a headline in the *National Enquirer* that said dead people weigh one three-thousandth of an ounce less than when they were alive a moment before. "Proof of Immortality!" the headline told. I didn't read it, but I guess the theory was that the soul flies off, weighing one three-thousandth of an ounce.

The last breath must weigh that. Little balloon let loose, disappearing upward.

Does she go on, in her next place? Does she have a soul, or is this loving memory of her all she's going to have of eternal life? If so, it's not much—when I die, it will be as though she never lived.

Maybe it's the other way around, that the life she lived, each moment of it, goes on and on, outside of time, like a radio wave, and once in a while, through some kind of divine grace, I tune in on it, and call it memory. Molly in the closet in her Dyn-O-Mite underpants, choosing her dress to wear, swishing her round bottom this way and that, singing at the

top of her lungs, *"Dat's* what you *get* for jumpin on de bed."
Shaking her finger jazzily. I can hear her voice. I can see her,
plain as day.

Proof of Immortality! What wouldn't we give for it? We
humans, who have to die, and know it. We've been setting up
a racket, we've been cracking our heads against that one for a
long time, that pane of dark, unbreakable glass, the split second when the creature breathes out and doesn't breathe back
in again and is gone. Just—gone. Right before our eyes.
We're touching her and she's alive. And then we're still
touching her, but she's gone. We're looking at her, but she's
not looking back.

Molly didn't know one thing about it.

But that's not right, because one night she came up out of
her sleep crying. "What's wrong, honey?" I asked. It took me a
while, but I finally got it out of her. "I can't go to heaven because I love my mama more than Jesus," she whispered, embarrassed. I hugged her and said, "Oh Molly, who told you
such a thing? Jesus doesn't care a bit. That's exactly what he
wants you to do, that's how you learn about love. Somebody
told you a dumb, scary thing." She listened and nodded, then
said, "That's what I *thought.*"

Where did she get that kind of talk? Those born-agains at
the festivals, maybe. Or maybe it's in some song. I was trying
to raise her to be a free girl.

I believe she's in the next place.

I was almost there myself, wasn't I? Or did I just make it
up, that shining behind the rocks, because I needed to?

The back door slams. I hear Ona shout, "Get back, greedy
thangs." I rise, cross the room, raise the shade. In the stormy
light, there goes Ona, against the wind, holding a white basin
of scraps out before her with both hands, her head jutted forward to help her trundle along in her green sneakers, toward

the chicken yard. The chickens bustle toward her, tilted headlong, just like her. She's clucking, they're clucking. The dogs
and cats mill around her—she kicks out sideways at them to
clear a space to open the wire gate.

I know that years from now I'll think back to this dry place
and time when I heard not the one sound anymore but the
clear singing of each separate thing. The morning glories in
the wallpaper, the ridge's high crest, the stones along the
path. The evening light in the cedar trees, up the hill. All
singing *come back.* The shine of life in the low last ray.

But I know what I didn't know before: that shine is sharp.
The little white teeth bared in pain. The light will turn sharp
for some living creature every moment. The creature will
bare its teeth, or it may scream once, then it will be gone.

In the west, long juicy light seeps out from under the bottom edge of the dark mass of clouds. Distant lightning throbs
here and there, but a narrow gold alleyway sharpens before
my eyes between the barn and the tractor shed, as if God said,
Let there be light.

It's last light, but it looks like first light, light inventing itself, trying itself out, pulling itself all new out of the void.
And now the tractor rolls roaring and clanking into it, its
shadow thrown out in front of itself. Cap does a hook turn into
the dark shed and shuts off the motor. The air seems to throb
a little in the sudden silence. He sits for a minute in the darkness of the shed, and then jumps down and starts toward the
house.

Meanwhile, Ona has slung out the scraps and the chickens
have followed the arc. Now she latches the gate of the chicken
yard and heads toward Cap, banging the bottom of the empty
basin against her thigh like a tambourine. Cap puts his hand
on her shoulder and they consider what's left of the garden,
the permanent beds of strawberries, rhubarb, asparagus, four

tomato plants on stakes, all the rest plowed under. In the end they both raise their heads at the same moment, and catch me standing at the window looking down at them. I raise my hand and wave. Ona waves back, her face lit up, welcoming. Cap also lifts his face, but doesn't wave, doesn't smile. Still, his face is alight, too. Bright and tight with pure intention, is how it looks to me.

Now they start toward the house. I see them the same way I saw my life, earlier, as I moved through that field: as a kind of far-off shining, an afterimage. All us flimsy breathy mortal things, on our way into pure light through the solid dense world, stone and bone, creek bottom and hillside. Or into pure dark. We don't know which.

Maybe what I'm seeing is the world shining around our dark-prone lives.

There's got to be another part to this situation, that we pass through the world of light so quickly, and out the other side.

If here seems stranger to me than gone right now that's just too bad. *Here* is where I happen to be. I have to throw myself into the idea of it. I have to learn what to do about *gone*. Ona's seventy-four, but *she* doesn't seem to waste any time with *gone*. She's seen mother, father, husband, oh, and daughter, too, go out into death, but still she holds on to this world like she holds on to the white basin, with both hands.

Or maybe one hand is for *here*, the other for *gone*.

Maybe everybody in the world but me knows this. At the funeral, the preacher said, "In the midst of life we are in death." It came as a surprise to me. Before she died I was heedless. I was in death, but death never entered my mind. I was just playing the music, just rubbing chocolate off my kid's face with a dishrag, never stepping back to see that death is not a door to go through someday, but the room we are already in. Now I know where I am, but I think I'm called upon—not to unknow it—but to know it in some better way.

WHEN THEY LOOKED up at me, what did they see? I hang over the bathroom sink, hunting for a clue in the fluorescent-lit mirror. Ona wouldn't have smiled like that for just anybody.

As for Cap, he didn't smile. His face lifted and then it stilled. I see that tight look of attention again, the audience quieting as the curtain goes up.

The last time I really looked in a mirror, I was breaking it to smithereens, laughing my head off. So I come as a shock to myself. My lower lip is loose, as though it can't feel—I'm afraid one of these days I could be drooling and not notice. My eyes, that once had a lot of snap and flash to them, just stare out, *seen it all*, the color of creek mud. *C'mon, buddy, give us some of that old razzle-dazzle.*

I flash myself a smile, but it only goes up on one side.

Also, I can't help noticing, now, I've got lashings of poison ivy all up and down my legs, in spite of how much soap I used. There's calamine in the medicine chest; I slap it on. Chigger bites, long scratches from the brambles and rose bushes I ran into—thrashing around out there bare-legged like an idiot.

Back in my room, I pull on my hot-pink T-shirt, my painter's pants.

Ona and Cap, below me now in the kitchen, are yelling to each other over the sound of running water and the electric pump under the sink, fast staccato syllables like machine-gun fire, something about broken teeth?—oh, broken mower teeth. "Can't get more till Monday," Cap's saying, "so I'm out of commission, far as that goes."

"That was your lucky stars wanting you to get off before you fell off," Ona sings back.

"I need to get after that pond pump tomorrow, anyway, so it's just as well."

"I'll run in and get them teeth for you, honey. First thing Monday morning!" Everything Ona says is a glad, piercing cry, straight from the heart, now that her baby's here. No wonder Cap's spoiled, no wonder he's got the big head. "If it was just to take and pour down now. . . ."

"No rain for *us* up there, Granny," he says. "It's going west of us."

"I wisht you didn't have to fool with all this load of work every time you get to come home, baby. It tears me up. Seems like we could hire Claude Lemons to do a little more than what he does." A few ticks of silence, then, "I got such a pretty roast in the oven, won't that be good?"

Jesus, how long is he going to stay? I dig around and find my long bead-and-feather earrings from Gatlinburg. I stare at the wall where the mirror I broke used to be, threading the earring wires in by feel. The holes in my ears have about closed up.

I go back to the bathroom to fill the buckets. We have a system. Whoever's going down bails some bathtub water into a couple of the buckets and packs them down the steps. We throw the water on the roses and fruit trees and tomatoes. The next one going up brings back the empties. Ruth grumbles about it—"She'll turn us both into pack mules like her, if we don't watch out," she tells me. One of the three of us is always kneeling, bailing with a saucepan from the tub into the bucket, *scrape—splash, scrape—splunk,* that's the sound of the days going by. And Ona makes us use the outhouse, in the daytime, so as to save on the flushes.

There's old Uptown Ruth right now—I see her through the bathroom window as I rise up from beside the tub—coming back along the privy path, in her red silk kimono once more and matching mules and loose long hair—she looks like Belle Breezing, except for the red half-glasses and the *National Geographic*. Hustle bustle, as though she's got an appointment. The screen door bangs, and now she's coming up the stairs, mules slapping fast against her heels, gold bracelets jangling.

I catch a glimpse of myself in the bathroom mirror again, in the wrinkled pink shirt and blue feathered earrings. Hopeless—now I look like a decorated stiff. I could come this far and then the only thing that would ever happen would be a deeper and deeper glaze to my eyes. I turn on the faucet and bring water up to my face again and again, to wake myself up and let this face loose into the future. To clear my head.

What I've got to work with is twenty grand and a fiddle. A house all paid for, except just the loan I took out last year for the plumbing. I've got more or less permanent tenants who pay on time. Some good friends, some loyal fans. A decent-paying, interesting job I can go back to—I've got to decide about that pretty soon. A career in music about to take off. If I want it to.

I've got to make a plan. A hot-pink T-shirt ain't a plan. I'm hollowed out behind the eyes. That's the space that opens out when a fiddler leaves off fiddling. As for the hollowness in my heart, I just don't know. I pinch up my cheeks the way my mama does hers. "Look alive," I tell myself out loud. My cheekbones look sharp enough to cut through the skin.

Carrie Marie, Carrie Marie. Voices are calling me, down under the elms and at the edge of the wood. *Bring water, we need it, bring water, we need it.* They are really crying out to the rain up there, wherever it is, but I pick up the buckets and start forward in my small first plan, which involves relief from drought for toads.

I'm not who I was, but I leave the blue feathers from other

times hanging down along my neck, my lost birds, my angels, my flying time.

THE SOUND DRIFTING up the stairwell stops me cold. I lean against the banister, my heart banging, to hear that music. I haven't heard anything like it in so long. I thought he'd be back in the kitchen chatting with his granny for a while more. I thought I could at least get out of the house. But he's set himself down on the front porch. In my mind's eye, I see him out there balanced on the edge of a straight-backed chair, leaning forward over his guitar, his only true love, his eyes, hidden under the brim of his brown felt cowboy hat, turned down to watch his left-hand fingers move through the chords with the least amount of fuss, his right hand strumming the strings. Many's the night I've kept my eyes on that small angle of light and shadow, where the two tendons of the thumb meet the wristbone to make the hollow that appears and disappears with the action of the thumb. I know it by heart by now. I was so crazy about it that tears would come up in my eyes, that's the kind of fool I used to be. The run of notes rises up the stairwell. I cannot move down to it. I don't have the courage yet. Cannot.

I see Ruth across the hall now, her door swung open. She's kneeling on the floor of her bedroom, stacks and spills of paper all around her from her desk that has all the drawers pulled out. In the dim room, the lamplight shines down on her black hair, with just a few strands of gray in it, falling to the front and back of her shoulders, and on the gaudy red silk, where big, full-blown blue and pink and ivory peonies bloom. I am drawn across to the light. "Hi," I say, leaning in her door. The red-framed reading glasses have slid down to the end of her nose. She lifts her sharp black eyes over the lenses to glance at me. "What you doing, Ruth?"

"Getting my affairs in order—just in case." She gathers up another handful of papers and cocks her head back to look at them as she slings them one by one into the overflowing basket beside her. "If that plane went down," she remarks, "it would all be in poor old Ona's lap. You know her, she wouldn't pitch a thing, she'd think it was all important, but she wouldn't want to be nosy and look. It would all end up in a box in her attic, marked *Ruth*, and that's where it would stay for the next two hundred years, if you think my kids would ever come around to tidy up my effects—they don't want to know, honey. They feel like they know too much already."

"Looks like you could use a paper shredder."

"I've got a few things in here that could stand a little shredding," she admits, sounding grim—you never know if she's bragging or complaining. She uses a lot of wrist, like *get out of my life*. "You'd be surprised how little is worth keeping."

"Not me. I wouldn't be surprised," I tell her. "Anyway, that plane won't go down. It wouldn't dare."

"Oh, don't let the powers that be hear *that*, Carrie. They don't dare or not dare. They just go on and *do*. As you well know." She eases down off her knees to sit on the rug with her bare legs hooked to one side. "In case I wade out into the Sea of Galilee and forget to wade back, then. Or run off with a pretty Arab shepherd boy. Ha! Never be seen again." She looks down, arranges the neck of her kimono modestly against her cleavage. "You can't ever tell."

There's a litter of beauty secrets, discarded jewelry, spilled face powder across the glass top of the dressing table, which has a skirt made out of an organdy curtain. Maybe it was Cap's mother's, before she got married. The whole room is still a memorial to Sweet Sixteen—pink rosebuds in the wallpaper, white dotted-Swiss curtains with wide pink grosgrain tiebacks at the windows. It doesn't know what hit it. What's living in it now is no rosebud, more one of those kimono peonies, dropping her silky lingerie like luscious petals here and there, perfuming the world up with White Shoulders. She's got too much to do to be picking up after herself all the time. She hasn't done a thing to claim this room, except to get a closet built down one side, arrange some silver-framed pictures of Dawn and Daryl and their kids on the dresser, and stack her books up by the bed.

Every weekday morning, she sits down in front of the ruffle-framed round mirror to put on her war paint. I try to catch a glimpse on my way to the bathroom—it makes it almost worthwhile to get up, getting to see Lady Fullblown herself, perched in her peach-colored slip on the white wicker stool, leaning in towards herself, painting on that Really Red. "Lookin' good, Ruthie," she'll congratulate herself out loud, checking her French twist from the side, with a little silver hand mirror. "I just don't see how I could look much better," she remarked to me once. "Do you?" And gave her hand a big kiss.

"If you want an Arab boy," I tell Ruth now, "it's for sure you'll get one. The poor kid won't stand a chance. I already feel sorry for him."

"Mmmmm," she says, with her lips pressed together, going on with her work, meaning, Maybe you think you're kidding, but maybe we'll see.

She's a showy woman. That old Judge, her second husband, didn't have a prayer of keeping her, but I don't think he lost her to another man. I think he lost her to *National Geographic.* Once I called her Hungry Heart, meaning Bruce Springsteen's song, but when I told her that, she remembered a poem by Alfred Lord Tennyson she had to learn in high school. "For always roaming with a hungry heart, Much have I seen and known," she orated, with her head thrown back.

Ruth's been here for nearly four years, since she moved out on the Judge. She didn't mean to stay, but here she still is, like the cats and the three-legged dog and the old foundered pony that was also supposed to be just passing through. She was getting ready for this retirement life and all the travel she means to do, so I guess she figured it would be a lot easier to put her stuff in storage and come and go from Ona's than to have to worry about closing up a house of her own and leaving it empty.

And she's as much of a blessing to Ona as Ona is to her, not just for the companionship either, though that's a big part of it. Ona doesn't have much money, just her Social Security and the income off the little investments Ruth made for her with Luther's life insurance. Cap splits the income off the farm with her fifty-fifty, but there isn't much of that even in a good year, now that Cap's not right here all the time taking care of business. I know, from listening to Ona wail about it, that most of Cap's part goes to hire Claude Lemons to keep things limping along—feed the steers and help with the mowing and the tobacco-raising. It's all Cap can do when he's back just to tend to the emergencies, pond pumps and fences and mower teeth. Ona helps as much as she can—she takes the tractor out for a little mowing sometimes in the late afternoon, and strips tobacco in the winter, and helps set it in the spring.

Anyway, the rent Ruth pays and her help with upkeep is a blessing to Ona as much as Ruth's getting to live here is a blessing to Ruth. And if I came to stay here, I could help, too. And maybe I could learn to do things on the farm. I know I could run the tractor—I always was mechanically inclined.

Now Ruth leans back and lights herself a cigarette, to be sociable, I guess, drawing in on it as if she's thought of exactly what will please her most right now. She lets the smoke out through her nose and treats herself to a good look at me. She studies me like an expert. Sizing me up.

I put down the buckets and clasp my cold hands in front of me. In the silence, we can both hear Cap perfectly well, doing some fancy runs up the sweet key of B. "B for Bluegrass, Key of B for Bill." That's another song I wrote. You could say a whole category of music got invented around Bill Monroe's vocal range. We both lift our heads, one ear high, and hold still to listen, like hound dogs. *Lord, I love that bluegrass music—when I'm long gone, honey, don't you know I'll love it still.* "That's old trouble coming down the road," Ruth sums up, after a while, cheerfully.

"How long is he going to stay?" I can't help asking, in a furtive voice.

She raises one eyebrow suggestively, gives me one of her superior looks, to let me know how much more she knows about me than I know about myself. "No telling, Carrie—I was thinking you had the right idea, to stay asleep for a few days, till the coast is clear. I believe that boy's laying for you. Come back to get you while the getting's good."

My stomach lurches at the thought. I see him reaching out, the way he did that time he came to pull me up off the floor, drawing me toward him.

"Well, to get me back in his band, maybe," I say, to keep Ruth out of my face. I keep seeing his brown hand closing on my arm.

"Maybe. I wouldn't doubt they've been learning exactly what they got without you. I expect they're ready for you to come back."

"They've *been* ready."

"And well? Are you going?"

"I don't know."

Come back to get you while the getting's good.

He was ready for me to come back the last time, the time his hand closed over my arm, the time he pulled me off the floor when I didn't want him to. He held my arm so hard it hurt. He pulled me to my feet. The getting's already *been* good, I should tell her, since she thinks she knows so much.

To get me back in his band, maybe.

Maybe that's what that good-getting was all about. He pulled me up, away from the wall. I didn't want him to. I struggled against him.

Ruth regards me silently for a minute. She takes a third or fourth drag on the thin, ladylike cigarette, then stubs it out abruptly and grabs up another handful of papers. "Well, like I told you this morning, Hawktown's a fine group of musicians, but you're the one that's never been seen before. Don't you forget it." I cross the room, stepping over her papers and clothes, hug my arms in front of me, and lean one shoulder against the wall next to the window, ducking my head, to hear Cap better. "I wasn't kidding on that star-quality thing."

I close my eyes. I wish she'd shut up. I only want to hear Cap playing this song I wrote.

"You decide if you want to give yourself a try. If you do— I've been thinking about this. When I get back from my trip, I'll get on the phone and start hustling my Nashville connections from the bank. I didn't do this job as long as Christ lived—thirty-three years, Carrie!—not to come out of it with a few favors to call in. I *know* you've got a future if you want it—how much a one is up to you."

"Oh." The word *future* sends an actual chill down my spine. "Oh," I say again—and yet, I know I have to make my plans.

"Quit moaning, Carrie!" she says sharply. "I want you to *think* about this while I'm gone. Nobody's saying you got to go there. But you got to *imagine* going there. Otherwise you'll not have ahold of your choices. I got no ax to grind—what you decide is your own private business. But if you decide to give it a shot, I'd say it's time to make your move. You're as ready as you're going to get."

I suddenly hear the jazzy refrain of a Nashville tune, sung by Wynonna, maybe. Or maybe by me. The backups would go, *Are you ready to place your bet? Are you ready for something you ain't seen yet? Are you ready for that big jumbo jet?* And then Wynonna would come growling in, *I'm as ready as I'm going to get.* Or I would. The idea of me and Ruth hustling our miniskirts and spike heels through some hotel lobby or airport is so funny I throw back my head and laugh out loud.

Ruth laughs, too, just to be companionable. She bangs her papers down to straighten their edges and pushes her case a little further. "You could take those boys with you if you wanted to, Carrie. If you ain't sick to death of them. *Or* you could light out on your own." I look at her, the laugh still on my face, as I hold on to each of my sharp elbows with the opposite hand. "Anyway, you've got a lot of ways to go, if you don't want to join back up with the band the way it was before."

I nod. "What if I don't want to go *any* way? What if I want to just shut up?"

She jerks her head back, makes her eyes wide, and gives an insulted shrug. "I wouldn't get down on my knees to beg you. It's up to you."

"I mean," I go on, in a low rush, "what do you think about, for a while, if I just—I don't know—go back to my day job, maybe, play for myself on my own time, try to hear myself? If I just try to find out what kind of music wants to come out of me now? I feel like—I just don't know if I can come across. If I even want to. I think I need to listen to myself. Pay attention to myself, for a long time, maybe. In case I've changed—I feel like I have. I don't know what it's going to do to my music."

She leans over and massages her toes, thoughtfully, as she hears me out. "My old foot's gone to sleep," she comments more or less to herself, then raises her wide optimistic face to me. "What I think is, it's a free country, Carrie. That's all. Just never stop singing, darlin'. Or playing that fiddle."

"That's sort of what I've been thinking."

"Where *is* your fiddle?"

"Home. I guess."

"Home, you guess." Her black eyes cut up over the thick lenses at me. "What about that insurance money? Ona said the check came. You made any plans for it?"

"I'll invest it, probably. I haven't thought."

"Well, you better think now."

"I will." I cross the room—she's started on another drawerful. Now it's photographs. Harbors, houses, her ex-husband the Judge with two English setters, out they go. "You'll be sorry you pitched those snapshots someday," I say. "For someone so crazy about history."

"Naw—that's just my life."

I pick up the buckets. "I need to take these down before the light's gone."

She doesn't even look up. "Well, have at it," she says.

I start down the stairs with the buckets. Now he's playing that most lovely of all bluegrass songs—it goes straight through me, especially the way he plays it, bringing up the serious bass line. And especially also the way he sings the crazy, sad words: *If the ladies were blackbirds and the ladies wore thrushes/I'd lie there for hours in the chilly cold marshes.* His voice rises clear and true and easy as the melody ranges high. It thrills my soul. But then I hear the words. I've been singing them for years, ignoring what they mean for the beauty of the melody, ignoring how the song comes home, settles down into grief and bitterness against women that's as old as the hills and one of the things bluegrass music is about. I let the dreamy words into my understanding as he sings them in that sweet, pure voice, a dream about shooting women in their high bushy tails with rock salt and nails.

Maybe he's not listening to the words either. Maybe he's singing it because it's a song he knows I love, maybe the words haven't got anything to do with it.

Maybe the song is just about *catching* them, *bagging* them.

I feel it's true, what Ruth says. Cap is laying for me. He's come to take me back with him.

We're all waiting to see if I'll go.

Thirteen

The lights spill down the hall, onto the dark wide floorboards, out of the kitchen. Comforting smells, cooking fruit and roasting meat, rise up the stairwell. At least *some*body's taking care of business around here, banging lids on pots. Guess who. I should go in there and help, but I've got this one project I want to accomplish before dark. I slide out the side door with my buckets into the storm-colored twilight, catching the screen door with my foot so that it doesn't bang behind me.

We've heard all this before—the absentminded thunder, way off, the leaves hissing like water on a griddle whenever the wind hits. When I move out of the shelter of the house, the wind slaps into the side of my face. The leaves fly along the ground all in one direction. In the toolshed I get the shovel and some old basins and take them out to the tilled-under garden. I throw a shovelful of dirt in each basin, kneel to break apart the heavy, cloddy clay and smooth it with my hands.

I'm not a damsel in distress.

I'm just a plain old girl in a plain old mess—

Hey! That's pretty good! *Don't need no*—what rhymes with armor? Farmer? No—*Don't need no charmer in armor charg-*

ing in to rescue me. Ha! That's two songs I've got a start on in the last five minutes. *I'm not a maiden tied to the tracks. I'm just a something something facing the facts....*

I pour bathwater in each container and crumble the dirt a little more. I'm excited by what I'm doing here—some good. Some good for toads—it's a start. A woodpecker drills into a hollow tree suddenly, as though the world gave a sudden loud yell. The birds sing, "Take cover, take cover." The cedar trees bend sideways, the rain's so close you can smell it.

I feel myself quieting down, getting interested in this smoothing of dirt. It's honest work. I want to pack it just enough—they have to be able to dig into it, but then they have to have enough to hold the moisture on top of them, once they're settled.

"Mud Pie Mullins, they call her." I jump. I didn't hear him. His voice goes through me like electricity. I look back over my shoulder, with my hair blowing all around my face, and he's standing there, grinning down at me, his hands in his pockets. I know it had to happen sometime. Circles under his eyes. He's been to hell and back, that's what he looks like. "What're you planting, Carrie?"

"Nothing. It's just dirt." I stand up, because looking at him from a kneeling position reminds me too much of my life. Eye level is bad enough. His eyes take me in, flash of blue blue blue, birdwing in the woods. The thunder rumbles all around the sky. He's exhausted—rough around the edges, bleary-eyed, from driving all night and mowing all day. I want to run my dirty fingers tenderly along the lines baked into his skin. He doesn't shine like once he did, up close. He looks a little beat-up at the edges, like an ordinary human being. "It's for the poor toads," I explain. "They don't have anyplace to go anymore."

He nods. "You think they'll find these things?"

I shrug. "They must know something about water."

I stoop and pick up two of the basins and hold them out to him. He takes them, one balanced on top of the other. "Flop-houses," he says, grinning helplessly at his joke.

I grin back, the best I can. "That's pretty good, Cap." I get two more of the basins. He walks along beside me as I choose places to set them down. "Who's been playing fiddle for you?" I blurt out finally. "Andy?"

He doesn't answer me for a minute, as if his mind's caught on some other complicated thing that he has to remove it from one strand at a time. "He flew in and played with us in Ohio, yeah."

"And then what happened?"

"Up through Pennsylvania and New York, we just put one foot in front of the other. We got Beider Johnson for a couple of weeks, and Dice Dawson came over and played a few dates with us—that was fun. Sometimes we just did without. We got by with it, some way."

I swallow and say, "You must be about ready for a regular fiddler."

"Well, we'll wait on you." He gives me a little sideways smile, now, like a shy man. "Andy can make most of the rest of our dates, through the South, so don't worry." He looks over my head at the sky, then comes back to me, hopefully. "Unless. . . ."

Oh, absolutely. I've been thinking I'd ride back with you next week. I'm ready to get started, let me at it. Wouldn't that take a load off everybody's mind, including mine, if I could say that? *Oh, for sure. For sure, Cap.* They've hung around all summer, waiting, not crowding me—I want to express my gratitude. I want to make it up to them. I could just run into town and get my fiddle, throw a few outfits together, pack my bag, ride in the van with Cap, taking my turn to drive, to wherever the next place is. I'd hug the boys——wouldn't they be surprised to see me? I'd climb the steps to the stage, tune my fiddle, then lean into the mike, in my gauzy purple dress and boots, to begin my life of music again. I want to say *yes* so bad I take a breath to do it, riding some wave of energy, but then it disappears underneath me, and I get that falling-through-nothing feeling again and say in a hurried dizzy voice, "I'll tell you what, Cap, I don't know about me. Maybe——"

"We're playing the IBMA Fan Fest at the end of September—they asked us to close the Saturday-night show."

"They did? Fantastic!"

His face is taut, his bloodshot eyes bright, alert. "Yeah, but Carrie, they didn't know when they asked us that you might not be with us. We have to tell them, as soon as we can, if you're not going to be ready. It wouldn't be fair not to."

"They'd think they were lucky—they'd be getting a bargain. Andy's hot stuff. They love Andy."

"*Yeah* they do, but I'm not sure it wasn't you they had in mind when they asked Hawktown. You're hot stuff too, honey." He grins suddenly, like the Cap of old, the dazzler. "Everywhere we played, somebody'd yell out, 'Whar's Carrie?' in the middle of a tune. I won't say how insulted we got."

I've been thinking of myself here lately as a woman who sleeps and gets up and looks at her shadow sliding around corners, one who hauls the buckets down the stairs, one who doesn't dare touch china. I can't quite get connected to the old show-business part of me, the star-quality girl, the one being yelled for. "Gosh. Oh well. It's probably just some old drunk——"

He goes right on. "It's your decision—you can come on back with us anytime you're ready to roll. Andy's loose about it—he don't care. He knows we need to get back to our regular band again, without no guest fiddler. He's just doing his

old buddies a favor—he owes us, considering how he left."
Now he sniffs and resettles his hands in his back pockets and
looks at the ground, then up again at me, squinting in a busi-
nesslike way. "Anyway, that's the last gig Andy could do with
us, the end of September. He's in rehearsal for Jez's tour after
that. So the IBMA is the end of the line, for him."

He gives a few little kicks at the dirt. "I see it as a big occa-
sion, like a celebration—you and him could both play. Everybody'd be so glad, Carrie, if you came back in with us that
night. You don't know how much people love you, honey.
And feel for you."

"I feel like they do," I tell him. "And like you do, and the
band does—you've been so patient with me. I hear you, Cap."
But the truth is, I *see* him better than I hear him. Through
the darkening air, I see his strained face, the lines, the circles
under his eyes, I see his eyes full of questions. "But. . . ."

When I say that word, he blinks. There is a sudden taking
back of light in his eyes. I hesitate, because I can't find a way
to explain myself yet. I can't find the courage.

He forces himself to go on talking. "I didn't mean to get off
on this, Carrie. But I reckon you need to know how things are
shaping up. I'd say we don't need you to come back right
away." He's pulled a brisk, cheerful voice out of his hat. "But
we need to know pretty quick when you *are* coming back.
There's bars and clubs from here to Colorado wanting to book
us—I'm not kidding, we could work all winter, we could play
every night of the week, if we wanted to. We could make it
just on our music now, we really could. But—we need to
know what to tell them about you."

"Of course you do. I'll make you a promise, Cap. I'll figure
out what I'm gonna do before you leave. You've done so much
for me, honey. . . ." There's a watchful, quiet look on his face
that makes me hurry on. "I'll make up my mind, I promise.

Before you leave. When are you leaving?"

"Wednesday morning."

"All right. I'll tell you by Tuesday night."

"What'll you tell me?" He's forcing himself to say it, a stiff smile on his face, painful to look at. "When? Or if?"

And I force myself to answer. "If would be first, I guess."

He opens his mouth, then runs his teeth over his lower lip and shakes his head once. He looks sideways at the sky with his eyes a little squinted, as if trying to do a calculation in his head. He folds his arms over his chest and finally says, "If we have to regroup, the IBMA would be a good place to introduce a new fiddler."

A pain goes clean through me at this—I see what I didn't see before: not Andy, or courtly portly old Beider Johnson, but another girl fiddler, I'm sure of it. It worked so well for them. And the girl fiddler that broke them in and got them to grow up and act human and did all the hard part would be out on her butt, too bad, only herself to blame.

I'm swaying a little with it, I guess. He puts his hand on my arm. "Or to let everybody know we got our old fiddler back."

We look at each other in mutual glazed exhaustion. He breaks off now, circles my wrist with his thumb and forefinger and raises it to look at. "You give up on food?" I look at it too. It's flat, the wristbone sharp and delicate. Skin, bones, little blue veins, that's all there is to me.

"You'll break her heart."

"I'm doing a little better, now," I tell him.

"You can't hold out forever against her biscuits." He looks at me for a moment, twisting his mouth around as if he's making a big decision, then gives my wrist a little shake. "You know why I came back this weekend?"

"To get your old fiddler back?"

"Naw. I figured you'd come back when you was good and ready."

I recognize this as a lie—he's been lying awake nights worrying. Anyway, he still has my wrist encircled and is sliding his thumb back and forth, back and forth, tenderly, over my pulse in a way that sends waves of feeling over me that I don't welcome.

"No—I came rushing back with all this real good news that I didn't think could wait a day, about the IBMA, and also, I might as well tell you right here. . . ." His eyes are shining with it like stars, I swear. "Carrie, John Kemp from Archer Records came down to Philly to hear us. I mean, that's why he came, to hear *us*—the whole band, but mainly you and me."

"John Kemp did?"

"I figured that would cheer you up, give you something good to think about. He came by the hotel before the concert. He was looking to meet you. He hadn't heard. . . . He said they've been keeping an eye on us for a year or so now."

"Oh," I breathe.

"They're especially interested in the duets, he said."

"The duets?"

"Right."

We look at each other while the words knock together. *Duets? Right. Duets? Right.* I'm beginning to get a handle on the true extent of that worried look in Cap's eyes.

"He said they think we've got a gorgeous sound. That's what he said—*gorgeous!* They've got hopes for us. He was really disappointed that you weren't there—me and Joe met with him and I explained everything to him, and he said to let him know when you come back in, and I said I would." He has let go of my wrist; now he hangs his hands over my shoulders. "I think this may be the big chance for us, Care. He wasn't just shooting the breeze, I don't think. He sounded serious to me."

He's looking down at me in a way that makes me rise through myself toward him. "I'll bet you're already thinking of a program," I say, with a smile that cracks my lips.

"Naturally. All the way back here, in the van, Joyner and me were rooting through the tapes, saying what about this, what about that. My guess is he came to Philadelphia with some kind of deal in mind, but when he found out you weren't with us, he decided he'd better can it till you were. He said it was all right, just send him our tour dates, so he could get back to listen to us, when you were on your feet again. I told him it might be a while—but I didn't know then it might be completely out of the question. . . ." His eyes brush up over my face. *It isn't, is it? Come on, it isn't completely out of the question?*

Oh, I don't want to tell him anything he doesn't want to hear. I don't want to mess him up. I don't want to disappoint him. I don't want to be difficult.

But deep inside me, *completely out of the question* sounds like a good description of where I am. God help me. I reach out and touch his arm, to get his attention. "I've been thinking maybe I just need to shut up for a while," I say. My heart is thumping, low and hard, shaking my voice. "Or play just for myself, off by myself, for—I don't know—as long as it takes. For a long time to come." I say it in a low, deliberate voice. He looks at me with a mainly puzzled face, like he can't quite get the drift because of my foreign accent. "I know this is the last thing you want to hear, but you've got to hear it. I don't know what I want to do, exactly—it doesn't have a name, as far as I know. But I need to do it."

I'm not saying this very well. I sound too vague, wifty. It's because I don't want to go against him. I feel his face wanting to draw up in irritation, I feel him wanting to say, "Aw, Christ." My thin uncertain fingers touch my throat.

If this ain't a damsel in distress, what is?

He keeps looking at me after I stop talking, the brightness not slipped out of his eyes yet. He flicks one of my feather earrings. Finally he says, in a rough, quiet voice, "Well, I'll tell you what, Care—I'm going to make it easy for you to stay and hard for you to quit us." He smiles a little with it, a hard, stretched-thin smile. "Can't blame me for that, can you?"

I lower my head from that smile in confusion, studying my bare feet facing his work boots, trying to absorb what he has just said. I have to confess that once upon a time I would have considered this a sexy thing to tell someone. That low voice, resonant with emotion and conviction. I would have admired his honesty. I would have been flattered. But I've been living with women too long, I guess. The women I've been living with would not say this. They would say, Figure out what you want to go after and don't apologize. But—to be fair—the women I've been living with aren't waiting to know if I'm coming back in their band or not, either.

I look up, to face him, to get to the middle of this. I steady my eyes, my voice. "Why would you do that, Cap?" My voice sounds flat, without any kind of grace.

He keeps his hands on my shoulders, but gives a bark of laughter. "*Because,* for Christ's sake, Carrie. Are you serious?" He gives me a little shake. "Because this might be our main chance, coming up. What we've been hustling our butts off for, all these years—playing F.O.P. benefits and bars where you're lucky if it's just a fistfight and not a knifing going on while you're playing 'Little Jimmy Brown.' Splitting a hundred bucks five ways. Driving all night and half the next day to play to thirty people in a Grange hall."

I am puzzled to hear our music life described this way.

We've hustled our butts off, it's true, but it's been a long time since we split a hundred bucks five ways, if we ever did—I can't remember. That might have been before my time. For sure, we've seen our share of drunks taking swings at each other, but, come on, there was only one knifing.

"Right in here's where we make it or break it, babe. Do you appreciate that? We could wake up some morning and find out we're famous. We could hit pay dirt. I'm not saying it will happen, but I'm saying there's a chance. I don't want to have to look back, twenty-five years down the road, and feel regretful. Wonder what would have happened if this or if that. I don't want to have no regrets."

He lowers his face so as to look into my eyes. "You've got to come back, Carrie. You've just got to." He laughs at himself, but goes on. "This is our chance. I feel like all we have to do is reach out and grab it. It's close enough to touch. If you ain't excited about Archer Records being excited about us, you got to be—" He catches himself. "I don't know."

"Me either," I murmur.

He's gazing down at me like someone on a tightrope, someone who requires balance above all else. He's performing an act of will and deep concentration. "This is our chance," he says again. "I don't know that we'll get another. Life don't hand them out like party favors. It says, You're a musician, be a musician. Give it everything you got." He breaks off now, turns, abruptly, away from me.

"Yes, but. . . ." I'm having trouble here—whatever he says, questions swim up around it. Is this truly the only chance we're going to get? Is that how the world works? How does Cap know? And then, what does life have in mind exactly when it says, Be a musician? How does Cap know what life says at all? Maybe it says one thing to him, another to me. And—above all—how much is everything I've got, and to whom am I supposed to give it? To Cap, to John Kemp?

I can't think of anything to say. My mind is clogged with questions. My quick wits have deserted me. I've been out here in the country too long with two women, instead of off on the road with four men. It's taken the fighting edge off me. Two women, being nice to me, cooking up a little chicken soup for me, ironing my nightie, and all the while talking revolution—for instance: *You don't have to be in no band to play the fiddle, darlin'.* And also: *It's a free country.*

All this time I've been thinking what a tough cookie I was, holding my own in there with the boys, standing up for my rights, slowly but surely getting my way, but all the time, I wasn't getting *my* way, I was getting Cap's way. I thought of myself as a free woman, walking down the street with my loose change jingling in the pocket of my denim jacket, my head full of music. But the last day I was free was the day before the night Cap Dunlap sat down at the back of Sweet's and listened and then came up and said come play with Hawktown for a while, and I turned my back on Pearl's Girls and went flying off to my chance to play in his wonderful band. There was no place for my will there. There was a place for my music and my music fitted itself into that place as if it had always belonged there.

I was in a box, calling it home, sweet home.

And now here's John Kemp up in New York wanting to put the lid on that particular box.

I know that version of the future. I know what it looks like: we'll sign a contract, put the album together and rehearse it, go into the studio for however long it takes to record it to suit ourselves and him, then start touring, getting the music out in front of as many people as we can, so as to sell the album, once it's out. Tour the stuffing out of ourselves, until we cut the next album. And the next. And maybe get famous. A big-name headline act, gigs on major television, money rolling in, a rack of CDs with our faces on them at Disk Jockey and Tower Records. Our main chance. Everything we do a step toward the greater glory.

All the time I'm getting this straight with myself, in the meantime, here's Cap in the gathering night, old Abracadabra, with his clean, lean chest and hard-pressed, hungry face lowered to me. "It's *you*, Carrie. Without you we got no deal," he says now, with a big puzzled smile. "Don't you understand? Someone's heard you. Someone knows what you've got. What *we've* got. And he's offering to get our music out in front of a lot more people than we ever dreamed of."

I'm beginning to understand that I'm the only one who can give him the only thing he wants. And what if I won't? For no good reason except I don't particularly feel like it? After all he's done for me.

"I'm asking you for about two years. Can't you give it?" he asks now sweetly. "Two years from now, when you've made your place in the world, you could go off for a year or so and play just for yourself, or do whatever it is you want to do. But right now—well, apart from everything else, it would be *good* for you to be on the road, not thinking about anything but the music. Good for you to be with the band."

"Don't get off on what's good for me," I say. The curtness of my voice takes me by surprise. "I'm the only one who can figure out what's good for me." I've got three ways to go here, as far as I can tell. I can stay with the band. Or I can leave it. If I leave it, I can try to make it on my own, the way Ruth wants me to. Or I can retire from public life, for how long I couldn't tell you, and play for the mice in the tobacco barn.

How in the world will I say *no* to him if it turns out I want to? And do I want to? The chance of my life? I don't know. I don't know, but I better know soon. I've got a feeling time's not on my side anymore.

"I'll let you know what I'm going to do before you leave," I say again, in a clipped voice. "You can wait till then, can't you?"

"All right," he says quietly. We stand there, at a loss. The last time we saw each other we were sort of falling together. I remember his eyes, closing. Where we are now we have no knowledge of. "Why'd you give me that stone, Carrie?" he asks, in a husky voice, as though he's not sure he should, but he's going to anyway, to get some solid ground under our feet.

"It was just a present." He nods, then fishes the little stone out of his pocket, holds it in his palm. My eyes go to it. Just a smooth little gray round stone. I don't even know why I liked it. "If you don't want it, give it back," I say. "I'll find you something else." There's a lump in my throat, suddenly.

"No." He slips it back in his pocket. "I'll keep it. Now I know it was a present. I got to thinking maybe it was a message." He gives me a cautious look. "If it was, I wanted to make sure I got it."

"It was just all I had on me." The inside of my mouth at the hinge of the jaw is trembling. I turn to go find the other basins in the dark that is still light enough to make you think you can see. I set both of them under the elm tree, where the squirrel went in, and stand there, with my hand against the trunk, swallowing, taking deep breaths, trying to compose myself. The dogs are barking, one here, one there, to pass the time as the night comes on.

When I turn, he's still right where he was, looking out towards the ridges folding off into the dark, security lights from distant farms tucked into the folds here and there. I go back and stand beside him. All that's left now of the light is the gleam of the tobacco fields, long and narrow down through the bottom, along the creek, the bare clay shining like snow. It's not going to rain. The rain's gone off. The wind's taken it west. What we've got instead is heat lightning against the horizon—our consolation prize. The mass of black trees against the pearly night sky. No sign of the full moon. Just that diffused light.

Standing a few inches from each other, not touching, looking at the same thing, not at each other, seems about right to me. Like what we should have been doing all along. Some relief in it. There are good reasons for never touching. Everything is so tangled now. Maybe in some other life we were brother and sister. What's really between us is simple, straightforward. If I were lost, he'd find me; if he were hurt, I'd help him. Is that not true? He brings his gaze back from the fields to glance at me. All the songs about the roamers and runarounds and pilgrims and strangers and poor traveling creatures mean him. We used to be perfect for each other. I wanted to want but not to have. He wanted not to be had. You can see it all over his body—that slight backwards lean into the left leg.

And now who wants what? I want to tell him there's nothing to be afraid of, we can go back to the way we were. But I can't look out for both of us. I've come out here to save a few toads.

His worried eyes scan my face, and he is on the point of speech. "You know what I'm afraid of?" I rush to say. "I'm afraid you're going to apologize. If you apologize, I'll come after you with a wrecking bar, Cap, I swear."

A deep, intimate smile lights his eyes. "You came after me the last time," he says finally. "And look where it landed us."

"I did not. You came after *me*. I just put up a fight. But I *will* come after you. So don't apologize."

He grins. "Well, it was a damn fine fight."

But then his grin fades out, and the thing I forgot while I was out here in the dark swings around like a two-by-four and hits me in the head: what I put up that fight *for.*

I WANT TO BE EXACT about it, I want to say it to myself so I'll understand it. When he came back to my house that second time, I might have been five minutes away from what I'd been struggling to get to—five minutes, five hours, what did it matter? I really believe I was in the grip of a process, when he bent so fast and closed his hand over my arm and drew me up, forever, away from it.

He thought he was rescuing me. He thought he was saving my life.

And also, a cold voice inside me now says clearly, *he was needing to know, were you or weren't you going to play the damn fiddle in his damn band.*

But that was urgent business!

And your business wasn't?

So that's what we're looking at each other through.

"I guess you saved my life, Cap," I say, to distance myself from that voice. It's true—there's a chance I might be dead now, my decisions all behind me, if Cap had not come looking for me that night.

But there's also a chance I would have sat there awhile longer, until I'd seen what I needed to see, and then gotten up and lived my life.

"I've wondered. That's what I thought I was doing, when I went over there. When I broke in." He pauses. I'm afraid to swallow or breathe. "At first it didn't worry me, when you didn't show up that night. I just thought, well, the wonder is she's showed up all these *other* nights." He stops again. He reminds me of a man stepping out on one of those shaky swinging bridges you see in jungle movies—careful, careful, one step, see if you're still hanging on, then another. "But after we'd played our last set, after the lights went out, and we were packing up, I broke a sweat all of a sudden."

"You did?"

"Yes. I couldn't get to the van fast enough. I don't remember driving to your house. All I remember was knocking on your door. And you not answering. The next morning, when you told me you were all right and insisted you were still going on tour with us—well, I guess I believed it. I know I *wanted* to believe it—for your sake, too, Carrie, not just mine—it did seem like the worst was over. I thought getting away from there would help you. I thought you shouldn't be staying there alone. Especially if we were gone.

"Anyway, I had plenty to get through that day, with us about to take off, so I pushed you to the back of my mind. But in the afternoon I had to stop by Joe's place, to go over some add-on bookings. I found myself heading out on Main Street, and I decided I'd just, while I was in the neighborhood, run by. Check on you. Carrie, if I hadn't showed up. . . ." His eyes search mine. I'm listening with my whole body. "I hope it was the right thing to do, to bring you back like that." He hesitates. "That . . . particular way," he says, with difficulty. He drops his eyes, then raises them like a man taking his medicine. "Or any way. If it wasn't right, you'll have to forgive me."

"Oh, it wasn't your fault," I say, sharp and bitter against myself. "I turned around easy, didn't I?"

"Is that what you think?" He puts his hand on the back of my head, still wanting to save me—oh, he's good. Cap's good! "No. You didn't turn around easy, honey. Like you say, you put up a fight. Believe me, turning back was the last thing you wanted to do." He stops, then plunges on. "You didn't choose it. I made you choose it. You fought against it."

I laugh without mirth. "For about a minute and a half."

"All I can tell you is, you didn't want to turn back." We're staring at each other. "I know you don't want me to apologize. And I don't apologize for . . . I've worried that I. . . ." he stammers, then gives it up. "I know it was just what happened. What's been bothering me is—I think maybe I got between you and what you wanted. I'm sorry for turning you back from where you were headed if you didn't want to be turned. I've felt bad. Like maybe I got in the way of your life—whatever it was going to be. Nobody has the right to do that."

We stand quietly for a minute, his hand still on my head, stroking my hair now and then. So. That's all right. He came back to check on me. He came back because he was worried. Because he loves me. Because he's tuned in to me.

But, as if some sharp part of me had broken loose and pitched itself outward, my clear voice says, "Why *did* you, though? Why did you turn me back?" He looks at me, his eyes glazing over with confusion. "I mean—if you knew all that. If you knew I didn't *want* to turn back?"

"Because—I thought you might do yourself harm."

"You could have called Kelly or Stony or someone," I say, reasonably, relentlessly. "Mrs. Stevens was right upstairs. Even Ruth—you know she would have come flying. That's what *I* would have done, if. . . ." I let it drop, then take it up again. "You could have gotten someone to come over and stay with me."

"I didn't think of it," he says in a stricken voice. "I'm sorry. I just thought I needed to get you away from that wall. You'd been there almost twenty-four hours by then. Maybe longer. Who knows. I figured that was long enough."

"It wasn't. It almost was, but not quite." My words are almost tender, regretful, against the coldness of that other voice inside me. "You did get between me and what I wanted, Cap," I tell him apologetically. "I won't kid you. You really did."

He looks at me through a haze of exhaustion and misery, nods, takes it. There's nothing at all but misery between us now. "And then," he continues, "it was too late. The rest of it—it was always getting ready to happen. As you know."

"Yes," I agree. But the flat, furious voice says, *I wouldn't have done what he did. I wouldn't have gone so far, if I had been the sane one. I wouldn't have—taken advantage of me. He knew I could never in a million years have drawn away from him. I would never have used my power that way. I would have sat down close beside him and tried to help him. Or gone off to another room and waited. I wouldn't have fucked a person on the edge of collapse.*

He was impatient. He wanted to snap me out of it, so that we could get on with the business at hand.

No. No. There were tears in his eyes.

Yes, there were. That too. Both things. Both things, tangled together.

He's only human. Isn't that what only human means? Both things at once? Nothing absolutely pure, everything mixed and tangled?

But the hard-nosed, implacable one won't back down. *Not necessarily.*

Maybe that's what's put those circles under his eyes. That it was both things, together. And he wanted to think it was only the one thing.

Later, he did what was right. He called his granny. He started making other arrangements. He didn't even once try to persuade me to pull myself together and go with the band. He had tried to talk me out of wanting to take the tour before, really, and I'd said no, I'm all right. I put him in a terrible position. When he saw then, really and truly, that I couldn't do it, he cared for me. He was dear to me. He brought me out here. He gave me to his granny. He took care of me, when he had so much else to do and see about.

And yet, and yet . . . he pulled me away from where I was headed. He interrupted me, he set me back. If he'd let me get on with what I was doing—

Well, maybe it would have been better. For both of us.

Instead, he worked his will on me. What he did was not right, in the sense of not working, if what he wanted was to get me on the tour. But also, what he did was not right, period. He messed me up, he sent me round the bend. I broke the mirror because I did not want to see the woman I was. The woman who hadn't learned her lesson. The woman who let herself be drawn away from what she truly, truly loved. And not for the first time.

Now I have to go through it all again, but in the world.

"Well, we can go back to where we were, before . . ." I say, in a worn-out voice.

"And where was that?" he asks.

"Where you said you weren't a faithful man. Where you said you'd break both our hearts for us."

He looks away from me, half smiling; then in a moment, he sort of sings, "Can't be done, Carrie." He shakes his head, stands with his body bowed over me, as if protecting me. "Really. It can't. That was another time. That was nowhere. I'm sorry I didn't know it sooner. Where we were—that day— that day we're talking about—that's where we're supposed to be. That's what's real. This right here is what's real. I'm not the man that said those things anymore. I'm better."

Now we both step back and nod formally. He smiles. I smile back. One smile catches the other, and goes deeper. Our eyes catch, the bright electric rising, oh love. "We can have anything we want. Anything," he murmurs, in a voice so low it is almost a hum.

Come back to get you while the getting's good, honey, says the relentless, bitter stranger. *We're waiting to see how far he'll go to get it done.* This bitter unbelieving voice is my own, no one else's.

"You understand? It's not too late, Carrie. It should have been sooner, but it's not too late, even yet. I'm begging you to see it's not too late. We can have—what people have, every bit of it."

The lights in the kitchen are yellow squares in the gathered darkness now. "Oh, here I am," I say, hitting my head with the heel of my hand, "letting Ona do all the work, as usual." I peel off, run ahead of him up the steps into the kitchen, hair flying, beads and feathers flying. Nowhere else to go.

Fourteen

Toward music. Ona's flipped on the radio, to keep her company while she cooks. Ruth's standing in the hallway, showing off her new outfit, bright periwinkle-lilac, she's not shy. Price tags hang off of it. "I saw it the minute I walked in the store," she's bragging to Ona. "I headed straight for it. When I see what I want, I don't ask how much. I was in and out of there in fifteen minutes."

"Why, that's wonderful, Ruth," Ona says, draining the steaming water off of the potatoes.

I'm trying to get on top of this sudden, fluorescent-lit kitchen situation. "It's nice," I say, feeling myself panting a little. It's all I can manage.

Ruth looks across the room at me, one fast toe-to-head assessment and a smile, mainly to herself. But she chooses to move on. She looks down at herself, severely, smoothing the jersey over her hips. "I think it'll be just right for those desert nights," she allows. "And it won't wrinkle."

"Desert nights," Cap says, banging the screen behind him. "She could have desert nights right here in Kentucky. Why don't she go someplace where it rains?" He's casual, under control, but there's a brightness under his cheekbones that it takes me a second to identify as a blush. Ruth looks from his face to mine, and back again, with alert interest.

Ona's mashing the potatoes, throwing her whole body into it, fanny jiggling. I turn to wash my hands at the kitchen sink—I feel all their eyes on my back, as I scrub my nails with the vegetable brush. "I think you ought to ask how much, myself," I say, my heart thumping, it seems like, against my vocal cords. I shut off the water and dry my hands and turn then, to look at all three of them looking back at me. "If you take that attitude into one of those marketplaces they show in your *National Geographic,* they'll see you coming and clean your bones for you."

I pick up the dishes Ona's set out. I thought we might use the good china because of Cap, but no, it's still the plates with no feelings. Mostly we eat in the kitchen. This is the first time since I've been here that we've had company. I spread the green-and-white cloth over the dining-room table. Old cotton, so thin you can see through it, but washed, starched, ironed. Then I put down the aqua Melmac.

Company. Listen to me. This is Cap's house, not mine. Ona's *his* granny, not mine. *I'm* the company.

I come back into the kitchen. Here's that old song I love by K. T. Oslin, "Hey Bobby." Asking and asking, like a cat rubbing against your legs. Cap is leaning against the refrigerator. He rakes his fingers back through his hair, his shoulders balanced carefully, boyishly, like they've just come to his attention.

I take a notion. I reach way down into the place in me that dancing used to come out of. Dancing and so forth. I try myself out. I dance real slow up to Ruth. She dances right back at me, price tags fluttering. It's coming back to me, though my body seems slack and sort of not all there. Ruth is doing her version. I twine my hands over my head. My hot-pink shirt lifts and my belly shows. That's all right.

Cap leans against his grandma's Hotpoint, watching, his fingers fitted into the pockets of his jeans, his brown wrists bent. Pulling the whole room in towards himself, as usual. I pull it right back, moving to the funny sexy words of this song, and the sly, sliding melody. "Watch out, boy," I'm telling him by the way I dance. "You came back to get me, but maybe I'll get *you.* Maybe you've met your match." Ruth and I are both strutting our stuff, faces mean and pouting, one shoulder forward, then the other, elbows out, hands cupped in the air in front of us, like harem girls showing off what-all we got. Ruth copies what I do, picking up some tips for her trip. Her hair, where she's pinned it up, falls along her flushed, excitable face. I dance sideways, putting my bare feet down toe first, high-stepping it, my expert bottom sliding to one side then the other inside my baggy pants.

"You take off them heels, Ruth," Ona orders. "You'll be punching holes in my linoleum." Ona won't dance. "No, get on away from me, Carrie Marie," she tells me when I slide myself in her direction. She waves a dishtowel at me. "I'm seventy-four and no fool, last time I checked."

Ruth kicks off her shoes. Her feet flash out across the blue floor, high arches and pink-nailed toes, don't think she doesn't know. Those cute pointy ankles with the diamond ankle bracelet giving off come-and-get-it glints. God knows what she gets up to on these tours she takes. Maybe I'll go with her, blow the whole damn insurance check. We'd do all right together, two hot numbers. I wonder if it's too late to get my passport. My own toenails, I notice, have traces of some long-ago polish. Cap lets himself off the refrigerator door when I come on to him, with my slinky shoulders and groovy hips. He holds his arms out like a bullfighter holding his cape, to go through his little moves. Ona dries silverware down into the drawer and says, "Good night nurse!"

Gulp you down, boy. Maybe that's all I want to do with my life now. Maybe I just want to follow you around, with my hand slid down the back of your jeans. I'll show you the true meaning of *duet.* I clap my hands softly beside my face, eyes closed, as K.T. talks the song home, straight-faced, promising Bobby she'll get him back early. When I open my eyes, I won't look at Cap—I'm overcome, once I don't have the music under my feet, by embarrassment. "Boy, we got the moves, honey," I say to no one in particular. I run off and get the bowl of gravy and the tomatoes.

But an early song by the Dirt Band comes on, and Cap has a broom in his hand. "Listen," he says. He's standing in front of a beam where Ona's iron skillets hang in a row. He's keeping time in the air with the raised broom handle. He's listening, and then he bangs out, with the broom handle on the skillets, the exact final three notes of the refrain. It's got to be some kind of miracle—he was just picking the skillets at random— but we aren't allowed to laugh.

"Listen," he commands, sternly, one hand in the air to keep our attention, the other beating anticipatory time in the air until he wants to hit a skillet with the broom handle, and unless my ears deceive me, every time he hits one, it's the right one. We all look spellbound at his raised intent face, his flat blue eyes wide open, his hand held up, to silence us, "Now listen!" and *bong bong bong.* When it's all over, he turns around and smiles magnificently at all three of us, the broom high in the air like a trophy. "There," he says.

"That was wonderful, how you did that, Cap!" Ona sings out. "You come in just right every time! I didn't know you was an old skillet-banger."

Ruth sits down and puts her high heels back on. She pats at her face and the sides of her neck daintily with a paper towel. "Watch out, Holy Land, she's on her way," Cap says.

Ruth laughs. "You better believe it, darlin'. One last fling."

"Oh, Ruth, you've been saying that whenever you've went off anywhere for the past ten years," Ona says, pulling the corn pudding out of the oven.

"One last fling," Ruth says again. "And then another." She throws her head back and her arms out into the air behind her, like wings.

Fifteen

Ona, low and lullabying, asks Jesus to bless our food. *For what we are about to receive, may the Lord make us truly grateful.*

To me, this sounds like a blind and desperate prayer, for who knows what we are about to receive? We might have to take it, but I don't see why we have to pray to be grateful. "Granny, Granny, you sure can cook," Cap says then, by way of *Amen.*

I feel mean and shy as a thirteen-year-old, scowling at my plate. Ruth's over there clinking her ice cubes, taking us in—I feel like Exhibit A. *Pass the potatoes. Here you go.* That's about the size of it. As long as we're all eating, Ona doesn't notice. Silence does just as well as talk. We butter our biscuits and make appreciative noises. Knife in one hand, fork in the other, she surveys our plates like an empress—serene, a little aloof, full of favors. "These greens is going begging, Cap—I bet you been living on corn dogs and funnel cakes out there." Finally, in no hurry, she comes to our rescue by trotting out her favorite conversational topic, ghosts.

"This night's giving me the willies," she begins, giving a little shudder and dipping a forkful of mashed potatoes daintily into her gravy. "It's exactly the same kind of night as when—"

The Evil Man, and how he stared at Ona through the window at three a.m. once upon a time at the full moon, when it acted like it was going to storm but didn't and she couldn't sleep and got out of bed and went into the parlor. We've all heard it before, but we don't mind. In fact, we're grateful. How he tried to make her get up out of her chair and come to the window, and the little feist's hair stood up all along his spine and first he snarled and then he whimpered and crawled under Ona's feet, the little feist named Hopeless, and Ona couldn't take her eyes off the face, which was the worst she ever saw—"Pale, with dark eyes, just a-burning with I don't know what. I could feel a force dragging through my body, wanting to pull me up off of that chair, but I held on to the arms with all my might and finally Hopeless fell to sleep on my foot and the sky was getting light. I felt like something had done let go of me. Throwed me aside in scorn, was how it felt. Like an old rag. I was the tiredest I've ever been, and went and crawled into the bed and slept till noon, which I never did before or since. And—I don't care if you don't believe me, Ruth—that really happened."

"I've been hoping for a ghost of my own," Ruth comments, examining her ring as she turns it with her thumb. "The woods out here are crawling with 'em, from what I can tell. I keep my eye out, but I guess they don't take to me."

"They don't take to anybody that don't really believe in them," Ona rebukes her. "They don't volunteer to look foolish." Then she adds as an afterthought, "And they don't take to anybody that's looking too hard for them, either."

"Where'd you walk today, Carrie?" Cap asks, like a polite stranger on a Greyhound bus, looking to turn the conversation, for my sake, I guess, but as soon as I describe the cabin I saw, Ona jumps back in, pointing her fork, and says, "Well, see, that's the place where Little Lady Kidwell lived at. I was the only one to see the Evil Man, but Little Lady don't mind at all who sees *her.* Every hunter that's been through that holler's had a sight of her."

"Granny," Cap says, grinning hard—I feel sure he's kicking her under the table.

"Don't stop on my account," I say. "I like to hear all these old stories. But all I saw was a barn owl—it flew out of the chimney. Was that a barn, off to the side?"

"Why no!" Ona cries, deeply surprised by the idea. "That was where they mostly slept. It probably looks poor to us now, but back then, well, it wasn't considered a *fine* house—this right here was what passed for fine—but nobody thought it wasn't a decent place to live and bring up eight or ten children or whatever they had. They was child-a-year people. Kids spilling out the doors and windows—my daddy said Kidwell was the right name for them."

She checks the gravy boat and nudges Ruth to pass it to Cap, slices more meat, talking all the while. "You'd walk over there and the walls would be just about bellied out with ruckus—those were rough and wild youngens. And their mother, Little Lady, right in the middle of it. I liked to go over there, to get in on all the hollering and wrestling and banjo-picking and laughing, I mean it was paradise. Sometimes me and Bonnie, the girl that was my friend, the oldest one—I don't believe she was much more than a dozen years younger than her mama—we'd break down the beds, without asking anybody's leave, and carry them out and scour the floor with creek sand till it was the cleanest thing you ever saw, and we'd hire Mr. Ben Hazel to fiddle and Lanter Kidwell would call and we'd dance all night—'Cage the Bird' and 'Open and Shut the Garden Gate.' Oh, we had a time."

"You made the poor man fiddle all night?" I ask.

"Well, it wasn't what you'd call fiddling exactly, Carrie—

he was just an old scratchaway—I don't believe he knew more than about a half-dozen tunes, but they was good ones—'Blackberry Blossom' and 'Martha Campbell' are two I remember. One called 'Glory in the Meeting House' everybody called for. He could keep up a beat. By daybreak, he'd be covered head to toe in fiddle rosum, from bearing down on them strings—come out looking like an old possum. Time we got done with him he'd be just about holding out a stump. Sometimes Little Lady or one of the older kids would join in with the guitar or banjo. Or somebody else would that knew how to knock out a tune. There was room for two sets in there, one side of the chimney and the other. The rest stood on the edge beating spoons or what-have-you, or went out in the yard to cool off. . . ."

She stops and dabs at her lips with her napkin. "That's exactly where I met Luther Barkley, out in that yard," she volunteers, then, shyly. "Or at least it was where I first got him to notice me, right where you was at today, Carrie. It wasn't no easy deal, either—I had to just about stand on my head to get it done." The idea of Ona upside down with her bloomers and chubby thighs on view and her skirt over her head makes me laugh out loud, and she laughs, too, flushing up like a girl. She picks up the white lamb salt shaker and shakes it all over everything, then arranges it, smiling, with its black lamb pepper shaker, so that they're kissing.

"And people have seen this Little Lady?"

Ona nods, pressing her lips together. "She's been known to walk."

"One person out here sees a ghost, six others have got to see it, too," Ruth says.

"Well, not the Evil Man. I was the only one seen that one," Ona corrects her modestly. "Little Lady ain't mean, like him, just stubborn. She died on the last child—she wasn't no age at all when it happened, either. Not much more than thirty, I don't believe. She looked like Bonnie's little sister, from a distance—she never got her full growth because she went to having babies so young. Anyway, she wasn't nowhere near ready to pass—she didn't aim to leave and I guess she ain't leaving. She probably can't imagine there's anyplace better to go to than the place she was already at, with music all the time and dancing and fun and sweet babies all around and a little white horse to ride on and Lanter to swing her around like she was his darling child. She had her a place that just suited her. So she probably can't make up her mind to pass. I don't blame her, and I hope she sees it the way it was and not the way it's come to."

"She must—she sure wouldn't hang around if she saw what it's come to," says Cap.

"Maybe she's stayed so long she's forgotten how to pass," Ruth suggests. We all look at her thoughtfully, and she shrugs.

"And Lanter?" I ask, then.

"Lanter run. Left the young ones to the older ones to raise. Just disappeared—not more than a couple of years after Little Lady died. I wouldn't be surprised if he didn't get tired of having a little ghost for a wife. He took the tobacco to market one day and never come back—they found the truck and wagon at the train station in Lexington, figured he caught the train to Alabama. I don't think they went after him—I reckon they thought he'd made his wishes known. After a few years, they sold the farm—Lanter must have made it over to them before he left. I remember my daddy trying to buy it, but it went too high to suit him—I wish we had it now, don't you, Cap?" Cap groans, rolls his eyes to the ceiling.

"Who owns it now?" I ask.

She cuts the pie and hands it around. "It's changed hands a couple of times, and now somebody not from around here has heired it. I don't know what their name is. It's a crime to let that creek bottom just go to brambles and sumac. It was some of the best land around in here, don't you think, Cap?"

"Somebody did run cattle over there," he offers, "but I don't believe there's been any cattle on it for two, three years."

"It ought to be mowed and harrowed and seeded down good in clover and fescue," Ona scolds, as if it's Cap's fault that it isn't. "They could let the steeps grow all up in woods, but they ought to mow out that bottom. It makes me mad, not to take care of something so pretty—when it wouldn't be hardly any trouble. It would be a pleasure." She stops and eats a few fast bites and you can tell she's imagining just how she'd go about it. "They lease out the tobacco base and let the rest go and anybody that wants to hunt in there, why nobody stops them—and then they just come on over the line fence and hunt the back of our place, too, while they're at it. So I don't know what Little Lady thinks about it now, but *I* think it's shameful."

"Maybe I'll buy it," I say. They all turn their heads and look at me, with flat polite looks on their faces. "As an investment," I explain. "I'll bet I could make a down payment out of the insurance money." Ruth gives me a languid, speculating look. Cap stares down fiercely at his empty pie plate, turning his fork over and over.

"Now what would *you* do with it?" Ona asks indignantly.

"I don't know—mow out the bottom to suit you, I guess. Try to keep the hunters away." I shrug. "It was just an idea. I just thought I'd try it out, hear how it sounded."

"I don't think it sounds so bad," Ruth puts in mildly. "Except you need to make some income off that money, don't you? What you planning to live on and make mortgage payments out of?"

Cap looks up then, straight at me, to hear my answer.

"I've got the rents coming in off the house in Lexington, that's one thing. And, you know, my leave from work is over at the end of August. And also," I think to add, after a moment, "anything could happen, with the band."

The silence continues for a few seconds. Then Cap falls to eating pie. "I've got to get some sleep," he announces, as he shoves his chair back and stands up. "I can't take all this good food." He squeezes the back of Ona's neck with both hands, a quick massage. "If I'm not up here tomorrow morning by nine, you give me a call." Over her head, for a second, his glassy, sleep-deprived eyes light on mine. He gives me the slightest one-corner grin, one-shoulder shrug, and he's gone.

We hear him back his van and turn and drive down the gravel road, towards his house across the hardtop.

The silence drifts down as the sound of Cap's van disappears. Molly drifts down. I'm remembering that time this past spring when Cap helped her catch the little bass. The last time she was here. After supper, Ona and Ruth and Louis and TJ and Joyner and Cap and Molly and I all had a walk down the Hawktown Road together. Cap lifted a bright blue plastic cup out of the weeds on the end of a tobacco stick. We walked, strung out in a line down the road, a straggly parade. The redbud was just starting to bloom, like pink breath around every tree, so maybe it was still April. Cap twirled the blue cup on the end of the stick above his head. Molly said, "Reach it way high, Cap. Maybe you could touch the moon"—because the moon was already riding up there, near to full.

Cap hopped up and balanced on the top rail of the fence and held the blue cup on the stick above his head. "Is it touching, Molly?" "Not yet!" He balanced on one foot and stretched up. "Now?" "Not yet!" she shouted in her flat, quacky voice, delighted with this game. She clapped her hands together and pushed them down, one leg raised a little, holding herself because she had to pee, not noticing, her head lifted.

"Come down from there, Cap," Ona said. "You'll break your foolish neck." He stepped out into the air, arms far apart, and landed with the cup still on the stick.

A truck came along then—it was near dark but it didn't have its lights on yet, I remember—and we all stood off to the side. I held on tight to Molly's hand. The truck passed, the driver leaned forward and waved and said something to Ona, and they laughed. Then Willy and three-legged Barney came racing up from the pond and shook water all over us, and we all screamed.

I want to see a ghost too bad ever to see one.

But I remember the time we all walked along the Hawktown Road together, and I held Molly's hand. I remember exactly what it felt like, in mine. I can feel it now. And then the dogs came and shook water all over us.

Ona takes her coffee and goes to the parlor to crochet some more squares for her church bazaar afghan and watch the Reds play ball. I clear the table, fast, and dive into the dishes, while Ruth changes out of her new suit.

I loved what Ruth did, how she threw her arms out behind her, like she was about to take a big old swan dive into the wide world.

Are you ready for that big jumbo jet? It comes over me—I could do it, too! I really could jump on a plane and take off! Where? Who in the world would care? Not me! I can practically feel the plane gain speed and sock into the air.

I can do whatever I want. I'm free as a bird, that's one way of looking at me. I want to be a footloose long-haired gypsy woman, like Ruth, half crazy but bent on living. Ruth's the vision of the future to me—the two of us with big shiny dark eyes and clear whites, our long gold and silver earrings glinting out here and there where our hair falls over our shoulders. We look a little alike. I could have been her daughter, before my face hit the wall.

She comes back down the stairs to help with the dishes. She's got on her glitter T-shirt from the Democratic Convention and pink sweatpants. I'm the washer tonight. I'm trying to be careful, but fast. I sling the silverware into the rinse water. "Now, watch out, Carrie," Ruth says. "You're getting wild with them knives."

Cap would be on the ground, waving. I'd be shooting upward through the clouds, fast.

"Let me go with you, Ruth," I say.

Ruth stops drying and turns right around to look at me, amazed. "What?"

"Let me go with you," I say again, not quite so certain.

"On my *trip*? What for?"

"I don't know—I got the money. And I got the time."

"No. No way. I should say not." She clunks the bowl she's been drying down on the counter and shakes her head. "Not on your life." You've got to hand it to Ruth, she makes herself clear. I blink back tears, blush, laugh. I feel like she's hauled off and slapped me.

"You wouldn't even know what you were supposed to be looking at," she continues gruffly, to cover up how much she meant it. "Holy Land. I never heard of anything so ridiculous. It never crossed your mind till you heard me say it. What's the Holy Land to *you*? Nothing but three wise men and some camels, I bet. You think of your own place to go, honey child. If you want a little joyride, take a cruise to Bermuda—that's supposed to be fun. But you need to be hanging on to that money and thinking about what you're going to do with it, not spending it like there's no tomorrow. You need to be planning your future. You're acting like some little old terrified rabbit in the road. Turn this way, turn that way."

"Maybe I'll just kiss the whole thing away—why shouldn't I? And when it's gone, I'll *have* to plan my future, won't I?"

"Fine. Spend it all," she says crisply. "But think of your own place to go."

I'm about done with these dishes. I wash the gravy pan and slap it into the drain and let the water out. I don't like being compared to a terrified rabbit, I'll tell you that. That's a new one. Nobody would have called me a terrified rabbit and lived, back in my roaring days. I wasn't scared of anything. What am I scared of now?

Anything that moves.

I think what happened was, when Ruth threw her hands up in back of her, I could imagine movement for the first time in a long time, and it was such a relief I flew right after it. In my grief, my soul's been wanting habits—beaten paths, ways to get from here to there. So the idea of movement swept me off my feet. I thought I should give in to it, because here lately I've found myself thinking about cows a little more than I'd like to admit—things that are slow and low to the ground. They just come into my mind. Cows. Rocks. Cedar trees, stubby and rooted. Myself, curling up in a little cove of rocks. The hummingbirds at Ona's sugar water make me nervous, their flashing nervous quickness. "Don't worry," I tell Ruth. "I don't even have a passport. It was just an idea—that I could get on a plane and close my eyes and let it take me somewhere."

"That's no way to travel. If you ain't asleep, don't sleepwalk." She reaches behind her head with both hands in a cheesecake pose to pull her yellow scrungy tighter on her ponytail. She's dressed to do her floor exercises while watching *Mystery*. She's in love with Chief Inspector Dalgleish. She gave up her bridge game at the country club to stay home and see him. She loves his ears—she'd like to see what would happen if you took and blew in one of them, she told us during last week's episode.

"I'll tell you something, Carrie—I've traveled towards and I've traveled away from, in my time. They've both got their advantages, but towards is better, because you're the one that's calling the shots. Keep your eyes open and make sure that where you're going is where you bought a ticket to." She nods over the wisdom of her words, then bends over, putting things in the cupboards. I dry my hands. "Here I've spent my whole life putting things in columns and adding them up. It was all right, it was what I did, I enjoyed it, but now I want my freedom time. I want things not to add up for a while." I open the pantry door while she's talking. "You'd just be trailing along after me, and if you weren't having a good time I'd have to bring on the entertainment, wouldn't I?" I take the keys to my truck off a nail where I saw them hanging, cross the kitchen floor in three strides, hoping to get out the door before she straightens up from putting away the Tupperware.

"And the thing is, *you* got serious business, too, right here, that you'd be running away from. That's all in the world you'd be doing.

"Carrie!" she says without turning. "You're not ready to take that truck out by yourself yet." I stop, dutifully, to hear her out. I practice opening and closing the screen door. "Especially at night." Now she straightens and turns. "Where you going?"

"I'll be careful. I just need to get out for a little while—I'll be back by midnight. I promise."

She examines me and then relents with a shrug—it's almost time for *Mystery,* after all. "You *be* back. Otherwise we'll both worry. And we won't know where to start looking."

"I just want to drive around, waste some gas."

The cab of the truck smells of old french fries. I get the engine to turn over after a while. This truck needs to be driven. And I need to drive it. I back it out, turn it around, turn on the headlights. Moths play in them, like little ghosts.

No, like moths.

I give my horse its head. It heads for the place I once called home.

Sixteen

I'm not a damsel in distress,
I'm just a plain old girl in a plain old mess.
Don't need no charmer in armor
Chargin' in to rescue me.

Chargin' in, bargin' in, chargin' in to rescue me.

I'm not a maiden tied to the tracks,
I'm just a railroad lady facing the facts.
Don't need no—

What? Hero? Nothing rhymes with that except zero. Lovelife with a Scout knife? Hell. *Slippin' in to set me free.*

Turn at the stone fence. Turn at the church. Cross the two-lane with the blinking light, turn again at the bridge. I'm driving to clear my head, know my mind. It seems everything about me is up for grabs.

I'm going home, back along the narrow forking roads through the thick night of the full but unseeable moon. I'm going home to get my fiddle. I don't want to play it, I just want to get it. Have it with me, where I am now.

I'm taking a drive to see my cheery yellow house, trimmed in white. My "property," as I once liked to call it, what I strove so hard for. It held us, it fit us about right, just close enough. A little room to grow. We could have stayed forever. I didn't have to think ahead anymore. I thought it would last us.

It had everything we needed—a window seat, radiators that frosted the long-paned windows. A screened porch, a maple tree, a streetlamp, a school I could have walked Molly to, this fall. Arches between the rooms, a fireplace. When Martha left for France, I painted her old room the color Molly wanted—purple—and stenciled neon-pink hearts around the window, by request, and put her bed in there, but half the time she still crawled in with me. I'd wake up and there she'd be, her knees in my back.

We could have taken over the whole house, if we needed it someday. If someday there had been more than the two of us. I felt we had the future covered.

Lexington lights the clouds ahead. The first night I came to town I got in about this time, and stayed in an old run-down motel the other side of the New Circle Road. It reminded me of the one Daddy died in. I don't know whether you'd call that nostalgia or what. The brown-and-yellow flowered bedspread, the smell of old smoke in the matted carpet—sleaze still gives me a thrill. It makes me feel I'm getting close. Bare light bulbs, cheap linoleum over rotten plywood in the bathroom.

I was in a high old frame of mind that night. I put on my fringed jacket and rushed right out to find the music, my fiddle in the backseat, just in case. I thought I was at the center of the universe, I can't get back the feeling of exactly why, looking now at the ordinary tame streets of Lexington. Eighteen-year-old adrenaline. Ignorance and fantasy, so that I thought every person I saw on Broadway played the banjo or the mandolin.

I loved where I'd gotten myself to—even though where I'd gotten myself to existed mostly in my head. I loved that I'd *gotten* there, pulled it off. I loved the way I felt—all one way and full of myself. I was eager to jump in somewhere and get cracking, show off my so-called technique. That's what I'd come for. I only couldn't figure out why there weren't any bands playing anywhere that night, I mean bluegrass bands. I thought there'd be one on every corner.

I settled for a bar with a blues guitar. I drank two Cokes and danced with a guy who was the brother of the wife of somebody who had once played with J. D. Crowe. The next morning I went out and got myself a cup of coffee and a doughnut and a newspaper, and by evening I had a job wait-ressing at the one bar I'd heard of that had bluegrass some nights, and I'd found a nice big room to live in, too, in an old run-down house right in the midst of things, on South Mill, that I could walk to my job from. That's the kind of girl I was—I knew how to make the best of a bad situation.

If I'd had the slightest idea what I was doing when I was eighteen, I would have stopped when I got to Knoxville. Or turned west on I-40 and gone on over to Nashville. Been the toast of the town by now, spangles, hair out to here, my own new album called *CARRIE!* Or taken a whole different road, up the coast to D.C., the bluegrass lover's paradise.

Not me. I heard Bill Monroe and the Bluegrass Boys and then I asked Mr. Millard where the Bluegrass was, and he said Kentucky. Where in Kentucky, I asked, and he said, Oh, around Lexington. I know he would have been more careful with his answer if he'd understood I was basing the rest of my life on it.

You can't help what chooses you. I *heard* that music, I heard the music in back of it. I felt it way deep in my heart. It was like there was some old grandma in my blood fiddling her heart out on some lonely front porch up in the mountains of Tennessee or Kentucky, to nothing but the moon and the Big Dipper, nobody around for miles to hear that fiddle sob and break and climb to the top of the scales. Nobody but me. It was a voice in me before I ever even heard that kind of music.

They say a fiddler's bound to fiddle. I almost think it must be a basic human urge—to run one taut string over another and see what kind of sound comes out: a bow made from a twig strung with a hair of the tail of your plow horse, sewing thread wound tight around two nails hammered to a cigar box or a syrup bucket. You can make a fiddle out of one cornstalk and a bow out of another. You can make a fiddle out of a gourd. It's like people just looked around, kind of wild-eyed, for something to put strings on and then for something to slide over those strings. I gave the pawnshop fifteen dollars and a guitar in exchange for that beat-up fiddle, and then my life began.

I'm sure that human beings are shaped sort of like arrows because for a million years they've been aiming themselves at what they thought they wanted.

Well, I aimed and let fly and hit what I was aiming at. Only, come to find out it wasn't just exactly the right target for bluegrass music, just for bluegrass *grass,* the kind horses eat. By the time I got that figured out, which was about twenty-four hours later, I'd used up my cash reserves.

But it wasn't exactly a wrong target, either. There was enough big and little action around town to satisfy me. There was some hot fiddling going on around Lexington, and I could get out to Monroe County and Magoffin County and Harlan and so forth, where I tracked down every old fiddler I heard about and tried to get them to show me the tricks they had up their sleeves before they went off to glory. I never drove anywhere without my fiddle and my tape recorder, so I could catch the songs that fly through the air around here like radio waves that you aren't aware of till you tune in. I tried to bring 'em back alive. You'd be surprised how full the world is of fiddle music, to its furthest corner, how much thought's gone into everything about it—getting that old elbow grease into the bowing, tuning a little sharp to give the music that wild edge, fluttering the first finger for a subtle slur, just this side of a trill. If I hadn't come to Lexington by mistake, I wouldn't have found, for example, old Bill Craven up a holler, to teach me how to play "Stoney Point" the way it was meant to be played.

If, if, if . . .

When all is said and done, this is the place I got to, and I made do. It was good enough for me. Maybe in another place, I wouldn't have lost my child, but what good does it do to think that? She wouldn't have been the same child, and there's the end of *if.*

And now I'm turning through the known streets of my thousands of nights since that first night, toward the street with the yellow house and the maple tree we thought was ours.

I park at the curb, not in the driveway, so that maybe nobody will notice I'm here, because I want so much to be alone now. The upstairs apartments are both dark—I'm glad it's Saturday night. Sometimes, around here, everybody is a little too close up against you.

Some nights, at Ona's, I would think of the way the street-lamp shone through the leaves of the maple tree and cast their overlapping, delicate shadows on the sidewalk, and now my shadow turns around my feet, skimming over the shadows I remembered, only now they're real, unless I'm dreaming.

Light shines through the front windows of my parlor. I can

hear the radio playing, to ward off burglars. I go up the two steps onto the front porch, and look through the living-room window, to see if Molly and I are piled together in the morris chair, reading *Uncle Wiggly*. When my father died, I let myself believe there was a life flowing along underneath *this* life, where things just went on forever the way you wanted them to, the way they always had—"where the soul never dies," as the old gospel song goes, but I didn't mean heaven, I meant *here*, in *this* world.

But nothing's going on in there. I look in, through the half-closed curtain, on an empty house where radio music has been washing through the air day and night for the past month. Washing it clean.

I've heard in my dreams the sound of the stiff bolt clunking back when I turned the key. My thumb remembered, even asleep, how hard it was to press down on the door latch, but now the lock turns easily because Cap fixed it, after he broke it, and the latch clicks down as if there's no reason to resist. I don't have to give the door my shoulder to get in. It just opens.

I was dreading coming back for the wrong reason. I thought the rooms would still be full of her.

But she's gone from here.

At first, in those first hours after the accident, the air trembled, moved, as if her soul were still moving around in the air of the house. As if she were holding on to the air, or it to her. I felt when I moved from room to room that I was moving through her life, her breath. I believed it was still partly the same air that had actually *touched* her. That had passed through her lungs. And that's how it stayed, to me—wavery, vibrating around people's movements and voices—until Cap showed up and took me to Ona's.

Now the light from the lamp Cap has left on seems solid as

a slab of marble. The life that once yelled and danced and sang and flew long-legged from room to room has drawn back to the edges. The echo of our loud sweet life together has contracted. It stiffens the walls. The rooms have turned into containers of ordinary, slightly stale, close air. I don't know where she is, but she's not here anymore.

And the fact is, neither is my fiddle.

I practiced that last afternoon. I put the fiddle in its case to take over to Justice's that evening. I think I put the case where I always do, on the window seat. But it's not on the window seat now.

I forgot about it, all this time, but now I hurry through the house, fighting panic. Maybe I brought it into the kitchen. Maybe my bedroom. I want to have it, have it with me, so I know where it is. So I can take it out of its case and hold it sometimes. Not play it. Not play it the way Cap wants me to. Or the way Ruth wants me to. Not ask it to do anything for me. Just hold it.

Doesn't take care of anything. Neglectful.

Oh, please don't let somebody have stolen it.

I knock into the ironing board, still standing in the bedroom. Long, long ago, I was ironing my red blouse. Then I lifted it off the board and put it on and couldn't get any further. I stop now and fold the board and lean it behind the door. *There.*

No fiddle anywhere. Maybe Cap picked it up and took it out to Ona's. But she would have given it to me, I think. She would have seen I needed it. Oh, I've been out cold.

Doesn't take care of. Doesn't protect.

No, I'm not going to hear that. I'm not.

Oh, I hope Cap came and got it and put it somewhere for safekeeping, and that somebody didn't just get in here and walk off with it. Anyone could have—half of Lexington has a key to the back door. It's all I've got left to protect. And I just forgot about it.

Lost that, too. Your fault. No excuse for. Your own fault.
All your fault.

Hanging laundry, deep in my thoughts. What of? Oh, I never want to say.

I had stashed Cap way down there where I couldn't hardly get *to* him. But sometimes, when my defenses were down, when the moon was full or my hormones were up or the music was especially fine, or whatever, I'd catch myself working over some little thrill, like one of those squirrels out at Ona's spinning a hickory nut in its paws. Spinning and chomping away on some damn thing that damn man had said or done. Somewhere along the way, the girl who reached out and grabbed what she wanted for as long as she wanted it had turned into a woman who couldn't let go of what she didn't have.

I guess you know by now we're not talking about a little crush. We're talking about serious obsession. Where does it come from, what is it for? What does it want? I stood at the clothesline, remembering some joke only the two of us had thought was funny the night before, and then that blue-eyed private smile. As my child aimed her trike down the steep driveway. I think I might have been practicing smiling back, right on my face, when I looked up, too late, and saw what I saw, and began the running that couldn't get there. It bends me double, right now, against the wall.

Pervert. Addict. Fool.

He was a danger to me. To my life. He prevented me from my real life. And I would choose no other. I chose him because he was a danger to me. Maybe I would have knocked it off, really and truly, if I'd known he was a danger to my child. Through no fault of his own. Through *my* fault, my terrible fault.

I slide down the wall, sit rocking back and forth, back and forth. When they tell me it wasn't my fault, they don't know what I know.

You *do* have to watch children that age every minute. A child like Molly you do, one that's quick and high-spirited and always on the muscle.

I was under a spell, hypnotized for years—I made him my religion. Made wanting him my religion, that kind of wanting that you do till wanting is the air you breathe and what you breathe it with. I wanted him from afar. Because no other man would do, I had a baby to break the spell. To have something real, not made up, to love. It would have worked, too, if he hadn't hired me into his band, not even a year after she was born. At the time I didn't take in the significance—you know, you don't. You never give a second thought to the timing of things. It's just the way things happen, it's just life. Molly brought me luck, I remember telling people, and then I made my adjustments, so that I could have everything I wanted.

If God were a woman, she would have seen the danger and cooled down that case of the hots, blown on it the gentle way a mother blows on her kid's soup. Instead I lay in my bed, wanting, wanting—with my little child that was mine to take care of curled against me. I did that with my life. It cost me what I held most dear. I ran, to save what I held most dear.

But it was too late.

I straighten and stand up. I run water in the kitchen sink and bring it up to my face, over and over. I dry my face with a paper towel.

I did get that bad angel wrestled to the ground, though.

I've got to say that for myself. It took a year or so, but I got it hog-tied. I felt proud of myself, older and wiser. I watched new women put the moves on Cap and my heart went out to them. I felt detached. I was otherwise occupied, at least as far as I knew.

But I gave myself too much credit, too soon. Because there I was, at the clothesline, playing back some smile like a love-sick teenager.

Having a baby didn't break the spell. Did losing one break it? I don't know. I am feeling him again, all around me. He's telling me it's real now, that we can't stomp it down again, must not. That we're in a different place now, where we ought to be, at last. That it's not too late.

It's too late. I've changed. I'm a person capable of framing a question in a killing way: Who do you love, Cap? Me or Archer Records? Can you tell the difference? I can't.

Some tangles you just have to back away from.

He bent over me this afternoon as if to protect me, and what I felt was his wanting to come down over me again. Wanting to make it easy for me to stay and hard for me to leave. I don't trust him, and I don't trust myself. Why should I?

All I know for sure that I can trust is: I want my fiddle and it's not here. I have half a mind to call him right now, wake him up and ask him if he's got it. But he was dead on his feet, the last I saw of him, and I have a heart. Surely, surely he has it. Surely it isn't gone. Surely he took it somewhere for safe-keeping.

THIS IS THE house of hearts. Heart house. Hearts everywhere. I was trying to raise her to be a wild-hearted, strong-hearted girl; she was wild for sure, but she was also a walking neon-pink valentine to the world.

Maybe what she liked so much was just the shape: the fat swoop outward, the sweet slide in, two opposite-curving hooks coming together at the upward cleavage and downward point. Sexy geometry of kindergarten hearts, shaped like Barbie's chest. Nothing like the real thing, that tough old muscle, forever clenching, clenching, to shoot the blood through the narrow passages. The heart's working day and night, too damn busy to break.

At least the plants haven't died, no thanks to me. Someone's been watering them. Mrs. Stevens, probably. Cap thought of everything. Stopping the paper, getting the lawn mowed, leaving on the lights and the radio. I turn the radio off and stand then in the dead cold failure of my plan to make a life for us.

The hooked rugs and baskets and prisms and candles in wine bottles, the bits of lace and cut glass, the jars of weeds and herbs and bath beads that seemed so comforting and lively and homey to me have no meaning at all. I gathered up stuff that seemed to me to have life in it to make a life for *us*. Lamps and bowls. Odds and ends, remnants of other lives. The morris chair doesn't care who sat in it. Nothing here remembers us. I could walk away and leave the whole damned mess, or fling it all out the front door. Nothing here has a thing to do with my life now.

I pass the phone, pick it up, and out of nervousness dial my mama's number. When I hear her prim startled voice, I say, "Hi there, Janette," jolly and gruff, to set her a good example.

"Oh, honey. I was just sitting here smoking cigarettes and praying. I *knew* it would be you when the phone rang. You at Mrs. Barkley's?"

"No, I'm in Lexington."

"At the house?" A little alarm pricking up her voice.

"Yes. First time I've driven the car since I went out to Ona's."

"Oh," comes a little flutter out of Mother. "You're not staying there by yourself again, are you, Carrie?"

"No, I took a drive and just sort of ended up here. I'm about to drive back out."

"You sound so far away, honey. So very tired." I can practically see the big tears coming up in her brown eyes. I wish I'd called Stony instead, if I had to call someone. Or put in an overseas call to Martha.

"You've been in that empty house by yourself feeling bad, haven't you." I don't think Mama was ever tuned in too good to my joy, but she homes right in on my sorrow. "Oh, I wish I was with you now. We could drink a beer and cry." She's crying now. We both laugh.

"I could *use* a beer. But I think I'll pass, on the crying."

"You're such a brave girl. I just think the world of you, honey."

"I know you do, Mama. But I'm not brave, I'm just cried out for now. You go right ahead, though."

She laughs and uses the side of her forefinger to slide tears off her cheeks. I've seen her do it a thousand times. She likes to cry, but she doesn't want to stretch the skin under her eyes.

There's a moment of silence, Mama poised on the brink of some drama, debating with herself. Then she announces, in a breathless rush, like she can't help herself: "Molly's all right, Carrie."

In spite of me, my heavy heart gives a dumb clumsy lurch. It knocks the breath out of me; I lean against the table.

"I was getting ready to call you about it." She takes another gulp of air. "I had a dream," she announces.

I hold on tight to the receiver, so as not to scream at her.

"Oh, Christ, Mom!" My eyes sting with tears. I could kill her.

"I came home from work tonight," she goes on, unnoticing, relishing her story, taking her time. "I was just beat, and I sat down on the sofa to watch the news and fell right to sleep and there was little old Molly walking along a beautiful, beautiful path—it went through woods, and then there was a meadow on one side, full of wildflowers. It wasn't like a regular dream—I felt like I was looking through a window at something that was really happening. She was having a wonderful time, Carrie. Looking at everything—strolling, you might say."

Her voice is rushed, but light and elated. It's the elation in it that terrifies me. "She was by herself, but there were lights flitting all around her. It reminded me of Snow White—do you remember when she wakes up and the bluebirds are flying all around her, singing away?" I clench my teeth and roll my eyes upward, for my own benefit. "I *think* it was Snow White," she chatters on. "Anyway, I figured out after a while that the lights were angels, keeping her company and helping her. Oh, I'm glad you called. You must have just felt it, that I had something to tell you."

I hear a kind of low growl coming from the back of my throat.

"I think it was a true vision, Carrie," she confides shyly. "It was so real it woke me up. I wanted to go right back to sleep and see if I could talk to her, but I was too stirred up. That's why I was praying. Saying thank you. She wasn't lonely or sad or lost or anything. She was full of—delight. And busy. I think she has a crowd of angels *all around* her to watch over her and teach her and help her."

"I hope so, Mom." She's waiting for me to be overjoyed, but I'm thinking, *You idiot.* "It'll probably *take* a crowd," I say in a snappish voice. "And they better be hard as nails. I don't think bluebirds are going to get the job done."

"Oh, don't, Carrie. Don't be sarcastic. It's like throwing my wonderful dream back in my face."

"I'm sorry, Janette. I don't mean to be mean to you. But I think we just dream what we have to." I know I'm cruel, but you have to watch this one. She told me, when it rained the day after the accident, that God had turned on his sprinklers for Molly to play in. She's one-third gloom and one-third unbelievable hokum. It's that other one-third that keeps me hanging on, her generous nature.

"Oh, maybe it *was* a true vision," I say, relenting. "Who am I to say it wasn't? I've had enough visions of my own like that. I just wish they could have spared a couple of those angels to come down here while she was alive. They should have seen she was too much for her mama. If they've got so many that they're swarming around her now. One good, full-time guardian angel, that's all I would have asked. I *had* Martha, but she ran off to the other side of the world."

"Oh, they *all* need one, Carrie!" This is the one-third I like of Mama, the one who goes right on to the next thing and doesn't hold a grudge, except against Daddy. "It's a miracle any child makes it to the age of six. I sure don't know how you did. I thought if a rattler didn't get you, you'd drown. I found you on the fifth step of a ladder when you were eight months old. Just grinning away. Connie and Dexter didn't give me anything like the trouble you did. You took after your father—daring. Some children *are* daring, and if they make it, they usually turn out good. But a lot *don't* make it. And she wasn't too much for you. You were right on top of things."

"Not quite, it looks like," I say, my jaw clenched so it won't tremble. "I feel like she'd still be here if I hadn't been neglectful." I'm surprised by how I can't keep myself from saying this out loud, to *Janette*, of all people, can't keep my voice from choking up when I say it.

"You *weren't* neglectful," she cries, taking up for me—I need it so bad. "You were never neglectful, you were a good mother! You watched her like a hawk. It only took a second, Carrie." I'm squeezing the receiver and taking deep breaths to keep from breaking into sobs. She knows this, and goes on talking to help me. "You know, baby, Molly got her little bottom smacked more than once for getting on that driveway, just the few times I was there. She wasn't exactly a *good* girl. In the sense of obedient. She was a little bit wicked, to be honest, always testing. I hope that doesn't hurt your feelings, but you know it's true. She had a strong will, and that was good, but it was dangerous, too. Listen to your mama, now. It wasn't your fault she went down that driveway, Carrie. She knew it was against the rules, and she knew why, because I explained it to her myself and I know you did, too. She was only five, but still."

"She forgot," I say, my voice still clenched, fighting tears. "She was having a good time. She was talking to Bootsie. She got carried away with herself. . . ."

"That's right, she did. I want you to stop thinking it was your fault, because it wasn't," she says, flat and certain—it surprises me, because almost every opinion she ever offers turns up at the end like a question. "Some things just mean to happen." She pauses to let me get hold of this, then goes on, "You were a wonderful, wonderful—" she searches for the right word for me—"single parent."

That makes me laugh, good old Janette, though it comes out sounding more like a sob.

"No, I don't mean that if she'd had a daddy she would have automatically been better off than having you by yourself.

There's daddies and daddies, aren't there. I just mean you did the work of two, and did it real well."

"Well," I say, embarrassed by how grateful I am to her. That's the main thing mothers need to do, it seems like to me—think the world of you and not be kidding. I don't know what fathers need to do. Show up once every three, four days, bring you a present about a month after your birthday, a pair of suede boots, even though your mother works in a shoe store and could have gotten the same ones in the right size on her discount. If the ones he brings you are a little too big, so what? You can wear socks. "But so did you. Do the work of two. With three of us. And a job."

"Yes, I certainly did. I did the best I could. The only difference between me and you, I was a single parent and didn't know it." She laughs, girlishly. "Your daddy did grace us with his presence every *once* in a while, so I got the mistaken notion we had a family together. So did you children. You knew you *had* a daddy, at least. And, oh, you thought the angels brought him in, Carrie. He wasn't for every day, but we could sure count on him for special."

"I've been thinking about Daddy some, here lately," I confess to her.

"Have you? What have you thought?" She wouldn't ordinarily inquire, but I guess she's looking to get me thinking about something else.

"What a good time he gave us, sometimes," I say shyly.

"Oh yes, he was real good at good times. He was the magic man." She says it with that brittle, light upward catch to her voice, so dry with disappointment and bitterness you could snap it like a twig.

"Yeah, he could disappear before your very eyes," I say.

But my whole life sharpens, for a second, as if somebody was fooling with the lens of a projector. What I'm thinking is,

No wonder. No wonder I'm the way I am. They ought to have Man-Anon, for adult daughters of women like Janette. Addicted to magic, to that dark wanting that beats all having. The only good man is a gone man, but it's got to be the right man that's gone, so that your life of listening will be well spent, your life of listening for the sound of that Riviera galumphing over the bump where the drainage pipe runs under the road, shoveling up the drive, spraying gravel. Listening for the sound that means the good times are going to roll again, for a day or an hour or a whole week, if you play your cards right. And I have to ask myself: Is that what I want? Is that what I want for my life? Could I change, and want something else?

Janette's voice is still all composed for passion, of a certain prissy, smoky sort. She was only about five years older than I am now when Daddy died in that motel room, not nearly old enough to give up on passion entirely. When I'm down there visiting, I notice she still stands one way and then another in front of the full-length mirror. She still comes out of the bedroom from putting on her makeup and high heels to ask Connie and me if she looks good. And we always say, *"Well,* now." Because the truth is she looks kind of wired together these days, her body jerky and angular-moving, like a puppet's, from too much holding herself upright, I guess.

"Still," she says now, "I still wish he was with us now, because he'd know exactly the right thing to do for you. You couldn't beat him in emergencies. He just had the touch." She thinks for a minute and then goes on less certainly, "But you know, I've been thinking here lately, I never really knew him. Too starry-eyed."

"Nobody really knew him, Mom. He didn't want to be known."

"His motel buddies. Maybe they knew him. I don't know. But they probably didn't see some of the sides of him we saw."

"Who knows? We were a starry-eyed crew. Even Dexter." There's nothing more to say, on the subject of Daddy, except Rest in Peace. He was just Cap's age, I think, when he died. "I wish he'd made it to my sixteenth birthday—he was going to sneak me into Dutch's, to hear him play."

"I wish he'd made it to your sixteenth birthday, too, sweetheart." We both sigh into the long-distance silence. "You going to stay out there with those old ladies awhile more?" she asks.

"They're not that old."

"They're sweet," she compromises. Then, casual: "Is Cap out there?"

"No. Well, he is this weekend." I make my voice neutral, offhanded. "He has to drive to Atlanta, I think it is, next week. They've got about another month on the road."

"I guess nobody's going to catch that boy," she says wistfully. "What a waste."

"Oh, now, *that's* my mama," I say. She thinks I'm giving her a compliment, egging her on.

She laughs her little throaty, man-hungry laugh. "There's something about him, *I* think."

"You and about six hundred others."

"Don't you?"

"I wouldn't want to hazard an opinion," I say, in a voice meant to close the subject. But then I have to add, "Except that I think *catch* is about the ugliest word in the English language."

Mama, given her experience with Daddy, should have helped us change our way of thinking about men. But no. At Christmastime to this day, I still get a box of sexy lingerie—

you know, teddies and silk bikinis and merry widows—with a card saying, "Love from Santa." What kind of mother is that, pray tell?

Something to catch a man with. I don't know why I can't just tell her to get me a Crock-Pot for a change. Afraid to hurt her feelings, trample on the one thing she thinks she's an expert on. I wonder sometimes why she didn't marry again, since she's so fascinated by this catching business. She had her chances, two or three of them that even I know about, maybe more. The one time I asked, when she was still bitter and hard about Daddy, she said, "I've had about enough marriage to last me. Dave Mullins took care of that. Both ways. He was the be-all, for me. But he was the end-all, too, baby. I'm looking to spend the rest of my life resting up."

But it's been sixteen years since he died, and things do change, or so I've heard. She could still find happiness with some sweet, decent, available man, if she wanted it. She doesn't seem any more interested in sweet, decent, available men than are her daughters.

"Well," she says now, teasingly, "I can see if anybody *does* catch him, it won't be you—you wouldn't stoop so low. How would you feel about singing at his wedding?" She doesn't give me long to decide before she answers for me. "You'd hate it. It would break your heart if he was to marry some other girl. How old is he, anyway—well into his thirties, isn't he? You'd think he'd be about ready to settle down."

"Everyone in the world doesn't have to settle down, just because *you* did. God knows *why* you did. Or why you'd want anyone else to—you ain't exactly a walking advertisement for wedded bliss with a musician, if you don't mind me saying so, Janette. Let the ones who want to get married do it and leave the others alone. Me, I hear wedlock, I think deadlock."

"Oh, Carrie, that's just talk."

I don't bother to reply. I'm hunting for a pencil and a piece of paper. I write down *deadlock, headlock, bedrock, gridlock, padlock.*

"You don't know what it's like to be lonely," she says.

"God! I wish you wouldn't be so downtrodden, Mom. You should be the one telling me there's nothing worse than catching a man that don't like to be caught. What's wrong with you?"

"You don't know he doesn't. He cares for you, I know."

Suddenly I'm overcome with heavy, thick exhaustion, as if my mother's voice had drugs in it. "Well, I got to shove off— so long, Mom," I say.

"Now, that's what I mean about you being brave," she observes. I hear a match striking. "When are you coming home?" she asks, meaning Lake Grace.

"It's going to be a while," I say. "I have a lot of decisions to make—like, about this house. And the band. And what I'm going to do with myself. Things I have to be *here* for. I'll come down later and spend a couple of weeks, okay? Once I get everything settled."

"I'll believe it when I see it. That's what I used to tell your daddy. And do you know what he'd say? You'll see it when you believe it. Like it was me not believing that kept him from showing up. I still get so damn mad I could slap him when I think of it."

I've been looking at a picture above the telephone all the time I've been talking to Mama. I found it at a yard sale and bought it for a quarter and put it in a frame. It's an illustration from some 1930s magazine, it looks like. In a dim room, with sheer white curtains drawn over a window, a woman, in dreamy profile, sort of blue-skinned, is sitting in the shadows, dressed in a flowered gauzy gown. She's turned in her chair, so that her thin arms are folded on top of one another along the back of it, her chin resting on her arms, a cloud of brown hair around her shoulders. She's looking out through the curtains. Behind her is a piano. There's a narrow bed with a suggestion of a headboard against one wall. A little girl sits on the edge of the bed, a square child with a broad face and straight orange hair, chopped off square under her ears, with red barrettes in it. She's sitting there, looking up through the gloom at the lady—I don't know whether it's supposed to be her mother or big sister or who. The child's got on a rose-colored dress, and an orange sweater, to match her hair, white socks and brown Oxfords—orthopedics, they look like. The dress is ladylike—smocked, with a bit of lace at the collar. The dress glows in the dim light; it's what your eye goes to first, before it notices the lady. The girl doesn't match the dress at all. She doesn't know how to sit yet—her stout little legs hang down. She's leaning forward, with her hands clasped in a ball between her knees.

It's the expression on the child's face that makes me keep looking at the picture after I hang up the phone. She's so jolly and all there and ready to roll. It's like she's saying, "So what are we going to do today, Ma? Huh?" And the woman is so blissed out, so dreamy or something, that she doesn't even hear her. She's probably going to swing around and play "Someday My Prince Will Come" in a minute, with many romantic trills. The girl reminds me a little bit of Molly, of course—that's probably why I bought the picture. But I see now that it's something else, more as if Molly reminds me of *this* girl. This girl is the first girl. Not myself, not the girl I was, but the image of the most familiar thing I know. Or used to know, and just now remembered.

And the dreamy, shining, beautiful, romantic lady, turned away from both the piano and the child, doesn't have a clue.

Doesn't have a clue what they're going to do today, because

she's only interested in what's going to happen some sweet tomorrow that she's given her life up to.

The world is full of these little girls, living and buried alive, visible and invisible, inner girls and outer girls. Squat, homely, excited, eager to know what comes next, comical girls who don't know how to press their legs together like ladies yet. How do they grow up into blind dreamers? The lady in the picture is a damsel in distress, she's under a spell. It's an evil spell, though it doesn't look it, with her dressed all in flowers, and light catching in her hair.

I would have given anything to keep Molly from falling under that spell. I wanted her to keep that look of being ready for whatever. She was willful, as Mama says, but she was already drawing hearts hearts hearts, even though I tried to interest her in horses and airplanes—she liked them fine, but it was hearts she had her heart set on. What in the world did they mean to her? To her imagination? I asked her once, and she said, as though amazed at my stupidity, "Love!" I heart Mama. I heart Teacher. I heart the cat. A world of love. It was only a matter of time, for Molly, till she hearted the wrong thing. I set her a bad example, as much as I tried not to, as bad as my mother set for me.

Most little boys don't heart things, I've noticed.

THE CARTONS ARE STACKED in Molly's bedroom. The ones Mama got from the liquor store when she was here. She wanted me to let her box up Molly's things, but I wouldn't hear of it. "Just leave every single thing the way it is. When it's time to do that, I'll do it. I want to be the one to do it."

It must be time, because I'm bringing Molly's clothes out of the closet by the armload and laying them on the bed. I fold the first dress carefully, so it looks nice, the navy-blue one with red embroidery that she wore for the portrait we had made at Penney's, me sitting down, her standing behind me with her hand on my shoulder, sturdy, bright-eyed, getting ready to laugh, both of us all teeth. I plump up the lace and tie the sash and put it down at the bottom of the first carton. Then I do another, paying just as much attention to the way I fold it, getting pleasure out of the way the plaid folds together, her school dress, for nursery school. Then her pink church dress. All her dresses together don't come anywhere near filling the carton, so after I've emptied the closet I start on the dresser, one drawer at a time, sorting through underwear, putting the worn-out panties, the unmatched socks and stretched sweatshirts and T-shirts and tights in the throwaway pile. My mind feels completely clear, but about the size of a ring box, the expensive kind with the plush lid that snaps down with hardly a sound. I work steadily, folding ever so carefully, packing just so, until every drawer is empty.

I've got to leave soon, to get back to Ona's when I told Ruth I would. I stuff a couple of things in my purse—Molly's Mickey Mouse T-shirt, my old worn-out silky nightgown that she still slept with her hand clutched around, thumb in her mouth, in that fierce sleeping she did that she took an hour to come up from, flushed and grouchy, sucking that thumb, finally smiling a little around it, when she was about ready to rejoin the human race. I arrange the shoes on top—Mama kept her in shoes, good ones. I wrap each pair in tissue paper. Her new fuzzy elephant slippers she wouldn't take off even to go to bed.

I find some masking tape and seal the box and write "Girl's Clothes Size 5" on it.

I pack what I can of her toys and books in the second box. What I'm going to do with this stuff beats me. I've been thinking of giving it to Kelly and Joyner, for Mary Emma. Maybe the toys and things, but none of us could stand the clothes. I'll get somebody to take them to the Salvation Army. Somebody can buy them who thinks the child who wore them just went into a size 6, the way they do. Or maybe I'll keep them, put them in Ona's attic when no one's looking, so that if I need them, they'll be there.

Now I turn out the lights and lie down on her bed.

I close my eyes. It comes to me, it comes to me. The little bare helpless legs. The shut white face.

And right on top of that, a kind of dream, merciful. I dream I'm dressing her. Combing her hair, buttoning her pink dress up the back, its small pearly buttons. It feels ceremonious, as though I were getting her ready to be married, or to take communion or something. Something religious. She stands still, with her head down, while I clasp her locket. She buckles her own white sandals over her pink socks with lace at the cuffs. She is excited. So am I.

I lie still then, on her bed. I don't see the little lights that my mother saw.

Instead, Molly's walking, in her pink dress, on the path, alone. She's quiet. She's paying attention. I don't see the lights, but there are others with her, I can tell that. "The ones who know" is the way I think of them. Though I can't see them, I know they are tall. They are bending toward her, caring for her, teaching her something that I don't know. She's walking, head bent a little, listening to them. What she's learning from them is taking her into itself. It's not scary, but it's serious. She's listening, her face quiet, absorbed. Shining. What she's learning is taking her away from me.

Maybe they're not angels. Maybe they're just spirits who've gotten used to being dead, old hands, gathered to comfort and instruct the one who yearns still toward the living loved one, to comfort the *dead* griever, not the living one. She's walking on a path deep in pine needles or moss, or some other unreverberant softness. No sound of footsteps.

She's not like Little Lady—Molly wasn't old enough to have accumulated much resistance to dying. She can go naturally, trustingly, where the path leads—deep, deep into the distance. It's simple, she wants to go on to whatever comes next. I feel myself as the one *down here*, her earthly mother, holding her back now with my heavy, strange, earthbound grief, from whatever comes next, even if it is just thin air.

I leave the boxes on the bed, close the bedroom door. I don't know whether I can really move in with Ona, but I don't see how I can come back here to live. I have to change everything. I pass the picture hanging over the telephone. I lift it off the wall and take it with me. That little girl would like to get up and dance, I think. If I can find my fiddle, I'll make some music she might dance to. That's a promise.

I close the windows, turn the radio back on, leave some of the lights on, lock the front door behind me.

MY MIND WENT to Cap for a moment, that day. That day she died. What I thought made me smile. Did she have to lose her life for that? I don't believe it! I won't!

I was a pretty good mother, I did the best I could. I loved her. That's all I know, for sure.

FOUR

Careless
and Gay

Seventeen

I lie flat on my stomach, with my head twisted to one side, trying to see up into the hole in the elm tree by the dim beam of my glove-compartment flashlight; everywhere I shine the light, no squirrel. But if it didn't knock down the board to get out, where is it? The heap of dry cat food Ona put in there for it seems untouched, the water cup is full. I can't tell how far up the tree the hollow runs—thin, vertical ridges of jagged dark wood back the narrowing space. Maybe there's a way up and out.

I turn off the flashlight, but I stay stretched out on my belly under the tree, my head on my arms. It's comfortable; I could stay here a long time. I'm in no hurry—I rushed back to get here before midnight so they wouldn't worry that I ran my car off a bridge, and here they both just went to bed. They left the porch light on for me, though.

Now here comes Barney, hopping around my outstretched body in a friendly, excited way, saying, "Come on, get up, you ain't dead, you can't fool me." I roll over and pat him—he's one of those dogs that know how to smile, part Border collie, part shepherd, the regular Oxford County mix, a lot of ragtag tail wagging a smart little dog. Willy, the yellow dog, isn't around. I don't know where he's gotten to. I sit up. The clouds have cleared off now to show the full moon high in the sky, white and kind of squinched up, as if all the moisture's been baked out of *it*, too. "The squirrel's not in there," I tell Barney. "Not that I can tell." It seems to me that if it were dead, we'd surely smell it by now, with this heat.

Barney sticks his nose in to have a sniff and wags his tail. I think he's on to something, but it turns out he's just after the cat food. I pull him away and put back the board, just in case. He sits down, leaning against me. His ears prick up and he holds his breath for a few seconds, listening—to what I don't know, one of the thousand things going on out there in the fields that I don't know about—then goes to panting again.

We lean quietly side by side for a minute; then I give him a pat and stand up and climb the porch steps and go in the back door. I turn off the porch light and find my way across the dark kitchen and into the hall. Ona's left a lamp lit on the upstairs hall table for me.

I hear her knocking it off up there. She keeps her bedroom door open, half for ventilation, half so she can hear me if I should have a fit in the middle of the night. Pictures called *The Four Seasons of Man* rise along the stairwall, youngest at the bottom, boys and girls and lambs and wildflowers all tumbled together in a meadow, then a young lady in a hoopskirt strolling along a country lane on the arm of her intended, then the wife and all the children gladly hurrying down the staircase to greet the husband, who's holding the baby high in the air, apples on the tree outside. The Last Season shows winter by the fire, snow outside, but everything cozy in the parlor, an old man in whiskers, a lady with gray curls under her bonnet, knitting.

Most people, their life is a progress, with stages. Mine just floats free. Maybe I'll get in on the last season: I see three old ladies in bonnets, knitting by the fire. I might need a little nip of whiskey now and then to get me through, is all. Maybe one old lady could crochet, and one could read *National Geographic,* while the other played them a tune on her fiddle.

I turn the light off in the hall. Without turning on the light in my room, I take the photograph of Molly and me out of my bag and set it on the bedside table. I prop the framed illustration of the dreamy lady and the little redheaded girl on the dresser, where the mirror used to be. Then I pull the Mickey Mouse T-shirt and the old nightgown out of my bag and sit down in the rocking chair, where the moonlight falls through the window. I bunch the T-shirt and nightgown together and hug them against me.

This is rocking country around here. I guess I rock myself to sleep. I dream something about China. I've been rounded up. I'm standing in a long line of students who are to be jailed, tortured, executed. We begin to sing our anthem, but the officials put their faces close to ours. They're serious. Deep in their dark still eyes, they mean to kill us. In the dream, I can hardly believe it, that they could look into our eyes and still mean to kill us. Their eyes are like walls. There is no way out. We have been caught and taken from our hiding places. We are as good as dead.

Now the wide night, where once our voices reached upward, looking for the dearest harmony, is flooded suddenly with the loud, hysterical midnight song of the mockingbird. I wake and listen, my heart pounding. One call tumbles out on top of another, with small buzzes and chirps thrown in, to imitate nestsful of baby sparrows, bluebirds, tanagers.

If this is the mocker I know, her nest is on the other side of the house. I think I understand what's happening: The yellow cat is creeping along the limb. The mother bird, having failed to drive him off, has flown to the oak woods on this side of the house, to try to lure him away. Her last chance. Nothing to put against those claws but songs. "Over here, come over here," she calls, urgently, moving from tree to tree. "There are many baby birds over here!" What cat would be taken in by this frantic incessant calling? *I am the oriole, cardinal, bunting, I am the wren, oh come here, come here, to this woods full of baby birds.* It's as if all the terror in the world is being funneled through that one tiny throat.

I'm out in the hall, soaking with sweat. Ona's there, too—the hall lamp goes on again, and she comes turning out of the darkness, reaching her hand out toward me. "You've had a dream," she tells me.

"It's the mockingbird," I say. "I think the cat's got her babies. I have to go see. I have to go out there and chase the cat away." She looks at me, stern and baffled, trying to understand. "The poor thing," I murmur. "Oh the poor thing! She's scared to death. I have to go find the cat, that bastard."

"That mocker's doing what every mocker does at the full moon, Carrie," Ona says, apologetic for the bird. "It's the male, not the female. He's just marking out his territory." Her voice is calm and means to soothe me, but she's looking at me as though I've misunderstood the whole universe. "He does it I guess as much out of joy as anything else. Or he just *does* it, anyway. It's the full moon and he feels like giving a concert."

I nod, my eyes on the floor, feeling ashamed but not convinced. I know hysteria when I hear it. But maybe it's my own hysteria I'm hearing. That's what *she* thinks, I know. "I'm sorry I woke you up, Ona," I say, giving her my regular broken-dish smile and turning, but then I turn back: "Do you know where my fiddle is?"

"Well, of course I do," she says promptly, glad for this opportunity to divert me. "Right in there in my closet."

I look at her with my jaw dropped.

She folds her arms over her chest—she's wearing a chenille

bathrobe the color of an Ace bandage, her hair in a gray thin braid down her back. "Cap said to wait till you asked. He thought it might be you needed to stay away from it for a while. And I think he was right—at the beginning it wouldn't have done you no good and it might have done you some harm—you or the fiddle, one—you were taken so hard then. You might have just got up one night and busted it against the wall. You weren't in much shape for *any*thing, let alone music.

"We should have told you before now, I guess, but it didn't seem like you was studying on it at all. I told Cap today I was fixing to set it down in your lap here one of these days, whether you asked or not. It seemed like you'd forgot about it. That wouldn't be right."

"I did forget about it. But I remembered it today. And then I thought I'd better go back and get it. I thought maybe somebody stole it. It scared me. When I couldn't find it."

"Oh, you poor thing. When Ruth said you'd gone off this evening, I knew exactly where you'd headed, and why. I wish I would have called you up on long distance, to tell you, honey." Long distance and Ona weren't meant for one another. When Cap calls her, from on the road, she yells, "But this is costing you money," after every sentence he coaxes out of her. "Come on and I'll get it for you now," she says.

So I follow her back into her bedroom, where every wall and almost every horizontal surface is crammed with photographs, some in frames, some just stuck up with thumbtacks. Her daughters, grandchildren, neighbors, school friends, Luther old, holding up a big fish and grinning, and Luther young ("To Ona my darling from Luther B./September 1938"), Luther and Ona in their fifties, sitting squashed together in front of the pastor's bookshelves, for their church picture. Ona's mother and daddy, I guess they are, stone-faced in oval gold-leaf frames on the wall. Cap in every precious stage of his existence, including Hawktown from earliest days, when he was nothing but a grin and a crew cut. Ona, young and brave in her homemade satin wedding dress, her round face sweet but unsmiling, her shining dark hair wound in a thick braid around her head; Cap's mother, who resembled the young Sally Struthers, in a big backlit studio portrait—her engagement picture, probably—tinted in pastels as though she were already an angel, with her mother's round face and big blue eyes. Cousins, nephews, nieces . . . "It will be quite a crew that gathers on the other shore when I show up," Ona said once. "Half not speaking to the other half. Half not speaking to *me*." Four generations of women on a lawn, including little four-year-old Ona in a starched white dress, looking about the same as she does now, with a broad face and deep quiet eyes, a tremendous white bow ribbon and black lace-up shoes.

And photographs are just the beginning—I get dizzy when I come in here. Every last cushion or framed poem about what makes grandmothers special that somebody has cross-stitched for her, every religious saying burned into a wooden plaque by a grandchild at church camp, every (unopened) box of talcum or bottle of perfume she ever got for Christmas. "You may not be rich in dollars," Ruth tells her, "but you got a fortune up here in cheap perfume." Plus jewelry boxes, music boxes, plastic flowers, figurines—a rich, cluttered life, as if the trick is just to treasure what's given and keep it dusted, make no distinctions, hold it all in one thought. Every macramé flowerpot hanger, every crocheted tissue box cover.

"He brought it out that next morning after he brought *you* out," she's saying. "On his way to Ohio. When he brought your truck. He didn't want to leave either one to get stolen. It's back in here." Her shallow closet has room for about six hangers, fit in diagonally. The first thing Ruth did when she moved in was to have a closet built into one whole side of her pink room. According to Ruth, Ona was so amazed by its shelves and arrangements that Ruth offered to have one built for her at the same time—but Ona told her, "Then I'd have to go out and get some duds that was fit to hang in there and pretty soon I'd be as bad a clotheshorse as you."

I see the fiddle case leaning against the wall in the corner next to Ona's stretched navy-blue church shoes. I duck down without thinking, sliding under Ona as she bends. I come up clutching the case to my chest, knocking into her as we both straighten up. We catch at each other to right ourselves. "Get out of her way, she's got that fiddle now!" Ona announces, as she straightens up by pushing in the small of her back with both hands.

"I don't want to play it," I tell her. "I just want to have it."

"Well, now you have it."

I kneel to unclasp the case. I open the lid, lined with white satin, and unfold a length of red velvet from around the instrument itself. I take it out, holding it between thumb and forefinger, by the neck. The feel of its smooth, precise lightness comes back to me, but no one could guess from what a distance it does. I see for the first time, it seems, how cleverly and completely the instrument is made—like something that took a thousand years to get right, through trial and error, all the wrong ways cast aside, to leave this one simple, perfect shape. I remember how to hold it, it fits exactly to that shelf that's made for it on my body. I unsnap the bow from its holder, I bend my ear to the strings, tuning up. Only I can't think of a thing in the world to play.

Ona stands with her hands clasped over her belly, watching. "Do us a tune, Carrie," she says.

"No—I've lost the oil in my wrist and elbow," I explain,

smiling. It's probably true. "You'd be surprised how fast it goes. When I get it back, I'll play for you. I don't want to mess up the first thing I try to fiddle."

"You poor girl. Going all that way for what was right here."

"I needed to go there anyway." I kneel to put my fiddle back in its case. "I needed to pack up her things."

"I wish you'd have let me help you," she says, in back of me.

I shake my head. "I feel like I've got to go on and face it now." I turn my head to look up at her. "I feel like I've got to look it in the eye."

"It hasn't got no eye," her low voice assures me. "If it did, it wouldn't let you look in it. It don't want you to, Carrie. It wants you to give up and live."

I nod. One rusty, jagged sob, deep in my throat, escapes. I wait with my head lowered until I can get my breath smoothed down again. Then I say, "I mean—not *death's* eye, exactly. Just. . . ."

She nods. "I know. But life's eye is what you need to be looking in. Life wants you to face the front and live, the first minute you feel able." Her kind face swings like a moon above me. I stand up now, holding the case by its handle in front of me. "Why don't you come on downstairs with me, now that you got your fiddle? I want some hot milk, and I'll fix you some too."

So I sit at the kitchen table. Barney slaps his tail against the porch floor to be let in; she opens the screen door for him, and he flops down right beside her feet, where she leans on the counter next to the stove, clutching the pot holder like a hankie, talking to me. "Carrie, I want to tell you something. You know I lost a daughter, too. You might think, yes, but Rachel was twenty-seven and Mollie Snow was only five. But you'd be surprised how little difference there is. Your daughter's your daughter, and you're the one left, and it was never meant to be. And twenty-seven is young, too."

It comes to me, for the first time, that I'm doing something for Ona, too, while she does everything for me. I don't look the least bit like Sally Struthers, but Rachel was only a few years younger than me when she died. The nights when Ona has rocked me and sung to me, *All right darlin' it's all right it's all right*, it's got to be partly Rachel she's holding on to. And also herself, the woman who lost her daughter. Who rocked Ona when she needed it? I hope somebody did. Who comforted her as she comforts me? I'm both her grieving younger self and her lost daughter, holding on to my own lost daughter, as though we go all the way in, echoing this grief, carrying it, grief within grief within grief.

The milk scalds and she takes it off the flame, talking as she pours it. "I feel like I know a little bit what you're going through. And I want to tell you it hasn't been but three months. It takes years. Two years, at least, to grieve out the hard part. It did me. To get to where it didn't just double me up. It's like sweating a fever. And *I* had something drawing me back—my other girls, and Cap, and the rest of my family, all over the county, and Luther, and the farm chores. We went right from burying her to stripping tobacco—it had to be done and that was that. I had to keep up with things, I had people depending on me—it was a blessing, to have my hands full."

We both look at *my* hands, those two useless strangers, as she puts the white mug between them on the table.

"I'm afraid if you're not careful you might get sucked into something you can't hardly get out of." Her eyes are on mine in earnest. "That's one reason it would be good if you got back to your music as soon as you can. To have something—you know—from *this* side, pulling on you, against the other. If you're in this world, you have to go ahead and be *in* it."

She takes a sip from her cup, then sets it down on the table, just so. "They don't like to be held on to, anyway, is how it felt to me. With me, I finally agreed not to try to call her back no more, because I got to thinking she was just being patient with me. You feel like they have forever to do whatever they have to do, so they can afford to let us hold on till we can stand to let go, but pretty soon you get the message that they're just being kind. That you're keeping them from their business."

I nod, and pick up the mug and hold on to it with both hands and blow on it and drink the hot milk, and we both hope it will let me sleep, so I can get up in the morning and start holding on to—whatever the next thing is, here on earth. "You know those monks who try to pray all the time? That's how I want to be. I don't want to hold her back, but I don't want to forget anything about how she really was. I feel like that's what my life is *for*, now. Like if I don't remember her, it will be as if she never lived. She was so young—she didn't leave anything at all behind but a few boxes of stuff. . . ." My throat tightens with tears. I have to stop.

She nods, her eyes searching my face.

"I want to concentrate just on her," I say, when I can talk again. "On Molly." Her name falls soft but heavy. The sound of the word *concentrate* calms me, a solid soothing word with *center* in the center of it.

Ona sits down across from me, her plump pink hands clutched on the table. She says hesitantly, "Yes. But you don't have to. She's part of you now—it don't hardly make any difference whether you concentrate or not." She looks at me quietly, almost pleadingly, leaning across the table towards me. After a while she tries to explain better: "She's in you. When you move, it's partly her, moving. That's just the way it is, no trying to it."

I nod again, but the idea makes me feel like howling, it's so much less than what I want, and all I can have, I know. "I don't want to forget anything about how she really was."

"You will, though. You can't help it." She cocks her head and rubs the edges of the smooth tabletop with all four fingers. "But you have *her*. You don't have nothing to say about it. You loved her and you have her, that's the way it is."

"I don't want to give up one single second of her life," I insist doggedly, fighting for it.

"But you already *have* give up a good many," she says, in a reasonable voice. I'm closing my mind to her. I'm wishing she'd shut up. "It's all right to remember her. But you can't hold things the way they were. You can't keep time from coming in and changing everything. There's no use trying. Life wants to go on and on and on—no matter how still you are, it keeps coming at you."

We look at each other across the round table. She hopes I won't curl my lip in the bitter smile of rejection of what she's saying; she keeps her eyes steadily on me, asking me not to do that, but they aren't apologetic or even sympathetic. They're just blue, holding me in their gaze. "It's just that I'm not done yet, Ona," I say at last. "I'll know when I'm done."

I take a deep breath and let it out, like they say to. "I know you're right, that life will move me on. But I want to pay attention to—I want to concentrate, right now, on—I don't know. I think it's important. I think I'll know when it's time—I think I have to trust myself to know. When it's time to let her go. I think I have to trust myself."

Then I laugh, a trembling drawing-in-breath kind of laugh. "I think I'm fighting the full moon."

She shakes herself loose from her concentration on me. "I

believe so, too. A sorry little old mockingbird, Carrie. You want one of your tranquil pills?" Ona keeps the pills and doles them out to me, on account of not trusting me to take exactly the right number.

"No, I'm going to try to do without. But no more naps in the daytime."

"That's right. You're going to get your days and nights switched if you don't watch out."

"I must have slept three hours."

"That poison ivy'll keep you awake, too. And all them chiggers."

"It never even crossed my mind, when I was out there wading around in the long grass. I'm so dumb."

"I've got to where the poison ivy don't hardly bother me—can't get through my tough hide, I guess. Does it itch yet?"

I pull up my pants leg to show her what's happened.

"Oh Lord, Carrie, what a mess. You're going to have to go in and get a shot. Anybody'd be restless. You got jumped on by every single thing that's out there."

She pushes herself out of the chair and finds some clear nail polish in a kitchen drawer. "Hike your leg up on the table and I'll paint them chigger welts for you."

"I can do it. You don't have to treat me so kind anymore." I take the bottle and prop my leg up and start to work on it. "And I don't want you all to be acting like I'm a mental anymore, either." I look up to emphasize my meaning, then down again at my chigger bites. "I've *been* one, but now I'm going to have to start being on my own two feet again, and you have to act like I'm normal and expect normal things from me. This is the last time I'm going to keep you up all night looking after me. After the day you put in."

"Oh, you haven't been hardly any trouble at all, Carrie.

And tomorrow's Sunday—well, I guess it's Sunday now. So we don't have to jump right up." As if to prove she's not a bit tired, she seats herself again and picks up her cup. "You want me to fix you some more milk?"

I smile and shake my head.

"Did you decide what you want to do about your house?"

"I don't think I'm going to be able to live there anymore."

"Well, you better come on and move in with us then."

"I don't know, Ona. I guess I'll have to run that past the man."

"What's he got to say about it?" she asks indignantly. "It's my place, I guess I can have whoever I want here with me. I can't see how it would make a bit of difference to him no way—plenty of granny to go around." She laughs and slaps at her thigh, to demonstrate. "If I was you, I'd sell that Lexington house, I swear I would. I wouldn't fool with renting it. You're liable to make some money, and if you put it together with that insurance, you'd *have* something. You could get Ruth to invest it for you, like she done for me. She'd make it grow for you. She wouldn't lose you nothing. You could little along on what it made for you for a while, till you decide what you want to do.

"You ought to let me and Ruth go over in the truck and get it all cleared out. Or the three of us together, if you'd rather. You could put your furniture in that U-Store-It, like Ruth done. You could use the barn for things that the mice and daubers wouldn't hurt."

I shrug. "It doesn't amount to a hill of beans, anyway. It's all just stuff I picked up. I'd as soon put it out on the street and let people take what they like." I can't remember anything I have that I want to keep—just Molly's Mother's Day card from nursery school still taped to the fridge, a horse and a mouse and a heart. "I want to travel light for a while."

She nods, with her lips pressed together, all business, as though she knows what traveling light means, and thinks well of it, Ona, who's never been a day of her life without a house full of solid mahogany and about four generations' worth of mason jars. "Of course, if you decide you'd rather rent it than sell it, you could rent it furnished, if you really don't care too much about what happens to your things. We need to get cracking before Ruth takes off on her trip, though—she's the organizer."

"Still—I need to get a few things settled with Cap first." I don't look up—I feel myself blushing and twist around to get at the bites behind my knees. "Give me a couple of days."

"Well, if you feel like you need to talk to him, talk to him. But I'm the boss over here, and to me you're welcome, and that's all anybody's going to say about it. Anyway, don't sell him short—"

I give a loud laugh at that. "I hate to tell you—my problem has *never* been selling old Cap short, Ona."

"I know he wouldn't begrudge you staying here, no matter if you're in or out of that band, if that's what you're worried about."

I give her a quick, cautious glance from under my bangs. She's not fishing around, as her buddy Ruth likes to do. She's got a serene pure mind, not given to speculation—in fact, maybe she should speculate a tiny bit more. What if he did begrudge my staying here? Couldn't he make us all feel it? And then what?

"He wants what's best for you," she adds.

"Mm-hmm," I say.

"Long as you don't mind living rough, the way we do."

"To me, this is the lap of luxury."

"You got the lap part right, honey!" She pushes herself up out of the chair with a little groan.

"Lord, Lord," she says, ahead of me, hauling herself by the banister up the stairs.

"You and me, Ona, we got to start working out."

"Honey, I'd founder on my first jumping jack."

I PUT ON my nightgown and this time get in the bed. The old boy out there reminds me now of a parking-lot banjo player running through a three-octave chromatic scale, showing off every lick he's got—until he abruptly stops, goes to sleep or breaks a blood vessel or flies off somewhere else. Or, if it's the mother, as I still believe, she gives up because the cat's got the nest now and there's no reason to go on.

The quiet lasts about two minutes; then from far off across the field comes a high run of startled, pained yips. It's Willy, and the barks are coming from the place where the skunk attacked us the other day. We ran as fast as we could. When I looked back, the skunk was losing ground but still barging along behind us, head low like a rampaging bull, till we rounded the curve. It was so ridiculous I threw my head back and laughed, but now it's not funny, because I'm afraid Willy's gone back there, like a nosy fool, and the skunk has bitten him. And no skunk but a rabid one would come after you like that.

I lie wide awake worrying about whether Willy's had rabies shots, because if not he'll have to be destroyed, and it will be my fault for not telling anyone about the skunk. Maybe it wasn't rabid. I don't know any more about skunks than I know about mockingbirds. Maybe Willy's barking at something else entirely.

So I go back to wondering what it would feel like to be a

student, nineteen or twenty years old, in hiding in China, knowing nothing much stood between you and death now but pain. Rifle butts and fists.

Finally, I get up again and sit by the window, watching the old moon, visible at last, sailing through the cleared-off sky without the least concern for all this agony down here on the earth—the sharp tiny white teeth of the squirrel bared in pain and terror.

I can hear Ona snoring again. In the dark, I put on a long-sleeved shirt and jeans. I pull heavy socks up over the cuffs— I'm that much smarter anyway than I was once. I pick up my moccasins and my fiddle case and steal down the stairs, feeling my way. Once I'm outside, I can see—the clouds have cleared off, the sky is glazed blue with moonlight. Barney's asleep in the kitchen. Willy isn't here to greet me, so it must have been Willy I heard.

The night is silent now. I go along the farm road to the place where we saw the skunk. "Willy," I call softly, up and down the road. If the skunk had bit him, she would have sprayed him, too. I don't smell skunk on the air, only moisture being pulled back, a faint hopeful smell of cut grass. So maybe Willy was barking at stray hounds, the way he sometimes does. Maybe the world isn't always dangerous.

Eighteen

What time is it? Don't know. Where am I going now? Don't know. Someplace where I can practice my music without being heard.

If a hunter saw me, he'd surely tell all his friends—Little Lady walks again. But I'm just an apprentice ghost, just ghost-hearted.

No, I'm not. I'm a flesh-and-blood woman trying to hack it. Trying to find a way to live the rest of my life, that's all.

Don't cry, Mama, I'm all right, just playing my fiddle in the middle of the night. Kind of a little jig.

All the frogs left in the world have gathered at the pond; I walk for a minute under the tent of their song. The moonlight makes the going easy; the gravel farm road is a white highway. The stars now shine clean and exact as notes in the bluish sky. I make out the constellations I know the names of as though I were reading music. The rest fill the sky without pattern.

I feel a little lift of my spirit into the night, as if heaviness could slide off of us, fall back to earth, making the earth heavy, as our spirits lifted up.

Now I pass into the field, following the path that follows the ridgetop, as the crest descends and meets the woods. The woods shut out the light. I have to stop and think, feel my way forward with my feet, stumbling over a root, slipping on a rock. I wave a stick in front of me to knock down spider-webs, I crash into brambles, this is no joke. Something takes off startled in the underbrush. Ahead of me, an owl nickers like a little horse; when I get to the owl's tree, I look up. The owl falls silent. I try out the sound, but the owl doesn't buy it.

I pass out of the woods at the line fence. Now I'm on the other farm, following the cow path through tall moonlit weeds into the heart of ghostland. I guess I'm hoping to fiddle my way into their affections. Hoping they'll come out and dance. I'll play "Root Hog or Die" and see if they'll come out knocking the back step, hand slipping from hand on down the line. I hug my fiddle case against my stomach with one arm, trying to follow the long-forsaken cow path, through sumac and ragweed, trying not to get tangled in wild rose bushes. No one is out here, I know, and yet I have to overcome a fear of something close. I keep shying back.

I can't believe I'm doing this.

The cabin at last is before me, tin roof collecting moonlight like snow. I come up on it this time from the creek, along the overgrown stepping-stones so many feet have felt for. I let myself in the wire gate, walk the few more path stones, and climb onto the porch. I cross it and shove open the door of the sleeping quarters; the window on the far side lets in a shaft of moonlight. It gives me courage. I use a tobacco stick to clear out the spiderwebs in the opening and then step down onto the dirt floor, stamp my foot, then listen to the faint panicky rustle of movement above me and all around me. "Get back, greedy things!" I yell, imitating Ona.

I can see the hearth standing up to where floor level used to be, one big slab of stone. There's a three-legged stool on its side in the dirt. I pick it up and bang it against the wall to knock the dirt and cobwebs and mouse turds off of it, then set it down in the shaft of moonlight.

Nothing left to do now but what I came to do. I get my fiddle out of the case, slide some rosin on my bow, and sit down in the moonlight where they all danced and banged spoons and made eyes at each other fifty, sixty years ago. I address my bow to the strings and try a few scales, listening to the sound with unaccustomed ears, like what is music, what is string, what is bow? How could music be made out of these skinny sounds? I sure can't think of any. The sound is painful to hear. My right wrist feels arthritic, the bowing uncontrolled, the notes harsh. My left wrist is weaker than I could have imagined. My fingers go through the scales, over and over. A month off can set you back a year, with the fiddle. I've got my work cut out for me.

That little upward, questioning phrase of music, *careless and gay*, comes back to me. I can't imagine the melody that came before or after, just those four plainting waltz-time notes I heard here yesterday at noontime. I put my fingers down as clean as I can on the four notes. It helps me to get over my shyness about being out here in the middle of the night calling attention to myself—I keep thinking what it would be like to be just passing by, say with your dogs, and you hear this fiddle music coming out of an abandoned cabin. I play the four notes, experimentally, this way and that, but I can't think of any melody on one side or the other of the notes—the emptiness of not hearing any music feels like hunger.

I go back to my scales, doggedly, until a bird at last rises in the dark air, a thin wing rises and falls—the song I sang here yesterday, against the window. *Oh! The moon shines tonight on pretty Redwing.* This is the first music I have made. To call music. Relieved, I remember how it goes, and play the chorus over and over, stopping each time I come to the end of it, to listen to the strange, tight silence.

Because I am unused to melody, each line seems miraculous to me, the inevitable but unexpected way it moves and changes and repeats and comes to rest. I sing the grieving words then, stopping after every line, letting my voice sail up into the rafters, up into the listening, empty air. But I think ghosts wouldn't be tempted by the sad way I can't help playing this song. They can be sad on their own time. They want to romp—why else would they come back?

So I move to a better idea:

> *Buffalo gals won't you come out tonight*
> *Come out tonight*
> *Come out tonight*
> *Buffalo gals won't you come out tonight*
> *And dance by the light of the moon?*

I wait, then try it again, launching into it with a shuffle and a slide. I don't know what I'm expecting. Some of those old Buffalo gals, I guess. I'd like to play for every one of them dead old dollies. If I was good enough.

> *Gonna dance with the dolly with the hole in her stocking,*
> *Knees keep a-knockin', toes keep a-rockin',*
> *Gonna dance with the dolly with the hole in her stocking,*
> *Dance by the light of the moon.*

Now I'm remembering, now I'm getting it back—my notes are flying around, a little fancy. If I were someone who used to dance here, I'd come back and dance again, I would—it's got to be as good as what that Mr. Ben Hazel gave them. But when I stop, there's nobody home, nothing doing. They better hurry, if they want to dance by the light of *this* moon. It's not waiting around for them. It's lowered, through the window, even in the little while I've been here. I play the chorus through again. Oh, now I think I could make a cow dance with this tune, but no one's dancing here, unless it's spiders. I give them one last chance to have a good time. . . .

And finally I do see something, some kind of movement, like that pretty Redwing rising, the edge of something, skirts atwirl, skin flashing, flashing spoons. I throw the verse out like a fishing line to see if I can catch anything. When I look up, my breath goes out of me and my heart flies up, for it's Molly I've caught. She's over on the other side of the chimney, over on the dark side of this dancing room, in her dark blue dress with red flowers embroidered in the skirt and around the collar, the hand-me-down dress she loved and tried to wear every day. She sways, self-consciously, hanging near the wall, not dancing, just smiling down at the dirt and holding her skirt out, sturdy knees shyly locked. She's granting me something, she's come, for my sake, a long distance—I've called her away from something. She wants to do what I want her to do, but she doesn't remember dancing, dancing is long ago.

I want to fly to her, gather her to me, but I know that if I so much as whisper her name, or look straight at her, she'll be gone. My only way to touch her is with the music I play.

I play; the movement of my bow feels like a kind of breathing, like a singer's breath. The music rises on the pure breath of the bowing.

She doesn't know what I want her to do, what is required of her. She takes a small skip to one side, then back, where she hesitates. She is so close over there, so solid and everyday, so much what she always was, in the curve of her cheek, her hair, her elbow, her expression of trying to keep a straight face, that I almost expect her to look over at me and say "Gink gank," her all-purpose pleasantry for sticky situations. It almost seems the world could breathe her back into itself, that she could turn away from death as if it were a dream, and come to her senses singing "Johnny B. Goode." But I must not think it. I must not want it. Because she's not what she was. She's set apart. Unreachable, by me.

She moves the one time, but not again. I go on playing my heartbroken song, because it's all I know to do, but she is separate from me, she doesn't know what to do, connected to this ceremony only by impersonal, distant kindliness.

But then another girl is there with Molly, to show her how, a fast dark girl, a little older, a little taller than Molly, with sharp elbows and a wide mouth and a ponytail high on her head. She skips and twirls. The sharp unfettered way she moves shows she has a charge of energy in her she hardly knows what to do with. Molly forgets her shyness with this other girl. They step toward each other, faces shining, latch onto each other, Molly blond in her dark blue dress, the other girl dark in yellow, with lace sewn into the hem of the skirt— and then I recognize my own six-years-old Easter dress that Grandma Shorter sewed, with the wide gored skirt that twirled out.

The two children, fingers hooked, swing themselves in a circle, feet in, heads back, bright spots of color in each one's cheeks, little white sharp teeth shining, eyes shining, blue and brown, hair flying, blond and dark, as they lean back and swing out in their circle, and now, as I fiddle them on, here comes the redheaded girl from the picture, doing some ungainly wild made-up dance, knees high, clumsy little orthopedics flying in a goofy way, elated, beside herself with joy, to be let out of that room of the lady who wouldn't get off her butt. She dances around the edges of Molly and Carrie swinging round and round, until they stop and catch her hand and let her into their circle. I cover them with rollicking notes, I play for all I'm worth, play till they throw themselves around, doubled over, till I can hear the three of them laughing—helpless chortling loud peals, child's belly laughs, ringing out one on top of the other.

So that the only way I know when Little Lady comes is that the sound is abruptly gone and the children gone, my girl is gone, vanished, evaporated, like a trick my mind played on me, like sweet dreams, like wishful, wishful thinking, and Little Lady just stands there, in her long skirt, her bare small narrow white feet down on the dirt floor, stilled in the spill of moonlight from the window, making that other vision seem innocent and sentimental as—a valentine. She sends it packing, by standing there, sucking all the air in the room into a kind of inside-out howl, and it may be as Ona says that she loves this place so much she can't tear herself away, but her eyes are so blue they're white, so blue they make the music stop. Blue and fixed. She's still as a post, still as a ghost can get, looking at me, or through me, with a cold unloving stare. She stands, slight as a child herself, with a child's tidy round face and curved brow, sucking all this world into her round eyes until she is the only thing.

She opens her full-lipped, mocking little mouth and in a high thin voice with absolutely no resonance to it, she sings, like a synthesizer approximating the human voice: *Careless and gay, hear the old fiddler play. Under the ashes till the break of the day.* There's a rustle of that threatening, raucous laughter that I heard before. It's coming from the loft. Egging her on.

I don't look up. I don't take my eyes off of her. She stops and shuts her mouth and looks at me. I take in the blue flowers of her long-sleeved, round-collared blouse, the small white column of her neck rising out of it, her chin carried at a right angle to it. A bonnet sits on the back of her bundled-up curly light red hair. The ties hang down in front. Now she sings the verse again, exactly as she did before, as though taunting me.

Or perhaps resolutely teaching me. I feel bound to raise my bow, and play it for her, her ghost song. She stands unmoving and, as far as I can tell, unlistening before me; when I finish, she opens her mouth again and sings, in that high narrow soprano like wind through a crack. *Careless and gay, hear the old fiddler play. Under the ashes*—no, under the *arches,* I think she's saying—*Under the arches till the break of the day.*

"What arches," I whisper humbly, lowering the bow, thinking of the arches between the rooms of our house, Molly's and mine, where we used to leap and dance till the plates rattled on the shelves.

Under the arches till the break of the day, she sings again promptly, knocking all thought of the regular daytime world clean out of my mind. The arches of the old fiddler—I see them, as she sings, pale, rising back and back, into one darkness after another. Her voice is *devoid.* It is pure mechanical note, nothing to do with what I think of as music.

But I play it. I play it for her with all my heart. Nothing is left at all of the world I call home except my fiddle and the parts of my body that help me play music. Everything else has fallen into her moonlit eyes. She stands before me in her bare feet. She closes her mouth, her lips rest together, so I leave off playing. We face each other in the silence, until I lower the fiddle, hold it in my lap. Now, amazingly, her small upper teeth catch hold of her full pale lower lip, slide upward over it, let it go. One of her canine teeth, I notice, is broken.

She takes one step toward me. She raises a hand, and the air shudders as her hand moves through it. She wants my fiddle. She comes no closer, but she wants it. I rise from the stool now, my heart in my throat. No wonder Lanter ran away to Alabama—did she raise that hand to him, too?

Her hand is raised but she comes no closer. She looks at me out of those still, locked, whitish-blue eyes. It comes to me, from a great distance, that Ruth was right. Little Lady has gotten herself caught at the edge. She can't turn and go on. She doesn't know how to. With great effort—it feels like she's exerting some force on it—I bring the fiddle close to myself, I hug it to my breast. And she takes up the song again, obsessively: *Careless and gay, hear the old fiddler play. . . .*

I understand now that this is all she knows, the one verse of this song, but she is bound to hold on to it, to go on singing it, forever. All the good times, all the rowdiness and fun—the world has slipped away from her, she's lost it, like a dream slipping away. And she's stuck now at the boundary, with just this one verse of this one song to hold on to, this little fragment of the good times like the fragment of a dream you hold on to as the rest slips back where it came from.

I know what I have to do, what is given to me to do—for her, and for myself. For I am caught at the edge, too. *I want to look it in the eye,* I said. This is the eye. I am looking in it now. The eye at the edge, death in life and life in death, where ghosts walk. The next time she comes to the end of the verse, I take it up, I sing it. I sing it with my head thrown back and all my heart gone to music.

> *Careless and gay*
> *Hear the old fiddler play*
> *Under the arches*
> *Till the break of the day.*

And then the melody climbs up the first line in a beautiful variation. Words come to me. I sing them as I think of them:

> *Hear the old fiddler play*
> *Till the break of the day*

She will go dancing
Careless and gay.

I don't care if she likes it or not. Still standing, I put my fiddle under my chin. The tune is pure, plain, ancient, meant. I play it as though all my days and nights of music, all my listening and all my practicing, all my longing for music, were just for this moment. I play with a full tone, certain and restrained, but full of movement, to fiddle Little Lady out of the place where she's caught. I wonder if her white feet can move, down in the darkness.

I play the caught sadness of this melody, and then I put in the music of it, how it opens. As water to a thirsty person, so is this music to me. I wish I could drink it, just gulp it down out of the air.

Careless and gay
Hear the old fiddler play
Under the arches
Till the break of the day.

And then the rising sweetness, the inquisitiveness:

Hear the old fiddler play
Till the break of the day

And afterwards, the quiet resolution, the hand opening:

As she goes dancing
Careless and gay.

The hand opening. The hand letting go. I was afraid of her, but now she's in the music. I can see the strands of her red hair curling on her neck, I can see the large knuckles of her hand loosening in the folds of her skirt. I know that if she so much as sways to the music, something will take her. I play now for the tall friends to come to her as they came to Molly. I play for her to let them. For them to come from the other side, from the many-alcoved room, from the beyond of her.

In life there is singing, and it must also be in death, I tell her. Some kind of singing. We just don't know what it is yet.

Everything that ever lived is dead, I tell her. Except the things that haven't died yet. Would all the singing be just in this one part? How could it be? She sways, hesitantly; like laundry on the line she moves; the wind has got into her. And I move too. I sway to the lovely waltz time of this music.

The ruckus in the loft has stilled. There's nothing in the world now but this song. She's gone. They're all gone. I'm alone here, in this long-abandoned cabin, playing. And then it's over. I'm through playing, for now. I've fiddled Molly back to me for one last time, but she has gone on now to where she needs to be—into the leaves or the bright air or nowhere at all or the place where the path leads, heaven, the room with arches and alcoves and unfoldings. I've opened my hand. I won't try again to call her back. To hold her back.

And I've fiddled Little Lady into death, at last. I know it. She's gone, she won't be back. My guess is that death is a journey. From one opening to another. Not a resting in peace.

I've just about fiddled in the dawn. It begins to show faintly, a green rim at the east, lifting the lid.

On the path again, I put my foot down, heel first, on the hard cracked ground. I take a step, then another. Where my foot comes down is the world. Is real. As I start back to Ona's, it crosses my mind that there is just the one path; this earthly real cow path across an abandoned farm in Oxford County, Kentucky, is the same path that Molly is on. I walk carefully, down the meadow of ragweed and along the creek, and it seems to me as I walk that there is no difference—Molly is farther ahead on this path we're both walking. It runs over to the other side. She is a little way ahead of me. She will turn and wait, at the proper time, for me to catch up.

I remember the vision I had of her on the path, going deeper and deeper. I have to do that, too. Agree to go through, to go deeper, to be taught. And then do it again. That's what life is, too, not just what death is. The same path, the same tall friends waiting to help you. To help you have your life. Or your death, whatever. Whatever comes next.

I hear the voices of children shouting over the hills, a far distance. I stop to listen. It takes me a minute to understand that what I'm hearing is just dogs, just hounds running, off somewhere.

The light is coming now, it seems to rise from the ground around the large cedar trees. Out in the distance the light of a security lamp pulses through the moving leaves. Morning, what now? The pink light touches the world, and as it does, it seems to me that it isn't only heaven that has those arched alcoves. Each day of life is a cove of light, a curved completeness, a waking to light, a going forth in light, and a fall toward and into the dark. Maybe if you have one day, you have eternity; if you live one day and fall asleep and dream, maybe you know all there is to know, here on earth, so that it isn't so bad if you die as a child. I don't know.

In the distance I hear a rooster. It sounds like a young one, just learning, practicing up, pronouncing carefully, as if repeating a lesson: "Cock. A doodle. Doooo."

I walk through the field where Cap has mown. The dawn wind smells like grass, though the path of dry stubble feels like little swords through the soles of my moccasins.

The sun's top rim, red and immense, comes over the crest of the ridge. As the light comes on, the certainty that this path goes through to the other side slips away. It's just the path back to Ona Barkley's place from the Kidwell place. This is just the earth, and Molly is gone from it, who knows where? I am here and she is——gone. It happens fast, it happens over and over. Lives coming into and passing out of this world. Here and gone, birdwings flashing in the sun, here gone, here gone.

As I follow the tractor road, the house rises into view. It looks newly put down in that open valley. The old hills fold around it in the pink light as though they remember a time when no house was here, no fields either, as though this house, rising white and sturdy in the dawn light, has been on the land no longer than the shadow of a cloud passing over the hills. I think of the many lives that have passed through this house.

The white house, its many afterthoughts rambling away from the original square structure, simply holding around its people through the night, but welcoming them back into its high wallpapered rooms, come morning; I enter the deep quietness, tiptoeing up the stairs.

I get my suitcase and throw a few things in it—Molly's shirt, my old silky nightgown, where I let them drop on the floor last night when I got up in such a sweat to save the baby mockers. A few clothes. My toothbrush. The check and the stack of cards, still unopened, that Cap brought out to me. The picture and the photograph I brought back with me last night. I strip the bed and leave the sheets folded on the rocking chair, like a person with good manners.

I go quietly down the stairs and write a note on an envelope: "Dear Ona and Ruth, I ran into town again to take care of a few loose ends. I'll call from my house this afternoon. XXOO Carrie." I leave it on the round kitchen table.

I tiptoe out the back door and get in my car, start it up, hop-

ing it doesn't wake them, and drive down to the hardtop of
the Hawktown Road and along it for about a quarter of a
mile.

> *Oh, the Hawktown Road is seven miles long,*
> *Many a fork where a girl could go wrong.*
> *Come out and try it if you don't believe this song—*
> *Yes, the Hawktown Road is seven miles long.*

Heaven help me, I can't quit making up these songs!

I turn left at Cap's driveway and stop the car before the
bridge—I don't want the sound of the motor to wake him, or
the sound of the car rattling over the boards. I sit in the car
and compose a letter for him, too, this one on the back of a
Hardee's bag, with a blunt pencil that I find in the glove com-
partment. The dried-up eraser leaves red marks, so, after a
few messy smudges, I try not to erase anything: "Dear Cap," I
say,

If you've got to tell the IBMA and John Kemp something right now you better tell them I'm gone. I'm not saying no—I'm just saying I don't know and don't know when
I will know or what I'll know when I know something. I
need to get you out of the middle of my mind for a while. I
can't be thinking about you and your situation right now,
I've got my own situation.

If you decide to hire a new fiddler I won't blame you a
bit—you've got a business to run. Or we can take a reading
in a few months if you want to. But for now nothing's simple, though you think it is. Let's just walk away from it and
see how we feel in a couple of months. You need to think
too—about what you mean by *everything*. It seems sort of
like you've talked yourself into something because you're
seeing me as your best chance, at least that's how it came

across, and you can't blame me for saying no thanks if that's the way it is.

I don't see how I can stay here after messing you up so bad. It would come between you and Ona I know. So I'm going on home. Thanks from the bottom of my heart for all you've done for me, bringing me out here and giving me your dear granny and bearing with me all this time. I know it's been hard on you. I'll never forget it.

If I didn't have to do this I wouldn't, believe me. I'll call you sometimes, I'll let you know what's happening to me. You do the same. Love always from Carrie.

I get out of the car and walk across the wooden bridge over the dry creek bed and up the hill through the cedar trees. Five stone steps from the driveway to the path that leads to his front porch. I sit down on the edge of the porch, where it falls away into daylilies, close to the wall that forms one side of the porch. I lean my head against the rough boards. I feel his exhaustion and his hopefulness, through the wall. I can't bear the thought that our voices may never find the harmonies in the old way anymore, that our music may be over.

I could walk in that door if I wanted to, I doubt it's locked. I could walk in and lie down beside him. It would be the most natural thing in the world. I think he would move over on his narrow mattress and, half asleep, welcome me against his warm skin. I think we would both fall asleep together there, and when we woke up we would see what happened next.

Instead I weight my note under a chunk of stovewood and start back down the path through the cedars toward my car. Just as I start down the hill, I hear the screen door slam, and he calls, "Hey, Carrie!" I turn halfway around—he's standing on the porch in a pair of brown pajama bottoms. He bends down, straightens up with my note in his hand, smiling in a puzzled way. I smile back, give him a comradely wave, but I keep on going, down the hill and across the bridge. I get in my car and slam the door and start up the motor. I back down to the turnaround. I don't look back.

The light hangs in the leaves. The trees catch fire as the new sun hits them. This is a new day, full of all the old ones. The fall is coming, a season I haven't seen here. I haven't even seen this one day. But it's time to go, for now. I can see the smoke rising, in the months to come, from the stone chimneys of Ona's house, the low gray clouds rolling over, the leaves falling, the light stretched long and gold along the stone wall.

No peach cobbler round the winter table for me. Here I was thinking I could stay snuggled up with Ona and Ruth till I felt like I was ready to face the future. But that's not how it's going to be. I'm going to face the future right now, ready or not. The lady who drops things. I'm just going to have to stop dropping them, that's all. I could have paid my keep and helped Ona out that way. And I could have helped other ways around here, too. Learned to run the tractor. Taken the lawn mower and a weed hook and gotten after the pigweed and thistles growing up around the barn. Mended the fence rails where they're held up with baling twine, if I could find a drill—I know I couldn't drive a nail into those old oak posts without one. It would have taken a lot off Ona. And Cap. And I could have kept Ona company while Ruth went off to the Holy Land and wherever else she's got it in her mind to go. I could have practiced all morning and again after supper, I don't know where—in my room, or in the stripping room or somewhere. It would have worked out fine for everybody.

Instead, I'll be back in Lexington working my day job, practicing at night in the house where I came to grief, learning to live with my life, scrabbling around after my own meals and keeping up with my own housekeeping without any good buddies working along beside me, giving me directions. Hard choices. Sometimes you've got to make a choice that looks a little wrong, just to be free.

Sometimes you have to pay the piper.

I've got no idea how it will turn out. Maybe I'll learn to be happy in my yellow house again. Or else I'll put it up for sale, after a while.

Maybe I really could buy the Kidwell farm, and get a little trailer to live in till I put enough money together to build a house.

Or things might get clearer between Cap and me. Maybe in a few months I'll feel like going back to singing duets with him, and maybe, if I do, he'll still want me to.

Maybe, since he's the Magic Man, he'll figure out what to do to make me believe what he says when he says we could have everything. Or else he won't, and I'll decide to make that record anyway. For my own ends.

I suppose I could come back out and stay here, nights, while Ruth is gone. So Ona won't be alone.

When I was sitting on the floor in Molly's room, listening, I might have been on my way out of the world. Or I might have been on my way to a place where I could rest, some natural stopping place. I'll never know—what happened happened. But this time, I'm going on with my business—I don't know how much time I'm talking about, or if there's a name for what I'm trying to find. All I know is I don't want to be interrupted.

I'm not talking about stopping. I'm talking about going on. I'm talking about listening to myself. Listening to my own music. That's what I want right now, my own little music, whatever it is. I'm talking about being free.

It doesn't matter what I decide. Everything will be decided, in its time. I'll have my life, my life will take some form. I'll always have this grief in the center of me, but my life will grow around it. My life will be real. It will have its moments. It will have music in it.

The woman stood at the clothesline, dreaming, as the child wheeled her trike into the street. Nothing will change that.

Nevertheless, I drive up to the top of the hill where the morning sun colors the sky. I pray to something, "Bless this day, and bless me in it."

As I top the rise, and the house comes into view, down below me, I see Ona hurrying back along the path in her chenille bathrobe, eagerly, from the outhouse, Barney bumping along on his three legs beside her.

Acknowledgments

Thanks to Sue and Dick Richards for their friendship, one of the chief privileges of my fortunate life: for endless generosity, practical help, indispensable counsel in many important matters—and a lifetime, by now, of bracing ridicule.

To the National Endowment for the Arts, the Kentucky Arts Council, and the Corporation of Yaddo for crucial assistance. To Geri Thoma for believing in my work from early days, to Carol Houck Smith for giving me the benefit of her artist's mind and instincts.

Among the trusted readers who've helped me hone this book, I want to give particular thanks to Roger Rawlings and Sue Richards for extraordinarily helpful readings of the manuscript, and to Diane Freund, Barry Spacks, and Cia White for years of loving give-and-take.

Finally, I want to thank my dear companion, James Baker Hall, for his unfailing confidence and joy in my behalf, his love and clarity, his devotion to his own work (which helped me learn devotion to my own), his grace and resilience along this pothole-dog road.